"I can give you a hand with that." Christopher stepped forward.

Penny tried to pull a set of sheets from the top shelf of the linen closet but couldn't quite reach it. Christopher leaned in close to her and retrieved them easily. She turned to look up at him. "It's handy to have a tall man around here."

He smiled and shrugged a shoulder. "My mom always said that."

"Sounds like a wise lady."

"I always thought so. Even as a teenager, I saw her as the coolest mom who had the best advice."

Penny pointed to the stack of blankets next to where the sheets had been. "Take as many as you need for yourself and the kids. My aunt always has extras for company."

Again he leaned close to her, and her heart clenched at his nearness. Penny frowned at the reaction. She wasn't interested in Christopher. Not even the tiniest bit.

And she'd keep _____ until her heart believed what h_____ knew. At least... she'd try.

D1115638

Dear Reader,

Nowadays, there doesn't seem to be anything more important than family, at least in my life. I've been blessed to have grown up with a family that is close. Sure, we fight now and then, but we make up eventually. Parties in my family involve way too much food and noise, but it's all worth it. And if we're playing games after dinner is put away and dishes are washed, the competition gets fierce.

This is the first book of a series that deals with cousins and a matchmaking great-aunt, Sarah. Take a scoop of noise and fun. Mix in the tendency to meddle with a big ladle of helping others and you have the Cuthbert family.

Now add in a single father who is struggling to raise his two children on his own after his wife died. Mix in a young girl's Christmas wish that her dad would laugh again and the woman who could make that happen. This is a sure recipe for romance and fun, especially during the holidays.

I hope that your holidays are full of family, friends and especially food.

Syndi

HEARTWARMING

A Hero for the Holidays

—

Syndi Powell

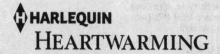

⬥ HARLEQUIN
HEARTWARMING

HARLEQUIN®
HEARTWARMING™

ISBN-13: 978-1-335-88991-1

Recycling programs
for this product may
not exist in your area.

A Hero for the Holidays

Harlequin Enterprises ULC
22 Adelaide St. West, 40th Floor
Toronto, Ontario M5H 4E3, Canada
www.Harlequin.com

Printed in U.S.A.

Syndi Powell started writing stories when she was young and has made it a lifelong pursuit. She's been reading Harlequin romance novels since she was in her teens and is thrilled to be on the Harlequin team. She loves to connect with readers on Twitter, @syndipowell, or on her Facebook author page, Facebook.com/syndipowellauthor.

Books by Syndi Powell

Harlequin Heartwarming

A Soldier Saved
Their Forever Home
Finding Her Family
Healing Hearts
Afraid to Lose Her
The Sweetheart Deal
Two-Part Harmony
Risk of Falling
The Reluctant Bachelor

Visit the Author Profile page
at Harlequin.com for more titles.

This book is dedicated to my cousins on the Hawkins side (Matt, Ben, Kelly, Christopher, Lindsey and Scott) and the Layher side (Sarah, Keri, Laura, Jessica, Mark and Dan). I love you all and miss the times we had at our family gatherings.

This is also dedicated to my cousin Keri and her family, whose own house fire inspired the story, as well as Mary Lynn Nancarrow, who suggested the heroine be jilted at the altar. Thank you for your ideas and for being a blessing to me!

CHAPTER ONE

MONDAY MORNINGS MIGHT be dreaded by most of the world, but in Christopher Fox's experience, nothing good happened on Tuesdays before noon.

This morning had been no exception. He opened one eye to peer at the alarm clock and then opened the other to stare at the blank screen. Hadn't the alarm gone off? Checking his phone, he saw that it was almost seven thirty, and he had to wake up the kids, then get them dressed and fed before taking them to school. Groaning, he jumped from the bed and ran down the hall to knock on their bedroom doors and rouse his children. "Get up! We're late."

His six-year-old daughter, Daisy, groaned and dived under the covers as he ran into her bedroom to wake her. "But I don't want to go to school," she whined. She'd gotten pretty good at whining lately. "Can't we start

Thanksgiving break today instead of tomorrow?"

"You're going to school. Now get dressed. And no cape."

Last year, Daisy had dressed up for Halloween as a superhero. Since then, she had worn the cape most days for at least a portion of the day. It was something that he and the family counselor had started to address with her in their therapy sessions. While he could understand her desire to live in a fantasy world where superheroes could save dying mothers, the reality was much different. People did die and nothing would ever change that. He gave his daughter his stern face. "I mean it, Daisy. Leave the cape at home, where it belongs."

She grumbled as she got out of bed and stood staring into her closet. Half convinced she would obey him, he poked his head into Elijah's room. The boy was still lying on his bed, covers up to his hairline. "Come on, buddy. Time to get up."

A groan from the pile of blankets and a stirring that meant his son would obey. Eventually. On his own timetable. He was only nine, but acted more like a surly teenager the closer he was getting to double digits.

Taking a deep breath, Christopher returned to his own bedroom and dressed in his typical work uniform: white oxford shirt, dark pants and one of the many ties he'd received over the years. He didn't even look as he pulled out one now and put it around his neck, then stood in front of the mirrored closet door to knot it. He barely glanced at his face, not caring what he looked like. Who was he trying to impress? The hundred or so senior citizens who lived in the assisted-living home he managed? Certainly none of the doctors or nurses who visited regularly. No, his heart had been buried along with his wife almost two years ago, so there was no one to dazzle with his appearance.

Downstairs in the kitchen, he pulled out boxes of cereal, bowls, spoons and the nearly empty gallon container of milk. The light bulb in the fridge was out. He'd have to remember to buy more milk and light bulbs on his way home after work. Footsteps above him assured him that his children would soon join him.

He glanced at his watch. No time for cereal even. He left everything on the counter, except for the milk, which he returned to the dark refrigerator. And then realized that he'd forgotten to make the kids' lunches last night like he'd planned. No time to make them now. He'd have to give them money for the school cafeteria instead.

Elijah was the first to make an appearance downstairs. His hair looked as if a brief attempt with a comb had been made, but a cowlick in the back kept the boy's dark hair from lying flat. It must be genetic, Christopher thought, as he reached up to smooth his own hair. "Where's your sister?"

The boy shrugged and started to sit at the kitchen table. Christopher sighed. "No time for breakfast this morning. Grab a box of granola bars from the cupboard and get in the car. I'll find your sister and be right behind you."

Elijah rolled his eyes and walked to the cupboards. Christopher left the kitchen and took the stairs two at a time to retrieve Daisy. He found her in her bedroom stuffing something into her backpack. "We're running late, sweetie. Let's go."

"You should have gotten us up earlier."

"The alarm didn't go off." He put his hand

on top of her head and herded her out of the room. "I'm trying to get better."

"You said that last time we were late."

Truth was that he meant to get better at being a single dad, but after almost two years, he still struggled. There was never enough time and always too much to do. "Things have been a little better since then, haven't they?" When his daughter gave him a look, he sighed and held up his hands. "I'm trying here, sweetie. Please help me."

He marched Daisy out to the car, where Elijah had taken the front seat. His daughter tugged on the car door. "It's my turn for the front seat, not Eli's."

Great. Just what he needed to add to this morning's fun. "You can get the front after school."

"But it's my turn."

"Daisy," Christopher said in what he hoped was an authoritative tone. "We're late. Get in the back."

Christopher didn't miss the look of triumph on his son's face as Daisy got in the back seat. He glared at his son. "You'll be in the back seat the rest of the week."

His son's jaw dropped. "But that's not fair. I got here first."

The children bickered back and forth as he backed the car out of the driveway. Looking up at the house, he saw their dog, Caesar, watching them from the front window. He raised a hand to bid the dog goodbye, then felt foolish for doing so. But in many ways, he wanted to stay home with the dog rather than getting the kids to school and himself to work. Just one day, he'd like to do something for himself.

But he'd promised Julie that he'd always put the children first, and Christopher never broke a promise.

Once the kids were dropped off at school with lunch money in hand, he headed to the assisted-living complex across the Detroit suburb town of Thora. Because of this morning's troubles, he arrived a half hour late. His assistant, Brenda, met him at the front door. Never a good sign. "We lost two residents overnight."

Though death was a natural part of working with senior citizens, Christopher still took it hard. "Who?"

"Mrs. Kensington in three-oh-one and Mr. Edwards in two-twenty-four."

He recalled the woman who had a fondness for chocolate and the man who always called him "Sonny." "I'll contact the families."

Brenda followed him into his office. "I already notified them. And EMS delivered the bodies to the funeral home."

"Still, I think I should call them. Express my own condolences." He hung his coat on the hook behind his office door. "What does today look like?"

She handed him a sheet of paper that listed his commitments. "And Dr. Watson wants a few minutes of your time at some point today. Preferably after she completes her rounds this morning."

The young doctor seemed to have taken an interest in him lately. Something he needed to nip in the bud. And quickly. He didn't want Brenda sending him those knowing looks, like the one she'd been giving him for the last few moments. "Stop looking at me like that. I'm not interested."

"But she obviously is."

A quick check of the schedule proved that a full day loomed, including a staff meeting at three. They needed to get their holiday rotation finalized so that everyone could spend some time with family and friends. Also, Brenda wanted to plan the staff Christmas party. He rubbed his face, frowning. "Coffee. I need lots of coffee."

"Bad morning?"

"We've had quite a few lately." He excused himself and walked to the cafeteria's beverage station to pour himself the first of many cups of caffeine.

By the time he met with Mrs. Tepperman and her daughter at eleven, Christopher contemplated quitting his job. He looked across his desk at the women sitting there, the older one frowning even as the younger one patted her hand. "It's a good place, Mom. And your friend Sylvia lives here. Didn't she tell you that she loves it?"

"I don't want to move out of my home. Your father and I lived there for fifty-two years." She glanced at her daughter again. "That's over fifty years of memories that you want me to walk away from, Deborah. I can't do it."

"You can bring the things from home that mean something to you," Deborah said.

The daughter peered at him as if asking for help to convince her mother to move into the assisted-living home. He took up the proverbial baton. "As your daughter stated, we encourage residents to bring items from home to make the apartment more comfortable and familiar. To put your own stamp on it." He leaned closer to the desk. "Our goal is to make you feel at home, Mrs. Tepperman."

He paused, deciding what tack to take with her. "What exactly does your friend Sylvia say about why she likes living here?"

"That she loves all the activities. She's even doing chair aerobics."

Christopher nodded. "It's a very popular exercise class. We also have game nights, live music on Sunday afternoons and planned outings to different places around Detroit. And if you're a knitter, we have a club that meets together and works on their projects."

Deborah touched her mom's hand. "You said that you wanted to get back to knitting again."

The older woman sniffed and glanced away. Christopher didn't blame her. He knew the fear of moving away from a place that held too many memories and starting over somewhere else. Even if he hadn't succeeded in doing it for himself, he was more than capable of helping others get to that point. That was why he'd been made director after almost four years of working at the home. He had what his former boss called "the touch" when it came to dealing with the doubts and worries of the older residents.

Mrs. Tepperman pulled the brochure closer to her and flipped through it. "I could bring my bedroom set here? My husband bought it for me on our first anniversary."

"Absolutely."

The daughter rubbed her mother's hand. "We'll hire movers to bring it over."

"Movers?" Mrs. Tepperman waved her hand. "Why pay for movers when I have grandsons with muscles?"

Christopher pulled out the application and handed it to Mrs. Tepperman just as his office door opened, and Brenda burst inside. "There's an urgent call for you."

Christopher motioned to his clients. "I'm in the middle of an appointment."

"You'll want to take this now." Brenda picked up the phone on his desk and thrust it at him.

Worried that it might be about one of the kids, he accepted the receiver. "This is Christopher Fox."

"Mr. Fox, your house is on fire."

He frowned, thinking this was some kind of sick joke. "Excuse me?"

"This is Sarah Taylor from down the street. Your house is on fire. You should get down here quickly."

Christopher bolted upright in his office chair. "What? On fire?"

"I've already called 911, and they're on their way."

He thanked the concerned neighbor, but she had already hung up the phone. He looked over his desk at the clients. "I apologize, but I need to cut our appointment short. There's been an emergency." He swallowed. "My house is on fire."

Mrs. Tepperman put a hand to her mouth. "Don't worry about us. Go."

He opened the middle desk drawer to retrieve his keys. What else did he need to do? He looked at Brenda and saw that she had his coat in her arms. He thanked her as he took it from her and promised to try to be back by the three o'clock staff meeting. She shook off his words. "I'll take care of Mrs. Tepperman and the staff meeting. Just go."

He gave a short nod, then rushed out of the office and through the lobby, taking the side door that led to the staff parking lot. He searched for his car, trying to recall what he drove. The red sedan under the maple tree beeped as he pressed the button to unlock the doors. Details of his normal life seemed to be fleeing from his mind as he put the car in Reverse and struggled to recall the best route home. All that his brain could focus on was the fact his house was on fire.

Before he turned onto his street, he could smell the fire and see the smoke rising in the sky. Emergency vehicles crowded the street, and he had to park a few houses down from his and jog the rest of the distance to the scene. Flames licked at the air from windows, while the roof and front door were also on fire. A firefighter in full gear stopped his approach, his arms spread out. "You can't go in there, sir."

"That's my house."

"We're doing everything we can to bring it under control. Is anyone inside?"

"The kids are in school." He paused, then pointed. "But the dog is in there!"

The firefighter muffled a curse, turned and ran into the inferno. Christopher watched the flames progress and wished he'd taken Caesar to the doggy day care like he'd originally thought. But they'd been running behind, and he had left the little shih tzu at home.

Seconds, then minutes passed as more firefighters directed water at the flames and others entered the conflagration with axes. More minutes went by as the fire seemed to be winning the war and eating the house with its fiery jaws.

How was he going to tell the kids that they'd lost their house and their dog in a single day? Caesar had found them at their lowest point just after Julie had died. A stray dog had stolen their hearts and made the grief a little easier. And now this? Christopher closed his eyes and hung his head.

A shout brought his head back up, and he saw a firefighter run out of the flames holding the still figure of the dog. Christopher broke past the barrier and gasped as the firefighter laid the dog on the ground, then removed his helmet and face gear.

Not his. Hers.

She started to administer mouth-to-mouth to the unmoving dog. *Please let him be okay.* Christopher knelt beside them, willing the dog to live. The dog's belly expanded as the firefighter blew her breath into the dog's nostrils. Once. Twice. On the third attempt, the dog's legs twitched. "Come on, Caesar. Breathe."

The woman blew for the fourth time, and Caesar opened his eyes and gave a weak yelp. Christopher broke into a smile and wiped at his wet cheeks. "That's it, buddy. Keep breathing." He looked at the woman, this blonde angel with bright blue eyes. "How can I ever thank you?"

The woman gave the dog's head a pat, then looked up at Christopher. "You'll probably want to take him to your vet to get him checked out, but I think he'll be okay. Just inhaled too much smoke."

"What's your name?" he asked, but she quickly placed her helmet and face mask back on and ran into the fire again, her ax in hand.

Christopher scooped the dog into his arms and cradled him close as he watched the fire consume the rest of his house.

Yep. Nothing good happened on Tuesdays before noon.

WITH THE FIRE now contained and her air tank running low, Penny Cuthbert took a second glance before walking out of the charred remains of the house. As she returned to the ladder truck, she could still hear her fire chief shouting orders, even as she removed her face gear and helmet to stow away on the truck. One of her colleagues thrust a cold bottle of water in her hands, and she took off her thick gloves to twist off the top and pour the water down her throat. Smoke gave her a sore throat and raspy voice if she didn't hydrate right away.

She glanced over at the distraught homeowner. Even though he was grieving over the lost house with a haunted look in his eyes, he was kind of cute. Tall and lean. Dark hair. Dark eyes. Totally her type. But he'd mentioned his kids being in school, so he was off-limits, married or not. She didn't date single dads. Not anymore.

Barnes nodded toward the homeowner. "I heard you saved the family dog."

"Yep. I'm the hero of the day." She took another swallow of water before focusing on Barnes. "Did you get an idea of where the fire started?"

"We'll have to wait for the official inspector's report, but my guess is the large chest freezer in the basement. Scorch marks seemed to radiate from there." Barnes glanced at the fire chief, who was still issuing commands. "Try to stay on Mac's good side today. I'm not in the mood to spend hours scrubbing down the truck."

Penny bristled at the suggestion. It had only been that one time, and she'd paid for her off-hand remarks more than any other newbie on the team. Could she help it if she wanted to prove to everyone that she had what it took to be the best firefighter in Thora? She had her father's big shoes to fill, after all.

The fire chief, Dale MacKenzie—or Mac, as the crew referred to him—crooked a finger at her. Taking a deep breath, she reminded herself that he was a longtime friend of her father's and had her best interests at heart. "Hey, Mac."

"Cuthbert, is it true that you ran into the house to rescue a dog?"

No use lying since he obviously knew the answer. "Yes, sir. The homeowner indicated that the dog was trapped inside. I assessed the risks before entering the home and found the dog hiding behind the sofa in the living room."

"And you gave the dog mouth-to-mouth?"

"Yes, sir." She'd been taught by her cousin

Jack, a veterinarian who had a soft spot for all animals, especially dogs. He would have been proud of her today.

The chief peered over his glasses at her. "Penelope, what am I going to tell your father?"

"That I'm one of your top team members, of course. I'm a hero. I saved that dog."

"To be the top and even to be a hero, you need to learn a little more humility, Cuthbert. And maybe a little teamwork."

Great. Here it comes. She knew that tone of voice. What would it be this time? Checking all the hoses on the truck and at the station by herself? Kitchen duty for the rest of the month?

He eyed her, then shook his head. "Let's see how heroic you feel after you clean the station's bathrooms with a toothbrush."

Penny frowned. "A toothbrush?" She'd be spending the rest of her day on her hands and knees cleaning, a task she'd never been fond of. When Mac raised an eyebrow at her, she gave a short nod. "Yes, sir. Happy to do it."

He grunted and walked off. She sighed. Her father had warned her that her impulsiveness would be an obstacle to her career.

It wasn't like she acted without thinking first, though. She assessed the risks, but teetered along the wrong side of caution at times. Saving the dog had been the right thing to do, and she wouldn't back down from that.

IT SEEMED LIKE he'd been watching his life go up in flames for days, although he knew it hadn't even been an hour since he'd gotten the call that changed his life. Again. He'd been working so hard to give his kids a new life after the death of their mom, and yet he didn't feel he'd achieved it. Now, on top of everything else, he had to deal with this loss?

At least he still had the dog. He nuzzled Caesar, closing his eyes and turning his back on the devastation that had once been his house. Thankfully that firefighter had saved his dog. He could rebuild a house. He could replace things. But knowing the kids were safe at school and him holding the dog in his arms—those were positives that he could cling to in the days, weeks, months ahead.

A hand touched his arm, and he opened his eyes to find his elderly neighbor, Miss Taylor, standing next to him. "Thank you for calling 911, Miss Taylor."

"Of course. It was what any good neighbor would do."

"Your house is half a block down from mine. How did you know it was on fire?"

Miss Taylor gave a shrug. "I was taking my morning walk later than usual, and I noticed the smoke coming from the windows. And where there's smoke—"

"There's fire." He turned his head to glance once more at the smoldering house. "I'm just grateful no one was hurt. It's only stuff, right?"

"And it can all be replaced." Miss Taylor looked up at him, her gray eyes seeming to assess him. "Where will you and the children go tonight?"

That was the big question, wasn't it? Where would he find somewhere for them to stay? It was two days before Thanksgiving. So many motels would be full of holiday visitors. And then he'd have to find a place that would take not just him and the kids, but the dog, as well. "I honestly don't know."

"Well, I have an idea about that. You'll all stay with me."

A generous offer, but one he should refuse.

Miss Taylor didn't need them all descending on her house. "I couldn't do that to you."

"Why not? I have a house with plenty of room. And I'm certainly not going to let you sleep on the streets."

"It's not as desperate as that. There are plenty of options."

"And most of those are booked for the holidays."

He had to admit she was right, but he didn't feel comfortable accepting her offer. He knew her in passing, but to open her house to his family? He shook his head. "I can't impose on you."

"It's not an imposition if I'm offering. Come on, Christopher. It's the neighborly thing to do."

"Neighbors loan out lawn equipment or give extra vegetables from the garden. They don't invite a whole family to stay overnight."

"Well, this neighbor does." She eyed him, and he felt as if he couldn't tell her no to whatever she said next. "And I'm talking about more than overnight. I'm talking about you staying until you can find proper accommodations for the long term."

"But that could be days or weeks." He

shook his head again. "Miss Taylor, I really
do appreciate the offer, but I don't think this
is a good idea. You're—"

"If you say 'old,' I'll kick you in the shins.
I'm not sick, young man. I'm not past it yet.
And besides, I would enjoy the company. I
haven't had anyone living in the house with me
since my sister died..." Miss Taylor glanced
away for a moment, and when she turned back,
she had a determined gleam in her eyes. "You
and the children will stay with me."

"And what about Caesar? Where we go, he
goes, too."

Miss Taylor frowned at him, then put a hand
on the dog's head, giving him a scratch behind the ears. "Then he'll come with you. I've
never lived with a dog, but I always thought it
might be nice to have one."

"A firefighter saved him, you know." The
image of the firefighter giving the dog mouth-
to-mouth resuscitation came to mind. "She
ran into the house to find him and saved him."

"She?"

"I never got her name, though."

"It's Penny Cuthbert. She's my great-niece."
Miss Taylor called to the woman, indicating she
should come over.

Penny. It seemed a fitting name for the blonde angel who had been a bright spot in an otherwise dismal day.

PENNY THOUGHT SHE heard her name and lifted her head to find her great-aunt Sarah standing by the homeowner. Sarah gave her a wave, which Penny returned. She went to join them.

"I was just telling Christopher here that you worked for the Thora Fire Department, and here you are." Great-Aunt Sarah beamed at her. "He told me that you saved little Caesar."

The dog in question moaned softly from his owner's arms. The man snuggled him closer and asked, "Is there any way I can repay you for saving him?"

Penny shrugged. "Just part of my job. No repayment necessary." She glanced behind her. The rest of her team had started to wind hoses and store the equipment on the truck. She didn't want to get called out for anything else by the fire chief. "I should really get going." She pointed at her great-aunt. "We're still on for dinner after my shift tonight?"

Great-Aunt Sarah nodded. "Would you mind picking up an extra loaf of garlic bread to go with the spaghetti? Christopher and his children will be joining us."

Penny wasn't surprised at the generosity of her aunt, since Sarah had a tendency to open her dining room to anyone who needed a meal. "That's really nice of you."

"Well, it seems like I should cook dinner for them since they'll be moving in with me. At least temporarily."

Wait... Penny snapped her head in the man's direction. "What?"

"He needs somewhere to stay, and I offered my house. You know I have all those extra rooms."

Christopher shook his head. "I never said I would, Miss Taylor."

Her aunt shrugged. "You didn't agree yet, but you will."

No. That was not going to happen. The last thing her elderly aunt needed was to be catering to some guy and his kids. "He'll move in with you when farmers can get chocolate milk from cows."

CHAPTER TWO

CHRISTOPHER STARED AT the woman whom he'd thought of as his hero. Why was she so angry at Miss Taylor's generous offer? He put up a hand. "I never said we'd move in with your aunt."

"Good. Because you're not."

Tempted to contradict her just to take the smirk off her face, he instead counted to three, like he'd taught his children, before things were said that couldn't be taken back. At three, he drew in a deep breath. "Your aunt is very kind, but I don't think moving in with her is the best idea."

Miss Taylor started to protest, but Penny cut her off. "Exactly. She has enough going on that she doesn't need to take on anything else."

"I understand completely." And he did. This was his problem, not Miss Taylor's. "I'll find other arrangements."

Penny nodded at him. "If I can help…"

Miss Taylor cleared her throat. "If you two are finished deciding my life for me, I'd like to add something." She pointed at Penny. "You don't get to decide what I'm able to do. And you." She pointed at him. "Stop being too proud to accept a little help. You have two children to think about."

"I haven't stopped thinking about them." He placed Caesar on the grass next to his feet, then glanced at his watch. It was just past noon, with hours to go before the school day ended, but he wanted to see his kids. Wanted to hug them and assure himself that they could face even this. At least they'd be together. "In fact, I'll need to go to the school and tell them what happened."

"And take them where?" When he didn't answer, Miss Taylor smiled widely at him. "It's a short-term solution. That's it. Take a few days over the holiday to figure things out."

She had a point. Once Thanksgiving was over, motels would have open rooms. He only had to get through the next few days. Then he could move the family out of Miss Taylor's home. The question of how long they'd be without a house made his head hurt. Finally, he nodded. "Okay. But just for a few days."

"No." Penny stepped between her aunt and himself. She looked like an angel ready to do battle. "I won't let you move in. My aunt isn't able to take care of you all."

Her aunt smiled at her. "Then you can move in, too, and help me out. I'm sure Shelby wouldn't mind if you stayed with me for a while."

"That's not the point."

Miss Taylor gave her niece a stern look until Penny finally held up her hands. "Fine. Temporarily." She glared at him before turning on her heel and joining the rest of her squad.

He felt as if he'd just made an enemy, but Miss Taylor laughed it off. "Oh, we're going to have so much fun. Now leave the dog with me, and you go pick up your children and bring them over to my house. I can watch them while you go shop for those essentials you'll need. Toiletries. Some clothing. Whatever you think you'll need for the foreseeable future."

The weight of all he'd lost settled on his

shoulders, and the thought of all he would need to now replace made him want to weep.

CHRISTOPHER EXPLAINED TO the elementary-school office staff that he had to remove his children from school early, then waited while the kids were paged. Elijah ran through the office door and looked around until he saw him. His son launched himself into Christopher's arms. "When the teacher said I had to go to the office, I thought…"

Elijah didn't finish the sentence, but Christopher knew that his son was thinking about another Tuesday that he'd been paged, when Christopher had had to tell them that Julie was gone. Christopher pulled the boy closer to him. "I'm okay."

"Then why did you come get us?"

By then, Daisy had joined them. He didn't want so many eyes and ears in the school office to witness this moment, but telling them their house was gone while driving to Miss Taylor's didn't seem like a good option. Instead, he knelt before them and held their hands. "There was a fire at our house this morning. The firefighters did their best, but the house is ruined. We can't live there anymore, so we're going to stay with Miss Taylor at her house down the street for a few days until I can plan where we're going to live next."

The children stared at him as if he'd spoken Swahili. Finally, Elijah frowned. "What about Caesar?"

"A firefighter saved him. He's okay."

Daisy let out a breath she seemed to have been holding. "What about all our stuff?"

Christopher shook his head, and her mouth drooped, but she didn't cry. His strong little girl. He squeezed her hand and wished he could make it better. And he would, somehow.

Elijah sighed and gave a nod, standing straighter. "It will be okay." He glanced at his sister. "Right, Daisy?"

She bit her lip, but nodded.

Christopher stood and put his arms around his children before coaxing them to the car parked in the visitors' lot. Elijah opened the front passenger door, but held it open while Daisy took the coveted seat before he got into the back. Pride and love for them swelled in Christopher's heart as he settled behind the wheel and drove them to Miss Taylor's place.

They were good kids, and they'd recover from this, just as they had from everything else in their short lives.

PENNY FINISHED CLEANING the last bathroom before checking in with the fire chief. He motioned to a chair in front of his desk. "Sit."

She paused, but then lowered herself into the seat, waiting for a lecture she knew was coming. He wasn't that much different from her dad. She crossed her arms over her chest before he could start.

"What am I going to do with you, Cuthbert? You've been here less than ninety days, and I've had you scrub the pumper truck twice. KP duty for three weeks. Now cleaning the bathrooms, and nothing has gotten through that hard head of yours." Mac tapped a finger on his desk. "I am the fire chief. Not you."

Not yet. She had her eye on his job within the next two years. She had the education and the training to lead a squad, if she could only get the chance. She looked at him as he continued his lecture. "You are to take orders from me or Lieutenant Buckner, but somehow you've gotten the idea that you can go off and do what you want."

"That's not what I was doing."

He raised an eyebrow at her outburst. "Did I ask you to go in and save the dog?"

She lowered her gaze to her lap. "No, sir."

"You were expected to back up Johnson on the hoses. But when you ran into the house and abandoned your orders, you let down your team."

"I didn't come here to back up a firefighter who doesn't know as much as I do." She sat forward in her chair. "Chief, you know my experience. I'm better than this. I should be the one getting backup, not Johnson."

"And that's the crux of the problem. You think you're better than everyone here."

She bristled at the suggestion. "Not everyone, but a few, yeah."

Mac sighed wearily and ran a hand through what was left of his hair. "I need you to be a team player, Cuthbert. Not a hotshot star who thinks she knows what's best. I decide that. So going forward, I will write you up when you abandon your orders. Do we have an understanding?"

She shook her head, not believing what she

was hearing. "When I joined the firehouse, you promised that I would have a leadership role on the team after a year."

"It hasn't been three months yet."

"Yes, but you haven't given me a chance to prove myself, either."

"You need to prove to me that you can be a team player first, because frankly, you're not ready to be promoted."

Penny left his office, wanting to punch something. She realized that her shift had ended while the chief had been yelling at her. She changed in the locker room, glad to get into her civvies, then plucked her phone from her purse. Her aunt picked up on the first ring. "You need garlic bread, and what else?"

"Could you pick up milk and eggs, too? I thought I'd make a frittata for breakfast tomorrow morning."

Did kids like frittata? "Fine. And I'll go to Shelby's and pack my bag after dinner. I'm starving."

"Good. We are, too. See you in a little bit."

At the grocery store, Penny collected the items her aunt had requested, along with a couple of boxes of sugary cereal in case the kids didn't like frittata. She turned down the aisle to look at snack options and she almost ran into Christopher, who held a basket over one arm. "Did Aunt Sarah forget something else?"

He frowned at her and shook his head. "I needed to pick up toiletries to replace what we lost, and I thought I'd grab snacks that the kids might enjoy while I'm here at the store."

"I was thinking the same thing." She pushed her cart forward and plucked up a bag of barbecue-flavored chips with ripples. "Don't judge me, but these are my favorite. I could eat an entire bag by myself." She picked up another bag. "Or two."

Christopher looked as if he wanted to smile, but had trouble raising up the corners of his mouth. "The kids are partial to pretzels."

Penny reached in and grabbed two bags of pretzel twists at the same time Christopher leaned over. In close proximity, they bumped heads. Penny put the pretzel bags in her cart, then rubbed her forehead where it had connected with Christopher's. "You have a hard head."

"I could say the same about you."

This time he did smile at her, and she

thought he might be more attractive if he did it regularly. Attractive or not, it didn't change the fact that he had kids. And she'd been burned by a single dad before. No thanks. Not going to happen again.

Penny took stock of her cart. "We need something sweet. Cookies or ice cream?"

"Ice cream. Definitely."

Penny tightened her hands on the cart's railing. "Race you there." She took off down the aisle before she could see his reaction. Turning into the frozen aisle, she zigzagged around other shoppers and stopped in front of the ice-cream section, where Christopher was already waiting. But how? She frowned at him. "How did you get here so fast?"

"I wasn't pushing a cart."

She noticed his long legs. She was no shorty herself, but she barely reached his shoulder standing at full height. "Hmm, you have an advantage over me in the leg department, too."

He gave her a nod, then turned to look into the freezer. "Chocolate or vanilla?"

She wrinkled her nose. "Boring." She stood next to him and surveyed their options. "Ooh, chocolate peanut butter. Definitely that."

"I'll get a vanilla, too. Just in case."

She shrugged, knowing that some people preferred the predictable. She was definitely not one of those, but it appeared that Christopher was. Well, the world was filled with all types. He grabbed the carton of vanilla ice cream and faced her. "I really appreciate you getting on board with us staying with your aunt for a while."

"I still don't think it's a good idea, but that's why I'll be there. To make sure she's not spreading herself too thin. She is eighty-seven, after all."

"I don't think you give your aunt enough credit. I'm sure she understands her own limitations."

"No, she's more like my nana was. They give and give and give until there's nothing left." She stared at him. Hard. "I won't let that happen to her. I promised Nana I'd protect her."

"You love your aunt."

"Of course. She practically raised me." Penny looked down at her cart again. "I'm set. Unless you can think of anything else."

"Nope. I'll see you at the house?"

She pushed the cart to the cash registers at

the front of the store. For a moment, she'd enjoyed herself with Christopher. She'd have to remind herself that he was off-limits.

CHRISTOPHER PULLED BAGS out of the car's trunk, then walked up the sidewalk to Miss Taylor's house. Unlike most of the other homes in the neighborhood that had a sameness about them, this was a Queen Anne that looked as if it had been built in the previous century. If not the one before that. When he knocked on the door, he could hear Caesar barking from inside. Miss Taylor opened the old oak door. "You don't have to knock while you're staying here. In fact, remind me to give you a copy of the front-door key."

He followed her into the kitchen, where Penny was sitting at the counter with Daisy, coloring in a book. She glanced up at him as he placed the bags of food he'd purchased on the counter. "Did you get stuck in a long line?" she asked.

"I had a few more things to pick up."

She nodded and returned to coloring with a dark blue crayon. He wasn't sure what to make of her. At times, she seemed to possess a maturity similar to that of the seniors at the assisted-living home. But at other times, she acted closer to Daisy's age. He had to admit that he liked her younger, playful side.

Like when she'd raced him to the ice-cream freezer at the grocery store.

Julie would have done something like that. It was that side of her that had made him fall in love with her when he was twelve. Her imagination had known no bounds, and he'd loved listening to her read to their children. She'd try on different voices for each character, making the story come alive. Even after she'd gotten sick and had lost most of her energy, she hadn't stopped the bedtime ritual. She'd told him that it was something Elijah and Daisy would always remember. After she died, he'd tried to do the voices like she had, but knew he failed miserably. But his kids loved it, and he'd promised Julie he'd do it, so he kept trying.

He put the ice cream in the freezer, then opened the fridge to put in a gallon of chocolate milk and several packages of cheese. Miss Taylor's refrigerator seemed to be packed with food, which surprised him.

Most seniors he knew had a few basics, like bread and milk, but little else since they ate their meals in the cafeteria or out at a restaurant. As Mrs. Wellman, another resident, had told him once, she'd cooked enough meals in her time that she had earned the privilege of having someone else do the cooking for her.

A large turkey covered in plastic wrap rested in a shallow pan. Christopher straightened and thought about his mom, who lived several hours away from them. He'd have to call her and tell her about the change of plans for Thanksgiving. Where would they go? Like the motels, most restaurants would be packed and have taken reservations weeks ago. He closed his eyes and wondered if his family could join the assisted-living home for Thanksgiving dinner.

Miss Taylor put a hand on his shoulder. "You'll join us for dinner on Thursday, right?"

He turned and looked at the older woman. "You in the habit of reading minds?"

"I've been on this earth quite a long time, so I've gotten good at reading body language. And yours is shouting." She patted his shoulder once more. "Now, if you'll move, I'll get dinner started."

Christopher stepped back as she took out

a package of ground beef. "Anything I can do to help?"

"Why don't you get the garlic bread started while Penny makes a salad? And I'll have the children set the table in the dining room, since I doubt we'll all fit at the kitchen table."

Given his marching orders, he pulled the package of garlic bread from the freezer and opened the cupboard Miss Taylor indicated to find a sheet pan. The kitchen became a bustle of activity as everyone contributed to getting dinner ready. Fearing that his kids would break a plate, he supervised the setting of the table.

In the dining room, Elijah carefully placed a plate on the table and looked up at him. "How long are we staying here?"

"I don't know, buddy. At least through the weekend, but I'll be finding us somewhere we can live soon."

His son looked skeptical as he placed the next plate on the table. Daisy skipped to the next place to lay a napkin next to the plate. "I don't mind if we stay here forever. I like Aunt Sarah. And Penny is really cool."

Elijah sent her a dark look. "She's not our aunt, so don't call her that."

"She told us to call her that." Daisy nodded at Christopher. "If an adult says it's okay, then you can, right?"

"If she said to call her that, then yes." He put his hand on top of her dark curls. "She'll be watching you tomorrow while I go to work, so you'd both better behave."

"We will. She told us we're going to help her bake pies and get ready for Thanksgiving." Daisy looked up at him with shining eyes. "She said I can roll out the dough."

"You're a lucky girl, then."

She hummed as she continued to help her brother set the table. Despite losing their house, she seemed to have bounced back in record time. But then, she'd always been his smiling, happy child. It was Elijah he worried about. His dark attitude seemed to be getting gloomier already.

Christopher pulled his cell phone out of his pocket and held it up. "I'm going to go outside and call Grandma to tell her about the fire. Will you two be okay?"

They nodded and continued with their chore while he stepped onto the front porch and pressed the number to his mother's cell. She picked up on the fourth ring. "Hi, honey. Are you ready for my visit?"

With halting words, he told her about the fire and their temporary lodging. "If it was my house, you'd be more than welcome, but I don't feel comfortable inviting you to stay at someone else's home."

His mother was silent on the other end, and he waited for her to say something. Finally, she sighed. "You're right. I raised you better than to assume that you could do that. But I'd hate to not see you and the kids for Thanksgiving."

"I know. We'll make it up next year in our new house."

"You're not going to want to hear this, but maybe this is the sign that you should move back up here by me."

"But my job and the kids' school are here. A two-hour one-way commute between here and Lansing is not best for any of us."

"And your memories of Julie are also there."

He stared at the large tree in the front yard. A few leaves clung to the branches as if stubborn will would keep them there another year. "Mom, I can only concentrate on the next few days. There's time to discuss longer term later." He didn't want to pull the kids away from everything they knew. Starting over was hard even when it was the best circumstances, which these were not. There had been enough changes in the past couple of years that they shouldn't have to deal with more. "I promised Julie that I'd put the kids first."

"And how is moving closer to their grandmother not to their benefit? Lansing has jobs and schools, too, you know. I could change my work schedule to babysit when you're at your job and they're off school. We could have Sunday dinner at my house." She paused. "Just think about it. That's all I'm asking."

"This spaghetti sauce smells wonderful, Miss Taylor."

Penny's aunt waved off the formal name. "Please, it's Aunt Sarah. And the sauce is from a jar, so I didn't have much to do with how wonderful it smells or tastes."

Penny took the bowl of spaghetti noodles from Daisy and put a good portion on her plate, since this was her favorite meal. For years, Nana had made spaghetti and meatballs whenever life had disappointed Penny. Breakups, betrayals and bad test scores were all reasons for Nana to make it. She passed the bowl to her aunt, who put a smaller portion on her plate before passing it to Elijah.

Once meatballs and sauce had been added to her plate, along with a healthy portion of freshly grated Parmesan cheese, she set to eating.

Over the meal, they talked about the upcoming Thanksgiving dinner, where her extended family would descend upon poor Aunt Sarah to be fed and entertained. Although, her aunt didn't look too stressed or upset about it. She and Nana had always made holidays special in this house. From the decorations to the music to the food, no detail was missed.

There were never too many guests, she admitted, and everyone arrived hungry and always left stuffed and carrying lots of leftovers.

Then there were the games. If the Cuthberts were anything, they were competitive. They made bets on who would throw the best roll at Yahtzee or who would draw the most cards at Uno.

"Are you working on Thanksgiving, dear?"

She straightened in her chair, thinking that she'd been caught sneaking the dog a noodle.

With those big brown doggy eyes of his staring at her, she'd been a sucker and had given in to his begging. Looking at her aunt, she shrugged. "I volunteered to do the shift to give Johnson a chance to spend the holiday with his wife and kids."

"That was generous of you."

Again, she lifted her shoulders. "I figure since I'm single, my colleagues might as well have a chance to be with their families. That means I'll be at the station on Christmas Day, too."

Aunt Sarah gave her a look that seemed to say that she didn't quite believe her. It was true that she wanted to give her fellow firefighters a chance to spend time with their families, but some of her reasoning also had to do with wanting to work and put in her time to get that promotion she'd been promised.

If she could prove she was a team player.

But didn't giving up the holidays mean that? Maybe it took more than that in the chief's eyes. She'd have to talk to her dad and get his perspective.

"How many people are you expecting on Thursday?" Christopher asked.

Aunt Sarah counted off on her fingers. "More than twenty with you three now."

Daisy looked across the table at Christopher. "What about Grandma? She was supposed to come here."

"It's okay. I talked to her earlier, and we'll spend Thanksgiving with her next year."

"It's not fair." Daisy pouted.

Aunt Sarah reached over and touched Christopher's hand. "She could join us. What's one more person when I'm already feeding an army?"

"I can't ask you to do that."

"You're not. I'm offering." Her aunt glanced at her. "And I don't want to hear a word out of you."

Penny wiped the corners of her mouth with her cloth napkin. "Not saying a word."

"But you're thinking it."

Maybe Christopher was right about her aunt being able to read minds. Didn't Aunt Sarah realize what the stress of a holiday dinner for over twenty people would do to her? Granted, her family would bring dishes to add to the meal and help Aunt Sarah with cooking, but the bulk of it fell on her shoulders. Under her aunt's scrutiny, she sighed and held up her hands. "It's your choice."

"Exactly. And I choose to invite Christopher's mother to join us."

"Thank you, Miss Taylor. I'll call her after dinner."

"And what did I say about calling me Aunt Sarah?"

Dinner continued with the kids sharing about their last day of school before the Thanksgiving break. Daisy asked Aunt Sarah about the pies they'd make the next day, and Penny remembered how she'd helped to roll out the dough for the crust when she was Daisy's age. And how Nana had let her sprinkle the dough scraps with cinnamon and sugar to bake on their own. The thought of Nana being absent from this Thanksgiving made a part of her heart break. How she missed her wonderful grandmother. She smiled at her aunt, grateful that she still had her around.

"Oh, I forgot something," Christopher said and rose from the table, breaking her focus on the sweet memories.

A moment later, he returned with a glass of chocolate milk and set it in front of Penny.

"Seems I found a cow that gives chocolate milk."

Penny returned his smile and lifted the glass in salute.

CHAPTER THREE

AFTER DINNER DISHES had been cleared, rinsed and put into the dishwasher, Christopher started the usual bedtime routine with his children. Daisy took her bath first, followed by Elijah, who preferred showers. While they washed, Christopher laid out the brand-new pajamas he'd bought for them on their beds. Superhero pj's for Daisy, while Elijah's sported the Detroit Lions logo. He hoped that they would like them. He'd also bought another copy of the book they'd been reading, hoping to establish some sense of normalcy.

Once pajamas had been donned, Elijah joined them in the room Daisy would stay in for the next few days. "This used to be Penny's room when her dad had to work overnights," she told them. "Don't you love the pink?"

Elijah appeared skeptical, but Christopher knew Daisy gloried in her favorite color. He reached over and adjusted her pillow to find a familiar silky cape. He pulled it out. "Where did you find this?"

Daisy dropped her eyes to the pink comforter. "I know you said not to take it to school, but I put it in my backpack." She looked up at him with a triumphant gleam. "And isn't it lucky I did? Otherwise it would be burned up with everything else in the fire."

Christopher wanted to groan. He'd thought losing the cape would be a small victory courtesy of the fire. And yet maybe it would help his daughter cope with the upcoming changes. He rested a hand on the back of her head and leaned forward to kiss her above one eyebrow. "Yes. It was lucky."

He gathered his children closer, putting his arms around their small bodies. Caesar rested at the end of the bed, watching them. Christopher gave a nod to the dog, then looked down at his children. "We need to talk about things that will have to change because of the fire. Staying here is only temporary, and Miss Taylor has agreed to watch you while I'm at work tomorrow, and I expect you to be on your best behavior while we're here." He glanced at his daughter, then gave a longer stare to his son. Elijah could behave when he wanted to, but often he used his attitude to talk back and complain. "You are to show her respect and do what she tells you. Am I clear?"

Elijah stared back for a second, then gave a small nod.

"Good." He pressed a kiss on the top of his son's head. "Things aren't going to be easy for the next few weeks, so I need you both to trust me that I'll take care of everything. I'll find us a house that is better than the old one. We're going to be okay."

Elijah made a noise at the back of his throat, but Daisy nodded vigorously. "It's going to be just fine, Daddy. I know it. Christmas is coming, and that's the time miracles happen."

He wished his daughter was right, but Elijah appeared as skeptical as he felt. He didn't want to dim Daisy's optimism, so he ran a hand down her almost dry hair. "Well, we certainly could use one." He pulled the book off the nightstand next to the bed. "Now, where were we in the story?"

He opened the book and flipped to the chapter where they'd left off last night before their lives had changed so much.

PENNY OPENED THE closet doors and studied the few pieces of clothing hanging there. When she'd moved back from Florida to live with her cousin Shelby in her condo, she had promised herself that she'd go shopping for more weather-appropriate outfits but hadn't found the time. T-shirts and shorts weren't going to cut it in the Michigan snow that would soon arrive. She sighed and pulled a University of Florida hoodie off the hanger and started to fold it and place it in her duffel bag.

A knock on the bedroom door made her turn her head. Shelby entered the room and took a seat on the edge of the bed. "So you're really leaving me."

"Temporarily." She placed a stack of jeans in the bag next to the hoodie. "Aunt Sarah's going to need my help."

"More like you're keeping an eye on the neighbor."

Maybe she was. No one was going to take advantage of her great-aunt. Not on her watch. "You know how trusting she is."

Shelby furrowed her brow. "Actually, she's not. Nana was the one who would believe any sob story, while Aunt Sarah dug deep until she found the dirt. If she knows that she can trust this guy, then my money says this guy can be trusted."

"She's mellowed in her old age."

"Not as much as you think. But then, you haven't been around much until lately."

The words brought a flinch of guilt, and Penny paused in her packing. "I was finishing my degree."

"I realize that. No one's saying you're a bad person or anything. I'm just stating the reality."

"Truth is I wouldn't be here now if Alan hadn't left me."

"I don't know about that. You've always wanted to come back and take over Thora's fire department."

Penny wasn't convinced. She'd fallen in love with Alan and would have blindly followed where he led her. Luckily, he'd shown his true character before they'd said their wedding vows. "That's certainly the plan now."

Shelby pulled one leg under the other. "It's going to be quiet without you."

"I was only supposed to live in your spare bedroom a couple of months until I found my own place." She went to the dresser and pulled out socks and underwear. "Besides, I'll be back once the family moves to a new home."

"I know, but I'm still going to miss your annoying chatter in the morning."

When Penny would have protested, she turned to find her cousin smiling, on the verge of laughter. She could give as good as she got. "If anything, *I'll* miss your nagging about wiping the counters down after I make a sandwich."

"What can I say? I don't like crumbs." Shelby rose to her feet and put her arms on Penny's shoulders. "I am going to miss you, Pen. It was nice having a roommate."

Penny hugged her cousin, resting her head on Shelby's shoulder. "You could always ask Jack to move in."

Shelby slapped the back of Penny's head. "Not likely. He'd bring one of his patients here and dirty up my beautiful condo." She wrinkled her nose. "Remember when he found the skunk that got hit by a car and nursed it back to health? Then was shocked when it sprayed him."

Penny shook her head. "I was in Tallahassee for that one."

"Trust me. It wasn't fun being around him then." Shelby glanced around the room. "What can I do to help you?"

"I'm almost finished." She looked at her cousin and tried to smile. "I don't think I thanked you for letting me stay here. If I had a sister, I'd want her to be like you."

"You're welcome. It's what family does."

"My dad didn't offer to have me stay with him."

Shelby shrugged as if it shouldn't hurt Penny that he hadn't asked her. "You know your dad. He probably thought he'd cramp your style or something. I'm sure he would have had you move in if I hadn't stepped in first and insisted you camp out here with me."

"You've always been bossy."

"It's gotten me this far, hasn't it?"

Penny zipped up the bag and slung it over her shoulder. "We'll do a cousins' dinner on Friday night?"

"You bet."

Back at Aunt Sarah's house, she walked upstairs to Nana's old bedroom and placed her duffel bag on the freshly made bed. "Thought

I heard you come back." Aunt Sarah entered the room and opened a dresser drawer. "I emptied one for you and made some space in the closet. I really should get in here and clean her things out."

Penny scanned the room that looked much as it had when Nana had been alive. "I keep expecting her to walk in and tell me to stand up straight."

"She worried about your posture."

"More than just that. She worried that I'd turn out like my father. Alone and obsessed about my career." She started pulling things out of the bag and placing them in the dresser. "Maybe she was right to worry."

Aunt Sarah helped her unpack, hanging a few things in the closet. "You are not your father. Just like you're not your mother. You are Penelope Mae Cuthbert, and you don't have to try to be anyone but her."

"Now you sound like Nana."

"She was my sister, after all."

Aunt Sarah stood beside her and put a hand on her shoulder, and Penny felt as if she'd gone back in time, to when she was almost a teenager and wondering what her life would turn out to be. She might be older, but she still wondered if she'd made the right choices to get where she was.

"Once you're finished unpacking, come and join me downstairs in the family room. I saved the latest episode of our show. I'll even make popcorn."

"Actually, I'm not in the mood for television tonight. I was thinking of taking a quick shower and going to bed early. We can watch it another night?"

"Okay. Towels are in the hall closet." Aunt Sarah headed for the door, then turned to face her. "She'd be proud of you, you know. She always hoped you'd come back and join the fire station here."

"Thanks."

Her aunt pressed a kiss to her forehead before leaving the room. Penny finished unpacking, folding her duffel bag and placing it on a shelf in the closet. She heard a door down the hall close and poked her head out to see Christopher leaving her old room. He gave her a nod, then walked downstairs.

The thought of going to bed early fled, so she turned off the bedroom light and joined Christopher and her aunt in the family room. Her aunt looked surprised when she took a seat on the sofa next to her. "I thought you were tired."

"Changed my mind."

Her aunt pointed the remote at the television and found the last episode of the police drama they were both addicted to. She paused the program before it began and spoke to Christopher. "I hope you don't mind watching this, but Penny and I are obsessed."

"I don't mind at all. Every Friday night, it was my job to get the kids in the tub and in bed, so my wife could watch it." He smirked. "Then I'd join her on the couch and cuddle." He looked away from them, seeming to be lost in memories.

To break the sad mood, Penny got to her feet. "I'll make the popcorn. What can I get you both to drink?"

They settled with popcorn and drinks in front of the television a few minutes later. Aunt Sarah started the show and fell asleep about ten minutes into it, the dog sitting on her lap and snoring, too. Christopher glanced at her. "Should we turn the program off so she doesn't miss anything?"

"Are you kidding me? She hasn't watched an entire episode since we started this season." She tucked the crocheted afghan over her aunt's shoulders. "She'll doze off and on the entire time."

As if on cue, Aunt Sarah's eyes fluttered open, and she took a handful of popcorn from the bowl on Penny's lap. Penny grinned at Christopher and brought her attention back to the show.

Once the show ended, Aunt Sarah had fallen asleep again. Penny stuck a finger in front of her mouth and picked up their bowls and glasses before tiptoeing into the kitchen. Christopher followed her as she started to rinse them off and place them in the almost full dishwasher. He looked behind him into the family room. "Will she wake up and go to her bedroom? I wouldn't mind, but she's sitting on my bed."

Penny filled the dishwasher with soap, then shut the door and turned it on. "Not a problem. I'll get you the sheets and blankets for the sofa bed, then wake her and walk her to her bedroom."

"I can give you a hand with that."

He followed her out of the kitchen and up the stairs to the hall closet that housed the linens. She tried to pull a set of sheets from the top shelf, but couldn't quite reach it. She tried to jump and get them, but Christopher leaned in close to her and retrieved them easily. She turned to look up at him. "It's handy to have a tall man around here."

He shrugged. "My mom always said that."

"Sounds like a wise lady."

"I always thought so. Even as a teenager, I saw her as the coolest mom who had the best advice."

Penny pointed to the stack of blankets next to where the sheets had been. "Take as many as you need. My nana always had extras for company."

Again he leaned close to her, and her heart clenched at his nearness. Penny frowned at the reaction. She wasn't interested in Christopher. Not even the tiniest bit.

And she'd keep repeating it until her heart believed what her brain already knew.

CHRISTOPHER LAY IN the darkness of the family room, Caesar sleeping next to him. He put his hand on the dog's head and ran his hand down his silky neck. This was not how he had pictured his day ending—lying on a strange sofa bed in someone else's home.

He rested his forearm on top of his head. If Julie had been here, what would she have done? Probably left it all up to him to take care of. She might have been a wonderful mother and a fun wife, but she hadn't been good at taking care of details. He'd been the one to find their house. To take care of the bills. To make sure there was food in the fridge.

The thoughts made him pause. He shouldn't be thinking like that about his dead wife.

"Daddy?"

He startled and turned to find Elijah standing next to the sofa bed. "What's wrong, son?"

"I had a bad dream. Can I sleep down here with you?"

"Sure." Christopher scooted over and pulled the dog closer to his side, then folded down the blankets to make room for Elijah. "Come on in."

Elijah got under the sheets and curled into a ball next to him. Christopher put a hand on top of his son's head and stroked the curls that he loved but Elijah hated. "Do you want to talk about the dream?"

"No."

The family counselor wanted Elijah to open up more about his feelings, but Christopher didn't want to push. He knew his son would share when he was ready. "Okay, buddy. Let's get some sleep."

He listened to his son's breathing until it slowed into a regular pattern. Then he settled into the pillows.

The middle of the night seemed to be when he'd think of his wife the most. Almost as if she waited until the kids were in bed before she visited his mind. Tonight was no exception. *What am I going to do, Julie? Where are we going to go?*

Unfortunately, she never answered him even though he could use her advice.

He rubbed Caesar's soft ears. Aunt Sarah's house was a temporary solution, as comforting as it was. He could see that the kids liked the older woman, and she liked them. Even the dog seemed to have developed a bond with her.

And then there was Penny. In some ways, she reminded him of Julie, especially her playful attitude. But that was a dangerous path to follow. Penny could never replace his wife. She couldn't be the spark of joy and light of life that his wife had been in their family.

No, he'd had the love of his life once. It didn't happen twice.

PENNY WOKE WITH a start when the alarm on her phone started blaring. She hadn't remembered to change it to a later time, since she had the day off and didn't need to be at the fire station.

She gathered jeans and a hoodie along with some clean underwear and peeked out into the hallway. No one there, so hopefully the bathroom was free. She walked to the door, but it was shut, with steam coming out from underneath.

Shoot. Probably Christopher getting ready for work. She started to walk back to her bedroom when the door opened, and the man in question appeared in the doorway with damp hair and wearing a shirt that still had the creases from the package. He flinched at her standing in the hallway in her T-shirt and boxers that she wore to bed. She glanced behind him into the bathroom. "Are you finished?"

"Yes. Sorry. I hadn't expected to see you up this early."

"Bad habit, I know."

He still stood in the doorway, blocking her access to the bathroom. She pointed at him. "So can I get in?"

"Right." He stepped aside to let her pass.

Before she shut the door, she looked up into his face and gave him a wink.

Resting her head against the closed door, she thought about her action. She'd winked at him. Winked. Why? She didn't need him getting ideas, but her eyes seemed to have other plans.

After showering and dressing, she went downstairs to the kitchen, where Aunt Sarah was sitting at the counter reading the morning paper and drinking coffee. "Penny, I wasn't expecting you up this early."

"We've got a lot to do today, right?"

"True." She motioned to the coffee maker with her mug. "Coffee's freshly brewed. I came downstairs to find that Christopher had already made it."

Christopher winced. "I hope that was okay."

"More than okay. Feel free to make it every

morning that you're here. I haven't had a man make me coffee since Jerry was alive."

"Your husband?"

"My grandpa," Penny clarified. "Aunt Sarah never got married."

Christopher raised an eyebrow at this statement, but Aunt Sarah didn't give any explanations. Penny added sugar to her coffee mug, then joined her aunt at the counter. Christopher took a final sip of coffee, then rinsed his mug and placed it in the kitchen sink. "I should be home at four. Four thirty at the latest. You have my cell phone if you need me."

Aunt Sarah waved off the suggestion. "We'll be fine. The kids are going to help Penny and I get ready for tomorrow. I thought I'd show them how to make a papier-mâché cornucopia for a centerpiece for the table."

"Thank you again for watching them today."

"My pleasure. Now, you go to work and don't worry a minute about us."

Christopher nodded and walked out of the house. Penny turned to her aunt. "I hope you know what you're doing with them."

"I'm being a good neighbor. If my sister was here, she'd be doing the same thing."

Penny shook her head. "You barely know the guy."

"I know him better than you. He's been my neighbor for six years, after all. True, we didn't do much beyond waving at each other, but that's all changed." Aunt Sarah folded the newspaper and placed it next to her coffee mug. "Now, get a pen and a piece of paper, and let's plan our strategy for today."

Penny narrowed her eyes at her aunt. "You're sounding a lot like Shelby."

"Where do you think she learned it from?"

PENNY PULLED THE crocheted afghan off the back of the sofa and laid it over Daisy, who murmured something in her sleep, then tucked her hand under her chin. Asleep, the girl looked sweet and innocent. Penny would never have expected her to be so…energetic when awake.

Not that the little girl was bad. Rather, she had a lot of "go, go, go" that required an adult's constant attention. Penny could use a nap herself, but they still had a dozen things to scratch off Aunt Sarah's to-do list before the next morning.

In the kitchen, Penny found Elijah sitting on a stool at the breakfast bar, doodling something in a notebook. When she tried to get a peek, he closed it and clutched it to his chest. "What are you drawing?" she asked in a low voice, trying to go along with it being a secret.

"Nothing."

"Nothing, huh?"

Elijah didn't say anything else. Instead, he silently scooted off the stool and left the room. Penny was disappointed. It was easy to find ways to connect with Daisy, but not with her brother. Penny had been an only child with mostly girl cousins, so she knew how to relate to them. Little boys were a mystery to her. Maybe she was making too much of it? After all was said and done, Penny wouldn't have to worry about trying to earn his affection. They wouldn't be around each other once the holiday was over and the Fox house situation figured out.

Aunt Sarah cleared her throat as she entered the kitchen. "You look deep in thought."

"It's nothing." Great. Now she sounded like the kid. "Nothing worth mentioning."

Aunt Sarah gave her a look, but didn't pursue the comment. She picked up her notepad, where she'd written down everything that needed to be done for Thanksgiving prep. "Dora down the street called. Her son and his family canceled their plans with her, so I invited her to join us."

"Of course you did." The more, the merrier was her aunt's outlook. "Did my dad say he's coming?"

Aunt Sarah nodded, but didn't look at her.

"Did you tell him I moved in here?"

At that, Aunt Sarah did glance at her. "No. I figured that's a conversation for the two of you to have. I can't keep being your go-between."

"Dad and I don't have conversations." She couldn't remember when they had stopped talking to each other. After the wedding that never was? Maybe. When she'd decided to come back to Thora, at least. Had he been disappointed in her giving up her seniority at the Florida station and coming home to start on the bottom rung? Truth was, they'd never been close enough to talk about things that mattered. Part of her hoped that moving back here would change that.

"We'll wash the good china tonight, and the linens are in the dryer. I'll leave it to you to iron and fold them."

Penny wrinkled her nose at that order. "Why iron them if they're just going to get balled up and washed again tomorrow after dinner?"

"Presentation! It might be kind of fun to try to teach the kids how to fold the napkins properly."

"If they'll even listen to me."

"Daisy listens."

"And Elijah ignores." She sighed and leaned on the counter, resting her cheek on her fist. "I'm usually pretty good with kids. But him, I can't reach."

"He doesn't want to be reached. He prefers being ignored."

"But why?"

"Then he won't have to get attached to someone who could leave."

"I'm just trying to be friendly, not be his mom."

Aunt Sarah made a noise that sounded like a tsk, but that didn't seem like her aunt at all.

Penny huffed. "Seriously. I learned my lesson. If I'm a mom, it won't be to kids who aren't mine. It's too much work."

"Since when did working hard make you stop from doing something?"

"I won't argue with you on that because I'm not going to be their mom. For that to happen, I'd have to marry their father. And that's definitely not going down."

"And why not? Christopher is a good-looking man."

Penny couldn't disagree with that assessment. "It takes more than good looks to make a happy marriage."

"He's also a good man, period. Full stop. One that would help you find a balance between being a firefighter and the rest of your life."

Penny peered at her aunt. "I'm doing just fine the way I am."

"You work too hard. Don't think I didn't notice that you agreed to do holiday shifts, instead of spending time with the family. Or is it your dad that you're avoiding?"

"What else is left on your to-do list?"

Aunt Sarah glanced at it, then up at her. "I understand that having your heart broken makes you wary of anything resembling a personal life, but how long can you use work to evade what you need? What will make your life better. Richer."

"What I need is to earn my promotion. Not

play mom to these kids or see pity from the family. And definitely not to bother talking to my dad."

She pushed off the counter and took the dog leash from where it hung near the door to the garage. At the sight of it in her hands, Caesar started tapping his front legs on the floor. "I'm taking the dog for a walk."

"Your problems will still be waiting for you when you stop running away."

Penny left the kitchen and bundled up before opening the front door. Outside, the air held a hint of the cold weather to come. She put one hand into her jacket pocket and started walking down the street, Caesar trying to pull her along faster than her legs wanted to carry her.

In front of the Fox house, she found Elijah sitting on the sidewalk, staring up at what remained of the place. Should she say something to him? He turned to look at her, then immediately looked back at the burned home, so that answered that question.

Still, she stopped beside him and stared up at the wreck before shifting her gaze to him. "You're supposed to tell someone if you're leaving the house."

He shrugged. "This is my house."

"You know what I mean, E."

He bristled at the nickname. "My name is Elijah." He scowled at her. "Are you going to tell my dad on me?"

She bent at the knees, sat on the cold cement next to him and looked up at the house.

Caesar lay on the ground next to Elijah and the boy reached out a hand to the dog.

"Sorry about the fire."

Elijah let out a grunt that she couldn't interpret. He rested his chin on his knee as he stared at the damage the fire had caused. "Whatever."

"I know that losing things, like a house or a parent, is tough. And you got a double dose."

Elijah frowned at her. "I didn't *lose* my mom, like I put her somewhere and I can't remember where. She *died* of cancer."

Penny started to reach out to him but dropped her hand when he leaned away. "My mom died, too, when I was a baby, so I know what it's like to miss a parent. You don't have to cope on your own, kid."

"You don't know anything about me."

Penny looked up at the house, then back at Elijah. "I do know we should go back to my aunt's. It's too cold to be sitting on the ground, staring up at a house."

"You go back. I'm staying."

"Why? It's not like you can change anything by just sitting here and doing nothing." Penny paused. The words had hit her, echoing what Aunt Sarah had been telling her about her own relationships. She couldn't change anything between her and her father by doing nothing. Nor would that help her personal life. She smiled, then put her hand on Elijah's shoulder. "Come on. I'll get you a snack at Aunt Sarah's."

He shrugged off her touch. "I'm not hungry, and I said I'm staying."

"It's freezing. We're going."

"You're not my mom. You don't get to tell me what to do."

This time she used her professional firefighter's voice, usually saved for telling folks to get to safety or to stay back from the scene. "I don't want to be your mom, but with your dad gone, you will listen and obey when I tell you to stand up and return to the house." When he still didn't move, she raised her voice just enough. "Now."

Elijah scowled, but stood and began to

walk toward the house. She got to her feet and followed him, the dog at her heels.

WHEN CHRISTOPHER LEFT work to officially start the holiday weekend, he didn't feel the usual excitement that a four-day break might otherwise give him. Instead, the time ahead stretched with confusion and uncertainty. He'd been able to reach the insurance adjuster, who would meet with him the following Monday morning. He'd called the fire chief, but he hadn't given him a definite answer about the cause of the fire. The inspector's report was still pending.

He turned onto his street and had to pass the shell of his former house before pulling into Miss Taylor's driveway. He noted that Penny's car was there. The thought of her made the coming evening seem a little better.

When he knocked on the front door, he heard a lot of activity inside the house, and his daughter shouted, "I'll get it!"

She opened the door and looked up at him. "Oh. It's just you, Daddy."

"Just me." He noted that she wore the silky cape tied to her neck. "Were you and your brother good for Miss Taylor?"

"Of course we were."

She grabbed his hand and led him to the kitchen, where all the activity seemed to be centered. The radio blared a Christmas carol as Elijah sprinkled cheddar cheese over a large casserole dish filled with macaroni and cheese, Penny bent over to check the oven and Miss Taylor placed a cookie sheet that held two pies on a cooling rack. Even from the doorway, the baking smelled wonderful. Penny turned to see him standing there. "Welcome to the madness."

The heat from the room had made her blond curls frizz up around her face even though she had pulled them back with a hair tie. With the frizzy hair and pink cheeks, she looked as if she'd been working hard, but a smile still graced her lovely face.

"You've been busy today." He took off his jacket and placed it over his arm.

And they had. Besides the two fresh pies, there were four more waiting on racks on the counter. A large pot of peeled and diced potatoes sat on top of the stove, waiting to be cooked. His children looked to be making dinner.

"I hope you don't mind homemade macaroni and cheese."

Mind? He'd never had mac and cheese made from scratch. Unless you counted one that came in a blue box with powdered cheese. "It would be a treat."

"Well, that's fine." Miss Taylor pointed to the dining room. "If you would set the table, we should be ready to eat in the next twenty minutes."

He left the busy kitchen and hung up his coat in the hall closet before entering the dining room, where it looked like they'd been busy, as well. On the sideboard, a homemade papier-mâché cornucopia sat beside handprint turkeys. He recognized his children's writing on them and figured they'd been productive on their day off from school. If the house hadn't burned down, they would have spent the time at the seniors' home, with Elijah keeping an eye on his younger sister and complaining that he was bored.

Maybe there was a small silver lining to this after all.

"DADDY, YOU WON'T believe all the stuff we did today—not just the art, although that was my favorite."

Christopher didn't want to dampen his daughter's enthusiasm, but her nonstop chatter meant her food was getting cold. "That's great, Daisy, but don't forget to eat your dinner." She had his wife's tendency to talk through dinner rather than eat. He put the napkin beside his son's plate in his son's lap and scooted his glass of milk out of the danger zone near the edge of the table. This was familiar even if the presence of two females was not.

Aunt Sarah folded her used napkin and placed it next to her plate as she looked at him. "Christopher, I hate to ask this after you worked all day, but would you mind bringing up the card tables from the basement after dinner?"

"No problem."

"And, Penny, maybe you could give him a hand with the chairs?"

Daisy sat forward in her chair. "I can help."

"They're too heavy for you, sweetheart, but I appreciate you volunteering." Miss Taylor put a hand over one of his daughter's. "You've got a very sweet girl here."

Next to him, Elijah muttered something too low for him to hear. He cleared his throat, and his son looked up at him, two dots of color on his cheeks. "Finish your supper, then help Miss Taylor clear off the table."

The boy said nothing until Christopher raised an eyebrow at him. Finally, he gave a terse nod. "Yes, sir."

"Such a helpful boy." Miss Taylor smiled down the table at Elijah. "Your children were amazing help getting ready for tomorrow's big celebration."

"I'm glad to hear they weren't any trouble."

"None at all."

"Can I get the special dessert now?" His daughter seemed to vibrate in her chair from the excitement of it.

"Once everyone has finished eating, dear."

Christopher placed a hand on his full stomach. "I don't think I have room for dessert after three helpings of mac and cheese. That was the best I've ever eaten."

"Trust me, Daddy. You'll want to have some." She smiled at him from across the table before looking over to Penny and covering her mouth and giggling.

Everyone seemed to be finished with eating, so Penny and Daisy disappeared into the kitchen. When they returned, they held a plate of what looked like pieces of dough twisted and dusted with cinnamon sugar. Daisy took the plate over to him and held it out. "Try one, Daddy. They're delicious."

He took one and bit into it. His daughter was right about it being tasty. He finished chewing and swallowed, then told her, "Very good."

"Penny and I made them with the leftover dough from the piecrusts."

"I helped, too," Elijah added, his brow furrowed at being excluded by his sister.

Penny put a hand on Elijah's shoulder, but the boy flinched and backed away from her touch. "He made perfect twists, don't you think?"

"You did. These are excellent."

Elijah's frown lessened as Daisy held out the plate for her brother to take a couple. Christopher swiped a few more before his daughter gave some to Miss Taylor.

"I'll get those tables, Miss Taylor." In the basement, Christopher looked over the paraphernalia that seemed to completely fill the space.

Penny moved aside boxes as she navigated

toward the farthest wall, then cheered. "Found them!"

He followed the path she'd made to find the card tables, which were resting against one wall flanked by several dozen folding chairs. He took a table underneath each arm and carried them upstairs to the dining room, where Elijah wiped off the first table. Penny followed him with another table and a chair and pointed at the entranceway to the living room. "We'll set some of these up by the fireplace. And put more in the family room."

He let her walk into the room first, then set up the tables where she indicated. It took a few more trips from the basement to bring up all the chairs, which Penny unfolded and set around the tables. She brought out a few more rags, and they wiped down the other tables before Miss Taylor covered them all with tablecloths that smelled of fresh laundry soap.

"How many did you say were going to be here tomorrow?" Christopher asked as he wiped down another folding chair and counted the seats.

"With the three of you and your mother, about twenty-six if everyone shows. And we always make room for stragglers." Sarah smiled at the number. "We haven't had a family gathering here since my sister died earlier this year. She'd be so happy to see everyone in the house."

"You hosted a lot of these?"

"My sister and her husband loved having their family around them. Lila would use any excuse to invite everyone over." Sarah tugged on one of the tablecloths to even the sides. "It might have been a lot of work, but she enjoyed it." She straightened and sighed. "And so do I. Can you give Penny a hand with bringing up the good china?"

Back down in the basement, Penny searched through more boxes until she found the dishes. "Thank you for doing this. I volunteered earlier today, but she insisted that we wait for you."

"It's a small payment for everything your aunt is doing for us."

Penny nodded and grunted as she lifted a box to place it in his arms. "You might want a refund after we carry these upstairs."

Several trips later, the kitchen floor held about a dozen boxes of china that had to be unwrapped, washed and dried by hand. Sarah put Penny on wash duty, while, by her side, he dried and stacked the plates, bowls and cups on the kitchen counter. He could hear the television program his children watched in the family room, and for a moment he had to stop swiping the dish he held.

It had been a long time since he'd been a part of a family like this. Growing up, it had been just him and his mom. When he married Julie, he'd inherited her parents and two brothers. They'd included his mom on the family holidays, and he'd spent many hours helping his father-in-law set up tables and his mother-in-law wash dishes. After Julie died, he'd gone to a few of the family holidays, but felt as if a chasm had opened between him and his in-laws. Eventually, it had gotten easier to have his own celebration with the children and his mom. He didn't keep his kids from their grandparents, but it was easier if he kept his distance.

Maybe he'd been wrong. Because helping Penny and Sarah prepare for Thanksgiving felt right somehow. And he looked forward to the holiday, rather than dreading those moments when he'd turn to find Julie and be met by an empty place. He cleared his throat to stop the emotions from overflowing.

Penny turned to look at him questioningly, but he shook his head. As if it was nothing.

But it was so much more.

Penny put a hand on his shoulder. "I've got the rest of these if you want to go sit with your kids."

He glanced at the stack left to be washed. "It's fine. I'll help, and then we can both sit and relax."

"Until Aunt Sarah finds us another chore." She shook her head as she rinsed a cup before handing it to him. "Don't think I haven't noticed how she keeps throwing us together while she and the kids work somewhere else."

He frowned at her words. "Why would she do that?"

Penny glanced over her shoulder, then at him. "No offense, but I bet she's matchmaking."

He sputtered at the idea. Matchmaking? The two of them together? He hadn't thought of being with a woman, any woman, since Julie. "I don't… It's not that… I mean, you seem…" He ran a hand through his hair.

"Don't worry. I'm not interested in you, either." She laughed and patted his arm. "Don't get me wrong. You're nice and all, but I'm not interested in you."

"Good." He glanced at her, hoping he hadn't offended her. "I mean, you're pretty cool, but I don't date."

"Ever?"

"Julie's the only woman I've been with. I wouldn't know what to do on dates now."

Penny considered him, then sank her hands back into the suds. "Let me guess. High-school sweethearts?"

"We met in sixth grade, actually, and that was it for both of us." He tried to keep his tone light. "I knew the moment she picked me to be her lab partner."

"That's kind of sweet."

"What about you?"

He didn't know why her answer would matter, but it did. And he waited to see what she'd say. Instead, she kept her gaze on the sink. "No boyfriend."

"Ever?"

She thrust a saucer into his hand. "Don't really want to talk about it."

"Hey, I just bared my soul to you. It's only fair."

She eyed him and then shrugged. "I was

supposed to get married this past August, but he changed his mind the night before, so no wedding."

"Ouch."

"Exactly." She rinsed another dish and handed it to him. "So, I moved back from Florida and started at the fire station a couple months ago."

"He was an idiot."

She startled and Christopher realized he'd said the words aloud. "I mean, you're beautiful. Smart. And you're great with kids. At least with mine, if Daisy's opinion means anything."

Her lips tightened into a straight line. "But not good enough for some, apparently." She thrust the next cup into his hands. "How about we finish these dishes and take a break?"

"Sure."

He dried the cup, and they completed the task in silence. He wished that he could comfort her since the pain seemed to still bother her. But she was tight-lipped and hurried through their chore.

Glancing at her, he realized that she really was attractive, with her big blue eyes and a mouth that was usually tipped up in a smile.

Her beauty went beyond the exterior, too. In fact, in different circumstances, maybe in a different world, he would have asked her out on a date.

When the last saucer was stacked on the counter, he put a hand on her shoulder. "I didn't mean to bring up bad memories."

"It's nothing I can't get over." She eyed him, then smiled. "Maybe Aunt Sarah's matchmaking efforts are working. There's nothing more romantic than washing dishes together."

She took a step toward him and looked up into his eyes. He felt his heart start to jackhammer inside his chest where she laid a hand on it. "Penny…"

And then she laughed. "Gotcha."

He wasn't sure if he felt relieved or disappointed as she spun on her heel, winked and left the kitchen.

CHAPTER FOUR

CHRISTOPHER WOKE WITH a jolt to realize that
Elijah had again joined him on the sofa bed
during the night. He pulled the covers to the
boy's ears. His curly hair reminded him of
Julie's complaints about her own. She'd hated
the natural wave that made her hair frizz during the humid summer days. He felt a sudden
overwhelming surge of both love and protec-
tion for his son. He'd do anything for this boy
and his sister.

Movement in the kitchen alerted him to
Aunt Sarah's presence. He slipped out from
under the blankets and padded barefoot to
find her struggling with the turkey in the
kitchen sink. "Here. Let me."

She jumped at his voice, but got out of his
way to let him pull the slippery turkey from
the sink and into the roasting pan.

Aunt Sarah put a hand on his arm. "Thank
you. I was able to get it out of the fridge, but

that's as far as I could manage." She pointed behind him. "I made the coffee extrastrength for today."

He retrieved a mug from the cupboard and poured the rich brew into it. He held the carafe high. "You need a top-up?"

"I'd love one." She held out her mug, and he topped it off for her.

"How long have you been up?" he asked as he returned the carafe to the machine.

"Since Penny left for work at three."

"I don't know how she does it." He grimaced at the mention of the early hour. Sarah chopped up celery and onions, then sautéed them before adding them to the cubed bread in a large bowl. She stirred before adding spices and stirring again. He'd never made stuffing himself, although he had watched his mother do it when he was growing up. But she'd used a box instead of making it from scratch.

"She's used to the long hours and early starts, but then, she grew up with a father who was fire chief. She knew what to expect when she took the job." She looked up from the bowl. "You want to taste it?"

She held out the bowl, and he plucked out a

hunk of bread and popped it into his mouth. The spices played on his tongue, and he nodded. "It's really good. Best I've had."

"It's not as good as my sister's was, but it's still tasty." She then poured broth over the mixture and stirred it again.

"What time are you expecting everyone here?"

"Shelby said she'd come early, probably about ten, but the rest will be here closer to noon, in time for kickoff. The Lions are playing." She paused her stirring. "What time did you tell your mom we'd be eating?"

"You said about two."

"Thereabouts. With this family, we tend to go with the flow. Unless Shelby is in charge, of course. Then we're right on time."

"And you follow her orders?"

Aunt Sarah gave a shrug. "That girl is a natural born leader who tends to take charge when no one else will. So we'll be eating at two. Trust me on that one."

"My family has the bad habit of running late."

"Well, every family's different. But what's important is the love, right? Doesn't matter if we're early or late. Big or small. Even when you get to my age, what matters is that we come together and celebrate. Spend time with each other. There's no bond like the one you have with your family." She took a long pull of her coffee, then set down the mug on the counter. "Well, this bird isn't going to stuff itself."

"Do you want me to do the honors?"

"Would you? I never liked this part, so my sister, Lila, always did it."

She stepped away from the turkey so that he could get access. Grabbing large clumps of soggy bread, he marveled at the fact that in eight hours it would transform into one of his favorite holiday dishes. He'd been known to eat leftover stuffing for breakfast the morning after, straight out of the plastic container. Aunt Sarah showed him how to put some in the neck area, as well as the cavity, then supervised as he put the rest in a large casserole pan to be baked separately.

He opened the oven to place the stuffed bird inside and frowned. "How are we going to fit all the side dishes in this oven?"

She waved off his worry. "Most will arrive already made, and the extra stuffing will bake once I take the turkey out of the oven to rest."

"Rest?"

"You don't cut into it right away or the juices will drain out and make the meat dry. Trust me. I've been making Thanksgiving dinner for almost sixty years."

"How long have you lived here?"

"My sister asked me to move in with her and her husband shortly after her oldest son, Mark, was born. It was only meant to be temporary, but I've lived here ever since."

"You never married?"

"Came close once, but it wasn't meant to be. He left me to fight in Korea. We were so young. It was more common then, not so much now. Now a lot of people wait. What for, I'm not always sure."

Aunt Sarah didn't expound on that, but Christopher felt there was more to the story. "Maybe Penny should have waited? She mentioned that her fiancé called off her wedding the night before it was supposed to happen."

Aunt Sarah shook her head. "The whole family flew to Florida to be a part of her special day, and then that weasel backed out at the last minute. I volunteered to track him down and make him suffer, but she insisted that she'd be okay. And she has been."

"She seems to be a strong person."

"That's how we make them in this family, as you'll soon find out." She removed her apron and refilled her coffee mug. "Now we can rest a little. I'd suggest watching the morning news in the family room, but you had an extra guest in your bed."

"Second night in a row he's come down and joined me."

"You're worried about him."

"I'm worried about them both. Elijah doesn't talk about what's bothering him, but lets it fester until he explodes." Christopher stared into the dark depths of his mug. "He'd been getting better, but this fire set him back. Daisy, too. I'm sure you've noticed the superhero cape."

"She wore it nonstop yesterday. I wondered about it."

"She claims it protects her."

"And you don't believe her?"

He looked across the counter at her. "Scraps of silk material don't protect anyone from anything. You know that."

"She believes it does, so what can it hurt?"

"And what happens when it doesn't protect her and she does get hurt?" He shook his head. "The counselor and I both agree that we need to break her dependency on it."

"All kids pretend things, but they know they aren't real. She knows the cape is just a cape, but pretending helps her cope."

"So you're a child psychologist now?"

"I have my master's in early childhood education and ran a preschool for almost fifty years. I'm sharing what I've learned from experience." She gave him a warm smile. "You're a good father, and they love you so much. Everything was 'wait till we show Daddy' and 'won't Daddy like this?' when you were at work yesterday."

"Sometimes I think I've got it all wrong. That I'm hurting more than helping them."

"Most parents think that at one time or another, especially single parents."

"If Julie was here…" He cut off the thought. "She was a wonderful mother."

"Who probably struggled with the same feelings of inadequacy at times, just like you are now." She patted his arm, then put her hands around her coffee mug. "You're doing a wonderful job with them. My concern is, what are you doing for yourself?"

"I don't have time to worry about me."

Aunt Sarah peered at him. "That's what I figured. When you went shopping after the fire, you had five bags of clothes and items for each of your children. How many did you have for yourself?" When he didn't answer, she held up a warning finger. "You've got to take better care of yourself."

"Before Julie died, I promised that I'd always put them first, and I have. I've taken care of them because they are my whole world."

"But who takes care of you, Christopher?"

SHELBY ARRIVED A few minutes before ten and thrust a bag of groceries into his arms, then turned and went back to her car for more.

Christopher carried the bag into the kitchen and started to unload the items onto the counter. Daisy bounced next to him, her cape tied at her neck. "What's all that for, Daddy?"

He glanced at the can of cream-of-mushroom soup. "I think that goes into a casserole of some sort."

"Green-bean casserole," Shelby answered as she entered the kitchen with two more bags of groceries.

Daisy made a face and left the kitchen.

"She's not into much of the green vegetables lately," he told Shelby. "Not that I'm a big fan of green beans, either, to be honest."

"Just wait until you try my green-bean casserole. It'll change your mind. Trust me."

Christopher smiled at her confidence, but he figured that he'd pass on that particular dish when the time came.

After the groceries had been unpacked and organized by menu item, Shelby brought out a chart that showed what needed to be made and what time to start making it. He was impressed. "How did you know how to do all this?"

Shelby grinned. "I was always my nana's little helper. She said that one day I'd have to take over for her." Her smile faded. "I just never expected it to be so soon."

Wanting to stay out of the way, he crept into the family room to watch the Thanksgiving parade on television with his children. He sat between them, putting his arms around their waists and pulling them closer toward him. Despite what had happened earlier in the week with the house, he was thankful that they were all healthy and together this holiday.

He frowned as he eyed Daisy's attire. "Why don't we leave your cape on the bed upstairs for today?"

"No."

"You don't want to get it dirty while you're eating."

"It can be washed."

He sighed, then tried another tactic. "You're safe here. Nothing's going to happen."

"But what if something does happen, and I need to use my superpowers?"

"You don't have any superpowers, dummy."

Christopher frowned at Elijah. "Don't speak like that to your sister." Then he turned back to Daisy. "We've talked about this, sweetie. It's just a cape. It doesn't have powers."

"Yes, it does. You just don't know it yet." She stood up and walked toward the kitchen in a huff.

Aunt Sarah stopped her at the doorway. "Just the person I was looking for. I need someone to roll silverware in the napkins, then put them at each place around the table. Do you think you could do that for me?"

Daisy skipped out of the room, following the older woman. Christopher turned to Elijah. "How many times have we talked about calling your sister names?"

"As many times as she's worn that stupid cape." The boy crossed his arms over his chest and stuck out his lower lip. "It's not going to save her."

"I know, but it helps her feel better."

"Whatever. I'm going to help Aunt Sarah." Elijah pushed off the couch and went in the direction of his sister.

He was still thankful for his children, obviously, even if he couldn't always change their attitudes. And he didn't know how to, despite what the family counselor said. Wisps of his earlier conversation with Aunt Sarah played in his mind. She'd called him a good father, but the evidence seemed to suggest otherwise. Knowing he should be helping, he rose and joined his children rolling silverware into napkins under Shelby's direction.

It was just before noon when the extended Cuthbert family started to arrive. First, it was Aunt Anna and Uncle Mike, with their grown daughter, Laurel, who had a little girl, Harper. Shelby introduced them as her family. Then it was Uncle Bob with Aunt Jeri. Their son, Jack, whom Penny had mentioned being a veterinarian, arrived soon after. They were followed by the baby of Sarah's four nephews, Rick, with his wife, June, and two of their four daughters, both college age. Their two other daughters turned up with husbands and seven kids between them in tow. Evidently, almost everyone was accounted for.

A small pack of children now ran around yelling and playing, having the time of their lives, it seemed. Christopher couldn't get over the noise. Eventually, the children, including his own, were sent outside to play, which helped a bit with the volume indoors, until the Detroit Lions football pregame show blared on the television in the family room. Meanwhile, more and more covered dishes were placed on kitchen counters already filled with food. Shelby wrote down on her chart who brought what dish and if it needed to be reheated before serving.

The roar of Lions fans from the TV told Christopher that the game had started. He poked his head into the family room, then echoed the groans of the Cuthberts as the TV flickered and went out. Uncle Bob got off the sofa and approached the TV, pressing the remote. Nothing happened. "Power's out."

Aunt Sarah entered, followed quickly by Shelby. "Mark, can you check the fuses downstairs? The electricity is out in the kitchen."

Aunt Sarah's nephew popped up from the couch and left the room while the others discussed what might have happened to have caused the blackout. One of the kids who had been playing in the backyard ran into the house, followed by Daisy. "The power's out all up and down the street," Poppy announced.

"How do you know that?" her mother, Kristina, asked the girl.

"Because we could hear the neighbors yelling about it," Daisy answered for her new pal.

Kristina hustled the children out of the room, muttering about getting the kids away before they heard any language that wasn't appropriate for young ears. Mark returned and shook his head. "I put in a call to the electric company. The power's completely out on the block and they don't have an estimate when it will be back on. It could be an hour. Or later tonight or tomorrow."

More groans.

"We could move dinner to someone else's house," Aunt June suggested.

"Whose house has enough room for all of us?" Uncle Mike asked.

Aunt Sarah seemed unflappable with the calm expression on her face. "No one's leaving. We'll make do here."

Shelby waved her chart. "How are we going to finish dinner without electricity?"

Aunt Sarah had the solution. "The turkey's almost finished, so we'll keep it in the oven with the door shut so that it keeps its heat. Everything else is pretty much cooked or needs a little reheating, but we'll be fine. We'll have to skip mashed potatoes, though."

Christopher held up a hand as if he was in a classroom. "I've got a gas grill in my garage that has a side burner. We could use that to boil the potatoes."

"Good thinking." Sarah winked at him. "Richard, get the grill out from the garage here, and we'll start heating things up on that. Michael and Anna, give him a hand. Mark, grab the casseroles and follow Christopher to his house to use his grill. Christopher, I'll have you take the potatoes."

Given their orders, Christopher took several covered dishes and led Mark to his lot. He tried not to imagine what the older man might be thinking as they passed the scorched house. Lucky for them, the fire hadn't spread to his garage in the back, so the grill had been spared, along with other items that he kept in storage. He placed the pot of potatoes on the nearby picnic table, then rolled out the grill and lit it.

"Hope you have enough propane in the tank."

"We should. I filled it up a couple weeks ago." Christopher shrugged at the other man's raised eyebrows. "I may not be much of a cook, but I know my way around a grill. I've even stood in six inches of snow to use it."

Mark grinned. "Nothing like a steak hot off the grill."

Christopher had a feeling that he was going to like Mark. While they waited for the grill and burner to heat, Christopher tried to keep his gaze off the house, but the other man noticed it. "I heard about the fire. Good thing you and the kids weren't home when it started."

"Maybe if I had been, I could have put it out sooner. Or at least saved some of our stuff."

Mark shook his head. "Nah, I read the report. An electrical short in the chest freezer in the basement sparked and the blaze caught. The fire was extremely hot and spread quickly."

"You've read the report?"

"I'm the state's fire inspector. I thought Penny would have told you."

Understanding dawned in his brain. "You're Penny's father. I should have known. She has your eyes."

"I heard she was on scene that day. Saved your dog."

"She was amazing that day. Definitely our hero. I don't know what my kids would have done if we'd lost Caesar, too."

"She's a hero, and I'm glad that she saved your dog. But that girl needs to start thinking with her head for everyone's safety. It could have gone badly for both her and the dog. She has too much heart and acts on her impulses. All her grandmother's influence. Hers and Aunt Sarah's. I was gone too much when she was growing up." Mark peered at him. "You know how it is, being a single father yourself. It all falls on you, and there's never enough time in the day to do it all."

"It's definitely not a job for the weak." The grill had started to smoke, so he put the potatoes on the burner, then a few of the casseroles on the racks before lowering the lid. "How did you do it?"

"I had help, and lots of it. I don't know if you remember my mother, but she was a formidable woman. You've met Shelby, and she's only a shadow of her nana Cuthbert." He took a seat on the picnic table. "I never had to worry about Penny when I was at the firehouse because I knew she was being well taken care of. It was only when it was just the two of us that we had problems. Especially after she turned thirteen."

"I'll admit that I'm not looking forward to the teenage years. Elijah is already rolling his eyes at everything I say. And if I hear 'whatever' one more time…" He blew out a breath. "I want to be there for them all the time, but I can't. And then when I am, I feel like a big failure. Like I'm not doing anything right."

Mark gave a dry laugh. "That's the thing. Years from now, your daughter will tell you that she just wanted you to be there. She sees you as a hero, even if you don't feel like one."

"I'm no hero. Just a worn-out guy trying to make things work."

"That's what we're all trying to do as parents, single or not. Sometimes you succeed and other times you learn from your mistakes. My big regret is that I wasn't there more for Penny, and now it's too late." Mark patted Christopher on the shoulder. "You'll figure it out eventually. And the kids will turn out just fine. Being there for your kids makes you a good parent."

Christopher hoped he was right. "Sometimes I think that we'll get over losing Julie. That our grief will subside one day. And then something else happens, like we lose our house, and we're back to square one."

Christopher could see Mark swallowing hard. "I lost my wife before Penny turned a year old, so I understand. Grief can be a strange animal." Mark looked him over. "You still love your wife."

He said it as a statement, not a question. As if he knew that Christopher still missed Julie. Still longed for her. Christopher could only nod.

They chatted some more, but stopped when a car pulled into the driveway. Recognizing the car as his mother's, he walked over to greet her. She looked at the ruined house and put a hand to her mouth. "I didn't realize it would look this bad."

Christopher hugged her as she shed a few tears. "It's okay, Mom. We can rebuild. The important part is we're all safe."

His mother sniffled, then pointed to the grill. "Why are you using that?"

Christopher explained about the power loss, then introduced Mark. "His aunt is the one who is letting us stay with her for a few days."

"Remind me to thank her. She's an angel." She shook Mark's extended hand.

"My aunt has a generous spirit." He patted Christopher on the shoulder again. "If you're okay for now, I'll go back and check on our progress at the house."

"We'll be over with the rest of the dinner shortly."

Christopher's mom claimed Mark's vacated spot at the picnic table. "How worried are you about the kids?"

"They're dealing with it the best they can. Daisy seems to think it's a great adventure and that we should stay there forever." He slumped on the bench next to her. "Oh, Mom. Why did this have to happen?"

"I don't know. I wish I had more answers for you." She put her arms around him and rubbed his back. "You've been through a lot in the last few years. The good news is that because of those experiences you're strong enough to handle what comes next."

He wanted to laugh at that idea. Him, strong? Out of place, yes. Clueless, definitely. "I wish I knew what I was doing."

"Christopher, darling, you are my son, and I love you. But don't you think it's about time you stop doubting yourself as a father?" When he started to protest, she held up one hand. "I know you feel like you're floundering, but most parents do. Your children are cherished, and, okay, they have some issues, but they are healthy and happy, for the most part. Take Elijah, for instance. What did the family counselor say about him?"

"That we have to take things day by day. But I don't want to wait for some breakthrough. I want Elijah to talk to me now about what he's feeling. I want Daisy to stop wearing that stupid cape." He closed his eyes for a moment. "And I want five minutes to myself for something that isn't about them." He rubbed a hand over his face. "How did you do it?"

"By sheer willpower and determination. But I'll let you in on a secret. I had plenty of doubts, same as you." She put her hands on the sides of his face and peered into his eyes. "You will get through this setback and come out stronger than ever. And do you know why?"

"Because you've got my back?"

"Exactly. How many times did I tell you that growing up? And have I ever let you down?" She pulled him into a hug. "I know things have been tough, and I wish I lived closer, but you're not alone in this. Whatever you need, call me."

He squeezed her tight. "Thanks, Mom."

They separated, and his mom strolled closer to the burned remains of his home, staring. He checked on the potatoes and the casseroles, then adjusted the temperature before putting the lid back down on the grill. He went to stand next to her. The charred walls of the house seemed like a sad ending to what had already been a sad story. "I've never been fond of starting over."

"I know. You like things to stay as they've always been."

"I meet with the insurance adjuster and the fire inspector on Monday afternoon to find out what happens next. I don't know if they'll have me rebuild or relocate."

"And in the meantime?"

"We'll stay with Aunt Sarah, but I'll need to find something long term for us."

"If I didn't live so far away…"

"I know." He reached over and took her hand. "You'd have us move in without a question, but the kids need to be here, where their school is. Their friends. I can't take anything else away from them."

She patted his hand and rose to her feet. "Speaking of, I need to get some grandma hugs in. I'll be back to help you carry the food when it's ready."

"Thanks again, Mom."

She gave him a warm smile, then asked for directions to Aunt Sarah's house before leaving him. He looked up at his house, pulling his jacket tighter around him. A chill had entered his bones even though the temperatures had been warmer than normal.

He put his head in his hands. *Oh, Julie. What am I going to do?* But no answer came.

If she was there, she'd probably rest her head against his shoulder and talk up their next house. Never mind the details of how to get there from here. He was in charge of the details while she kept the dream.

But this was no dream.

His mom returned a little while later with Elijah, who had volunteered to help carry the food. They checked on the potatoes and pronounced them done. Then his mom took the large pot back to the house to be drained and mashed. Elijah sat beside Christopher at the picnic bench. He put an arm around the boy's shoulders. "How are you doing, Eli?"

He shrugged. "Fine."

"Everything's going to work out, you know." He gave a soft smile. "Do you know why?" When the boy shook his head, Christopher echoed his mother's words. "Because I've got your back. Always."

Elijah didn't roll his eyes at this, but Christopher had the sense he wanted to. He leaned over and kissed the top of his son's head. "I promise that everything will be okay."

"You can't promise that, Dad. Even Penny said that losing a house is hard."

Christopher glanced at him. "When did she say that?"

"When I came back here to the house yesterday." Elijah sighed. "I figured she'd told you."

"Why don't you tell me now?"

Elijah looked back at the house, but didn't say anything for a while. When he did, his voice was tinged with restrained tears. "I wanted to see it for myself, so I came down here. Penny found me."

Christopher nodded, appreciating that she could be there for his son when he couldn't. "She made you feel better?"

Elijah shrugged and looked away again. "That's not the point."

"What is the point, then?"

"None of this is easy." He looked up at his father. "And saying it's going to be okay doesn't help."

"What would help?"

"I don't know."

Christopher put a hand on his son's shoulder. "I don't know, either, but I'm hoping that if we work together we can figure this all out."

He slipped his arms around his son and held tight for as long as Elijah let him.

Once the casseroles had heated through, he and Eli used kitchen towels to carry the hot dishes down the street. Chaos seemed to have only increased in the house. The turkey had to finish cooking on the grill since it hadn't reached the proper temperature, and some dishes had a distinctive char on them, but everything smelled delicious as they prepared to sit down to eat. Shelby did a final check of her chart, then nodded. "It's all here."

"Good. Why don't we all share what we're thankful for and then we can eat," Aunt Sarah said as she took off her apron and placed it over a kitchen stool. "Mike, why don't you start us off?"

One by one, the Cuthbert family shared what they were thankful for, going down the line until they reached Daisy. She twisted her mouth to the side, thinking, before she held up her finger. "I know! I'm thankful for Miss Penny, who saved our dog."

Christopher grinned at his daughter. "I'm thankful for my kids."

Elijah was silent next to him. When Christopher nudged him, he sighed. "I'm…" He stopped and shook his head. "I'm thankful for pumpkin pie, okay?"

Several of the adults nodded. "I'll take mine with lots of whipped cream," Uncle Bob said.

Aunt Sarah looked around the crowded room. "And I'm thankful that we're all still able to get together for Thanksgiving in this house."

As she said the last word, the lights flickered on to cheers from the family. "And for the power coming back on," she added. "Now let's eat."

Christopher helped his children with their plates and got them settled at one of the card tables in the living room before returning to the food line to make his own plate. He noticed that the television had also come back on, and Uncle Mike checked the score and announced the disappointing result to the groaning fans.

As he sat next to his children and mom, surrounded by this family and friends, he paused in eating to take in the moment. He'd never been a part of a big family like this. It had been just him and his mom growing up. And he'd spent time with Julie's family for holidays, but nothing like this, where a dozen conversations filled the room. Kids and adults alike were teasing and laughing and shouting to be heard. This would be a holiday he would remember for a long time. He looked across the room at Aunt Sarah, who was sitting at the head of the dining-room table. She spotted him looking at her and winked at him.

Thank you, he mouthed.

She gave a short nod and turned to Aunt June, who had spoken to her.

Then he tucked into his dinner and had to admit that the turkey tasted even better grilled.

PENNY WRAPPED THE man's burned hands as her partner, Wesley, lectured him about the dangers of deep-frying a frozen turkey. Knowing Wes's love of all things fried, he spoke from experience.

"The ice and the oil don't mix. Remember that for next time." Like her, Wes had volunteered to work today since he didn't have family in the area.

She looked over the man's shoulder at the scorch mark on his deck. Luckily, the man's son had called them as soon as the hot oil had caught fire, while his wife had tried to smother the fire with a bag of flour. This was their fifth call of the day for a similar incident, and Penny was ready to go back to the station and find some of her own Thanksgiving dinner. She'd heard a rumor that the fire chief had ordered dinner from their favorite diner, and she could practically hear a piece of pecan pie calling her name.

While the rest of the team rewound the hoses, Penny returned the medical bag to the appropriate compartment and checked the level of her supplies. Because she had EMS training, she'd been assigned the role of paramedic on these calls. Not that she minded. She'd gotten her certification in order to make her more valuable and versatile to the station.

"We've got another call," Lieutenant Buckner announced to the team as he listened to his radio. "Two streets over from here. Let's go!"

They hustled to the truck, dragging the rest of the hoses and supplies, then stuffing it all on the truck before jumping on and speeding to the next call.

Fortunately, the truck returned to the station after that response, a little after four, and

Penny's stomach growled louder than the engine. Buckner shook his head. He was in the front passenger seat and turned to look at her, smiling. "Hungry, rookie?"

"Starving, sir."

"I could go for some of my wife's stuffing. No one makes it like her."

"I'd put mine against hers any day," her teammate Carter said.

His brother, Charlie, laughed. "Forget the stuffing. I want a turkey leg. It's the best part of the bird."

The crew shouted out their favorite dishes as they rolled up to the station. The large glass door slid up as the driver maneuvered the truck inside. Before anyone could get out, the lieutenant reminded them they had to check the hoses and restock the truck before eating. Penny sulked, but knew he was right. If their dinner got interrupted, she needed to know that she'd have what she required for the call.

She hopped off the truck and opened the compartment that held the medical supplies. Using her checklist, she restocked what she had used. She didn't hear anyone approaching, but felt a tug on the hem of her turnouts. Looking from the clipboard, she saw Daisy smiling up at her. "Hi, Miss Penny! Happy Thanksgiving."

"Happy Thanksgiving to you, too." She quickly scanned the area, but didn't see Daisy's father or brother. "What are you doing here, sweetie?"

She pointed behind her. "Daddy's in the kitchen. We brought leftovers from dinner for you and the other firemen."

"That was nice of you." She looked over Daisy's head to see Christopher walking out of the living quarters. Her heart gave a flutter, and she put her hand to her chest to stop it.

Christopher joined them and slipped his hand in Daisy's. "Been busy today?"

She shrugged and tried to ignore how the light in his brown eyes seemed to warm in her presence. "How was dinner with the family? Thanks for the food, by the way."

He mimicked her shrug. "Aunt Sarah asked us to drop it off to the station and asked me to tell you that she kept aside your favorite pie for later."

"Please thank her for me."

"How long are you working?"

"Barnes takes over for me at midnight."

Christopher made a face. "That makes for a long day."

"It's the life I signed up for." She put her clipboard in the compartment and shut the door, turning the handle to lock it. "I have to admit it gives me a rush. I love it."

He nodded at her, his eyes locked on hers. Seconds stretched out as they couldn't seem to look away from each other.

"Daddy, why are you staring at Miss Penny like that? Do you feel okay, Daddy?"

She noticed a corner of his mouth twitch, but then the moment was broken. "I have to go. Thank you again for bringing over the food. Great to see you, Daisy. Did everyone like your turkey drawings?"

Daisy nodded. He gave her a quick nod and stepped aside so she could walk past them into the living quarters. She stopped at the door and turned to watch Christopher and his daughter leave the station.

What was she doing? She sounded like a soppy schoolgirl. But then he stopped and turned to look at her, and she found herself smiling and lifting her hand to wave goodbye.

It had been good to see him, and she looked forward to seeing him again.

Wait. This was Christopher. Single dad. Penny shook her head. The sentimentality of the holiday must be getting to her. For a moment, she had considered letting go of her vow of no more single dads. Muttering to herself about the danger of getting sappy at this time of year, she returned to the firehouse.

Minutes later, she filled her plate with food and took a seat with the rest of her squad. Skipping the turkey, which she'd have later, she took a big forkful of mashed potatoes and closed her eyes as she savored it.

"You could never resist potatoes in any form."

She opened her eyes to peer at her dad, who waved at a couple of the crew members who had worked under him before he'd left for the inspector position. She finished eating her mouthful, then asked him, "Now, what are you doing here?"

"You didn't think Christopher would be the only one to bring over leftovers from Aunt Sarah, did you?"

Actually she had, but he was right. It was more than a one-person job. "How was dinner with the family?"

He told her about the power outage and

Christopher's quick thinking to use the grill to finish cooking. "He's quite a young man."

"He is."

Her father watched her for a moment. "But he's not right for you."

She opened her mouth to protest, but shut it. Arguing with her father had never gotten her anywhere. Instead, she cut her stuffing into bite-size pieces. "I'm not interested, Dad. So don't worry about it."

"He's not over his wife. Maybe never will be with his broken heart. He said as much earlier today."

She ignored the regret that fluttered in her chest. "Like you were with Mom?"

Her dad waved his hand as if he could brush off the suggestion. "It's not the same thing."

"Isn't it? You never even dated anyone after she died. I don't think I ever saw you even look at another woman."

"This isn't about me."

"Well, it's not about me, either, Dad. I'm not interested in Christopher Fox, okay?"

"That's not why I sat down to talk to you."

She looked him over and sighed. She knew the lecture would eventually come. "Mac talked to you about what happened the other day."

"Of course he did. He's my best friend." Her dad tapped his front teeth with his thumb, a habit she knew meant he was trying to find the right words. He'd done the gesture enough when she'd been growing up. "I know that you think he's being hard on you—"

"Because he is."

"But he's got your best interests at heart, Pen." He scooted his chair closer to hers and leaned in, dropping the volume of his voice to avoid any curious ears around them. "I know you think that you're ready for more, but trust me when I say this. You have to learn the station from the bottom up. Hotshot moves like the other day only prove that you're too green. Experience will be a better teacher than your college professors."

"How can I get experience if Mac wastes my time cleaning bathrooms and checking hoses? I need to be on the front lines."

"You need to listen to your superior."

Penny pushed away from the table and rose to her feet, but her father put his hand over hers. "Sit back down and listen to me for once."

She wanted to leave her father sitting there, but several pairs of eyes had turned in their direction. Taking her hand from her father's, she sat down and looked over at him. "I don't want a lecture from you. Not here."

"Then how about a friendly reminder that you're a member of a team that depends on you to think with your head."

"I saved a dog. What's so wrong with that?"

"You ran into a burning building when everyone else was being evacuated. This isn't about being a hero. It's about being safe. You should have checked with Mac first. The rules are there to protect you, not stop you from doing your job." Her father ran a hand over his eyes. "What if I lost you in that fire? Do you really think I want to lose you, too?"

She looked over at him, surprised that he had shared so much. "Of course not." She paused, shaking her head. "I thought that coming back to Thora was the right move, but now I'm not so sure."

"It was really the best move." He put a hand on her shoulder and waited until she looked up at him. "I would trust Dale with your life. And your career. But you need to listen and learn from him. He'll get you where you want to go if you do."

A TAP ON his shoulder. Christopher opened one eye to find darkness. Now someone shook his shoulder. "Julie?" He'd just been dreaming of her and wondered if she'd appeared as if by request.

He turned over to find Penny kneeling on the edge of the sofa bed. "Come on. Let's go," she whispered to him.

"Go where?"

"Black Friday shopping."

He groaned and pulled the covers up to his ears. "No, thank you. But I appreciate you asking."

The other side of the bed sagged under Penny's weight. "We can get a lot of things for the kids at great prices, but only if you get out of bed and dress."

"It's still the middle of the night."

"Exactly. If we wait until dawn, the good stuff will be gone. Now let's go."

He grumbled as he got out of bed, but he knew she was right. Julie had loved getting up early to get the best deals on Black Friday. She had shown him with pride how much she had saved. Didn't matter that he pointed out to save two hundred dollars she had to spend five hundred. "Fine. Fine. Just give me a minute."

"You have sixty seconds. Then you better be in the passenger seat of my car."

"I need coffee."

"It's taken care of. I brewed some for us. Thermoses are ready and waiting."

"And my wallet."

"Don't need it. This is our treat. Aunt Sarah collected money at my suggestion yesterday from the family to help you out, so you don't have to worry about a thing."

"I can't accept that."

"You can, and you will. Cuthberts can be very stubborn when it comes to helping out other people."

"I don't need your charity."

"It's not charity. Now get dressed."

"I'm not dressing in front of you."

"Fine. See you in my car."

It took longer than the minute to pull on his jeans and the sweatshirt he'd worn yesterday. Maybe Penny was right about him needing to get some things for himself. But his focus had to be on the kids. He could get by with very little.

When he got into the car, Penny had the

heater running full blast. The interior was warm and cozy. She waited for him to buckle himself into the passenger seat, then backed out of the driveway. Penny turned to smile at him. "Don't look as if this is torture. This is going to be fun."

"You couldn't shop without me?"

"You know the kids better than I do—they're your kids—so I will defer to your judgment." She paused. "Well, mostly I will."

The radio blared with Christmas music as Penny drove them to a large shopping center in a nearby suburb. Despite the early hour, cars filled the parking lot, and they had to hike toward the entrance of the department store.

Penny stomped her feet as Christopher sipped his coffee. She glanced around the crowd. "There's a lot of people here at this hour. Once they open the doors, the plan is to go to the left. Most people will start on the right, so we can avoid some of the crowd. That will take us by the home department, and they have those towels on sale that Aunt Sarah likes."

In a few moments, the doors opened, and the crowd surged forward. She grabbed the bottom hem of his jacket in order to stay together as they entered and went to the left inside the store. Penny pointed to the shopping carts ahead of them. "Let's both grab one. I figure we can get a majority of our shopping done here based on the online ad."

Christopher grabbed a cart, then followed Penny through the home department. They picked up items from different displays with large signs above them shouting out a great deal to be found there.

After the home department, they entered the kids' section. Christopher found a steal on boys' jeans and picked up several pairs and put them into his cart, along with a Detroit Lions jersey with Elijah's favorite player's name on it. He added a few T-shirts, then Penny called him over to a rack. Holding up a bright tie-dyed sweatshirt against herself, she said, "Think this is too loud?"

Christopher cupped his ear. "What was that? I couldn't hear you over that top."

She laughed as she placed it back on the rack and raced ahead of him into the girls' section.

Penny chose a pink tutu and smiled. "Don't

kill me, but this screams Daisy's name. Ooh, and here's a matching sparkly top."

He smiled. "She'd love it."

Penny returned his smile, and he wondered that he might have missed out on Black Friday shopping with this special woman.

His cart had started to fill up when they stopped next at the men's department. Penny plucked a blue button-down shirt from a rack and held it up to his body. He stepped back, his hands raised. "We're not here to buy for me."

"We took up a collection to help out your family. And as head of the family, you need things just as much as the kids do." Penny pulled another shirt from the rack and shook her head before replacing it. "Now, will you tell me your size or do I have to guess?"

"You really don't need to do this."

Penny put her hands on his back and pushed him farther into the department as she plucked more items off the racks. Shirts. Pants. And a sweater in his favorite color, navy blue. How had she known?

When they reached the fitting rooms, she handed him a stack of clothing and pointed. "Go try them on."

He almost saluted her before obeying. Knowing he had little choice, he tried on the navy sweater with a pair of jeans. He exited the fitting room to find Penny with her eyes closed as she leaned against one of the carts. When he cleared his throat, her eyes fluttered open and she did a slow journey with her eyes from his toes to his head, then whistled. "Not bad, Mr. Fox. Or should I call you 'foxy'?"

He shook his head, but smiled at her compliment, then turned to look at himself in the long mirror. "Looks good, then."

She approached him and smoothed the material against his chest. "Looks a little loose. Maybe a size down?"

"I don't want it too tight."

"Don't want the women to notice your pecs, huh?"

He returned to the fitting room and put on one of the red shirts, a color he wouldn't normally wear. Pairing it with a pair of black pants, he stepped out of the fitting room once more. Penny nodded at his outfit, then snapped her fingers. "I saw a tie that would look great with that shirt. Stay there."

He watched her run to the accessory section and she returned with a Christmas tie with laughing Santas and leaping reindeer. He cocked his head to one side as he stared at her. "Really?"

"Why not? It's the season for ties like this." She held it up to him under his chin. "Your seniors would love this. Not to mention your daughter."

He stared down at her and swallowed, his smile getting lost in a tumble of feelings he was afraid to explore. "Pen—"

"Fine. I'll go find the most boring tie in the world."

She left before he could do something crazy, like putting his hands on her waist and pulling her close. He opted to return to the fitting room and put on the next outfit. This time when he stepped out, she held a handful of the ugliest ties that had ever been made. He winced. "This has gone from bad to worse."

She smiled and put one tie against his chest that had a shade of blinding yellow. "That is definitely not for you." Then she held up one with neon rainbow stripes. "This one, however…"

"I don't think so."

The next tie she held against him had a

navy background with cream-colored sail-boats. "Call me crazy, but I like this one."

He liked her. He put a hand over hers. "I'll take it."

Her smile faded as she looked up at him, then slowly removed her hand from his. Taking a step back, she gave a nod. "Maybe I should let you pick them out yourself."

Right. He wasn't supposed to be touching her in the middle of a department store and thinking about kissing the smile off her face. "I'll go change."

When he returned in his own clothes, Penny had added more things to her cart. "It's time to hit the toy store," she announced. "What do you say?"

They moved to the long lines at the cash registers. As they waited, they talked about the upcoming holiday events in Thora. He knew Daisy was excited about the town's Christmas-tree lighting the following night, which co-incided with the arrival of Santa. "My cousin Shelby's shop has an excellent view of the tree, if you want to stop by before the ceremony."

"Which one is her shop?"

"Shelby is the new owner of the mechanic's garage on Main. Cuthbert Motors."

While he might have guessed that Shelby was a business owner, he'd never take her as a mechanic. Penny shrugged. "It was her dad's shop, and she grew up working in it. Now that he's retired, she left the accounting firm and took over. She likes being her own boss."

He could see that about her cousin. "Her dad is Mike, right? I remember him from yesterday."

She shot him a grin. "How did you like meeting my boisterous family?"

He paused a moment, thinking of everything he had experienced the day before. "They're loud and they talk over each other and…" He smiled. "It was the best Thanksgiving I ever had. It must have been hard for you to be so far away from them when you were in Florida."

"I missed them a lot."

"And now you're back in town, but you still weren't there yesterday."

She gave a half smile. "You know how families are."

"Actually, my experience with big families like yours is pretty limited."

"I love them, don't get me wrong, but they tend to interfere in my personal life." She held up the envelope with the money they'd collected yesterday. "But they have good hearts."

Once they had paid for their purchases, Penny took a few bags while he carried the rest to her car and placed them in the trunk. "So can we go home now?" he asked.

"We're not done yet, mister. Just you wait."

CROWDS JAMMED THE toy store's aisles, and Penny brushed up against Christopher to allow a fellow shopper to pass behind her. Looking up at him in such a tight space, she thought that the Barbie aisle was a strange place to start falling for the single dad.

Maybe it was the lack of a Ken in her own life, but she hadn't minded standing so close to Christopher that she could smell his sweet scent. She also hadn't minded how he put his hand on her back as if protecting her.

When the aisle cleared, she took a step away from him and grabbed a Barbie dressed as an astronaut. "What about this one?"

"Daisy prefers superheroes."

"I might have guessed." She put back the astronaut and scanned the shelves. "We'd have better luck in the action-figure aisle."

Christopher plucked a box from the shelf and held it out to her. "Look. It's you."

Penny looked down at the doll that was dressed in the turnout gear of a firefighter. Even her blond hair had a wave that mirrored her own. "Well, what do you know? I'm a Barbie."

"She even has your big blue eyes."

Penny blinked at him several times. He'd noticed the color of her eyes? For a brief moment, she wondered what else he might have noticed about her.

Then questioned why she would care. She couldn't date the man. No matter how handsome he was. Or how good with his kids.

Or how a small, teensy part of her imagined what it would be like to kiss him.

He raised his eyebrows at her. "Something wrong?"

"Why?"

"Because you're staring at me."

She had been? Placing a hand to her belly, she shook her head. "I must be hungry."

"And you're imagining me as a large turkey drumstick?"

She laughed at the image. "More like thinking that we should get breakfast after we finish here."

"Sounds good to me." He put the firefighter Barbie into the cart. "I think we can find a few things for Eli in the next aisle. He does love his plastic building pieces, otherwise known as torture instruments on his dad's feet when he leaves them on the floor."

They found several building sets that Elijah would like and added them to the other toys in the cart. After paying for the toys, they dropped off the shopping bags at the car. Penny nodded with satisfaction that the trunk was filled. "Now we eat."

The walk to the diner next to the shopping complex was quick. Ever the gentleman, Christopher held the door open for her, and they entered the crowded restaurant. Penny looked around the room and saw Shelby and her friend Melanie, who waved them over to their booth. "You want to join me and Shelby? We just put in our orders, but there's plenty of room for you two at our table."

Shelby stood and joined Melanie on the same side of the booth, while Penny scooted across the bench seat, and Christopher sat next to her after Shelby introduced him to Mel. The fit was tight, and her shoulder rubbed against his, sending unwanted frissons of joy to her nerve endings. They were just friends.

Just friends.

To distract her traitorous body, Penny picked up the menu and perused it even though she'd known what she was ordering when they'd walked through the door. She needed that wall around her so that she could stop thinking about him. About kissing him, especially.

Once the waitress poured their coffees and they'd ordered their food, Shelby looked over at the two of them. "How did the shopping go?"

Christopher added cream to his coffee. "Very good. I can't believe all the stuff we were able to get for the kids." He looked across the table at Melanie. "This is going to sound a little strange, but do I know you from somewhere?"

Mel smiled over at Christopher. "The bookstore on Main is mine."

"You're Mel's Books? That's why you look familiar, but I couldn't quite put my finger on where I'd seen you. My kids and I love your bookstore."

Mel glowed at the compliment, and Penny tried to ignore the snake of jealousy winding around her belly. She was tempted to kick Mel's leg underneath the table. Not that she and Christopher were a couple. Not at all. But he was becoming a friend, and she didn't like the idea of sharing him with anyone. Not even Mel.

She stopped those thoughts in their tracks. They made her sound like a jealous girlfriend, which she definitely wasn't. And, keeping her gaze on Mel, she could admit that the woman would be a good match for Christopher. He seemed quiet and devoted to his kids, who obviously liked to read. If she squinted her eyes, she could see the two of them together. Maybe she should play matchmaker. Then he might get out of her head.

The waitress brought their meals and re-filled their cups of coffee in record time. Shelby lifted her cup of coffee. "That's why I like this place. The food may not be fancy, but it's good and the waitstaff is quick."

Over breakfast, they discussed the up-coming holidays. Aunt Sarah planned on having family and neighbors over for the annual Christmas Eve blowout that had been a neighborhood tradition since the sixties. Since Mel didn't have much family in the area, she had been invited, as well. She sighed as she poured syrup over her waffles. "Some Christmas I'm going to show up for that party with a boyfriend. Unfortunately, it won't be this year."

"You never know what could happen between now and then." Shelby put an arm around her friend's shoulders. "Don't give up on Mr. Wonderful."

Mel smirked at her, and Penny turned to Christopher. "What about you? What are your Christmas Eve plans? I'm sure Aunt Sarah would love to have you come."

"We usually visit my wife's parents in Lansing, then spend the night at my mom's."

Mel narrowed her eyes. "You're married?"

"Widowed."

"Oh." She gave him a sympathetic look. "Sorry to hear that."

He nodded and switched his gaze to his breakfast. "It's okay. I don't wear a button announcing my wife died."

"People might look at you strangely if you

did," Penny said, then covered her mouth. "Did that sound insensitive?"

"Yes," Mel answered as Christopher said the opposite.

"Sometimes I say things out loud before thinking about how they might sound."

Christopher nudged her shoulder. "You also pick out horrible ties."

"They weren't horrible."

He grimaced and spoke to the other two women. "Neon rainbows. Do I need to say more?"

The two women laughed as Penny's mouth dropped open. "I'll have you know that I like rainbows."

"Julie did, too." Christopher's mouth twitched, and he dropped his gaze to his plate.

Penny put a hand on his. "It's okay to miss her."

He turned and looked at her, his eyes glistening. "Thanks."

She nodded, then turned to find Shelby watching her with an amused grin. Before she could ask her cousin what was so funny, she checked her watch. "We'd better get eating if we're going to finish our shopping."

When the waitress brought the bill, Christopher brought out his wallet and waved off their protests. "You've done more than enough for me and my family. I insist on paying for breakfast."

They thanked him, then got their coats on before heading back outside. The sun was starting to rise above the shopping mall. They escorted Mel and Shelby to her cousin's car— Shelby had to drive her friend to work—then walked to Penny's car. "Shelby's offered to join us in our shopping. She needs a gift for her yoga instructor. Hmm, that might be a tricky one."

Christopher agreed and looked a little worried he'd be having to try out a yoga mat or two. "Thank you for your generosity, but I'm done with shopping for the day. I'd like to go see my kids."

Penny was disappointed her time with Christopher was being cut short, but she understood. She kind of missed the kids herself. "I'll text Shelby and meet up with her after I drop you off at the house, then."

She had been insisting all morning that she and Christopher weren't a couple, so what was she expecting? She needed to get her head in the game and shake off these feelings for her aunt's houseguest.

"There's still money left in the envelope." She pulled it out of her purse and handed it to him. "Maybe you can use it for things that you need once you find somewhere to live. Pots and pans. Towels. Sheets."

He didn't seem to want to take the envelope, but she pushed it into his hand. He stuffed it into his coat pocket. "Thank you."

Penny pressed the button to unlock the doors, but Christopher stopped her from getting inside the car. She shook her head. "Don't you dare thank me again."

"Wasn't going to."

She sneaked a quick peek at his face. "Then what were you going to say?"

"That I've enjoyed this morning with you. I'm glad you insisted that I come out with you."

Oh. "I'm glad you did." And she meant it. She might have resisted when Aunt Sarah mentioned it, but she'd had fun with him.

He returned her smile. "Are we becoming friends?"

"I'm afraid we are."

"I should warn you. The last woman I was friends with, I married."

"That will never happen with me."

CHAPTER FIVE

AFTER SHOPPING FOR the rest of the day with Shelby, Penny returned to Aunt Sarah's house to find her in the kitchen baking cookies with Daisy and Elijah. Flour dusted the counters as Elijah rolled out dough with a rolling pin that was older than Penny herself. She took a seat on a stool next to Daisy, who was searching through a box of metal cookie cutters. "Hey, short stuff. Need some help finding Rudolph?"

Daisy opened her mouth into a perfect little O and started to dig harder through the different cutters. When she found him, she held Rudolph high. "Got him!"

Elijah nodded as she handed it to him so that he could cut out several Rudolphs into the dough. "See if they have a Frosty, too."

As Daisy continued looking through the cookie-cutter box, Penny picked up a Santa mold and pressed it into the dough. "Having fun making cookies?"

Daisy nodded vigorously as Elijah stayed silent. Penny looked over at him. "You're not having a good time, E?"

He shrugged. "I guess it's okay." He offered a soft smile. "I'd rather be eating the cookies, though."

Penny placed a hand to her chest. "A man after my own heart. But decorating them in frosting and sugar can be fun, too."

Aunt Sarah pulled a tray of baked cookies from the oven. "Are you going to join us in the decorating?" her aunt asked.

Penny yawned and stretched. "Wish I could, but I think I'll take a quick nap, then shower before I meet the cousins for dinner."

"What time are you meeting?"

"Seven." She checked the time on her phone and frowned. She could fit in a nap if she only slept for fifteen minutes, but between working yesterday and the early morning shopping, she'd probably fall asleep in an instant and not wake up until tomorrow. "Maybe not a nap, then. Just a shower."

"Oh, before you go upstairs—" Her aunt

stopped whatever she was about to say, then waved her on. "Never mind. It's all right."

"Everything okay?"

"Perfect. Better go upstairs. You don't want to be late for dinner."

Her aunt smiled a little too widely, which left Penny curious. She pondered her aunt's reaction as she walked upstairs and into her room. Where a very large male was sleeping in her bed. She had a sudden, fleeting idea of joining him there.

So that was why Aunt Sarah had been thrilled that she was coming upstairs. She should have known that her aunt would continue her match-making schemes, but this time they weren't going to work.

She crept to the closet and opened the door, turning the small light on to see. After pulling a red sweater from its hanger, then glancing at her jeans to make sure they were clean, she started to tiptoe toward the door.

"I heard you when you came in."

She jumped at the sound of his voice and clutched the sweater to her body. "I didn't know you were sleeping in here."

"That's what you get for waking me up at oh-dark-early to go Christmas shopping." He rolled over and sat on the edge of the bed. "I'll get out of your hair. By the way, you missed the fashion show."

"What did the kids think of the clothes you got them?"

"Elijah grunted at his clothes, which I interpreted as a good sign. And Daisy loved that sparkly pink top you found."

"I figured she would."

"She said it would be perfect if it had also been in purple, too." He ran a hand through his hair. "I have no idea what to do with a girlie girl like my daughter. Julie would have, but…" He stood and glanced at the sweater in her hands. "Date tonight?"

"Dinner with the cousins. Black Friday tradition."

"You spend all day shopping together, then have dinner together, too? You must be close."

"As an only child, they were like my brothers and sisters." She gave a shrug. "Besides, this is usually the last free night we all have for a while as the Christmas holiday approaches."

"Your aunt mentioned something about a charity toy drive that your family sponsors every year."

"My pops and nana were really involved in the community, so they started it when my dad was a kid. Shelby and I were shopping for it today."

"That's admirable."

"It's tradition. There's a big dinner. Dancing. And we collect a bunch of toys for kids who might not otherwise get one. It's a really fun night. You should come with me."

He gave a shrug. "I don't know. Maybe."

She cocked her head to one side. "You don't have to dance if you don't want to. And if you do, you can ask me. I love to dance."

The words were out before she could take them back. Christopher colored and stared at her for a long time before glancing at the open bedroom door. "I should go check on the kids."

He brushed past her, and she closed her eyes. What had she been thinking? She had thrown herself at him, and being a gentleman, he'd let her down easy by sidestepping her invitation. She smacked her forehead with her palm. What was he doing to her resolve? She was supposed to be tough. To forget about him. Avoid him.

Even if he was hot, with that tall, lean body. And was kind. And he could be funny.

She found herself smiling, then chided herself. She couldn't be thinking about him. She should do her best to get him off her mind. They might be living under the same roof temporarily, but that didn't mean he could take up residence in her fantasies.

CHRISTOPHER FOLLOWED THE whiff of baking cookies. Honestly, he was glad to have escaped the uncomfortable scene upstairs. Had Penny really asked him to be her date to the charity dinner? He hadn't imagined that, right? He might like her and see a friendship developing between them, but that was all there could be.

Even if she was gorgeous. And funny. And sweet.

He stepped into the kitchen to get distracted from where his thoughts wanted to take him. Aunt Sarah looked up at him and smiled. "How did you sleep?"

"Great. Thanks for letting me."

She grinned and chose a cookie off a cooling rack. "Here. Try this and tell me what you think."

He bit into the still warm sugar cookie and sighed. "Heaven."

"I thought we'd finish baking these cookies, then indulge in another Cuthbert day-after-Thanksgiving tradition." She pulled a folder and thrust it at him. "After cooking all week, we get takeout on Friday night. You can choose the place."

He called and ordered their dinner, then took a seat at the counter to help Daisy put the last of the cutouts on the cookie sheet. "How many cookies did you make?"

Daisy flashed her hands several times. "A whole bunch, Daddy. And you missed it."

"I can help eat them. How about that?"

She giggled and leaned into his shoulder. He held her close and looked over her at Elijah, who frowned. It seemed to be a permanent look on his son's face these days. "How about we help Aunt Sarah clean the kitchen before dinner arrives?"

Together they put the kitchen back to rights, and Aunt Sarah pulled out the last trays of cookies from the oven when the doorbell rang. He waved off her offer to pay for dinner and walked to the front door.

Aunt Sarah had laid the good china on the

small kitchen table by the time he returned with the pizzas. She shrugged when he asked about it. "I usually use these from now until New Year's. It's easier than schlepping all those boxes up and down the stairs all the time."

"Or making one of us schlep them," Penny said as she stole a piece of sausage pizza from the box. Her hair still looked damp from her shower, and her face had been scrubbed clean. "I, for one, am glad we're using them more often."

Aunt Sarah slapped her hand away. "You're having dinner with your cousins. Don't ruin your appetite."

"Shelby's cooking for us. She was going on and on about some recipe she found on Pinterest that is low-carb, low-fat." She made a face. "*Low taste* is more like it."

"You might be surprised and like it."

"Doubt it." Penny stuffed the rest of the pizza slice in her mouth and grabbed a second before running back upstairs.

Christopher watched her leave, then turned to find Aunt Sarah watching him. She gave him a smile, which he returned, knowing what she was probably thinking. But she was wrong. He might find Penny attractive, but he wasn't interested in her.

At least he kept trying to remind himself of that.

He gave Daisy a hand with the breadsticks, then said, "Tomorrow night is the Christmas-tree lighting on Main Street, and I was going to take the kids. Would you like to join us, Sarah?"

The older woman pursed her lips. "I don't know if I'm up to standing outside in the freezing cold waiting for them to turn on a light switch."

"But you have to see Santa come. You just have to go." Daisy emphasized her point by waving her breadstick in the air. "And we sing Christmas songs. And Santa hands out candy canes. And it's the beginning of Christmas in Thora."

Aunt Sarah seemed to be amused by his daughter's insistence. "Well, if you say so, Daisy, dear, then I have to go."

Daisy cheered and took a bite of her breadstick. Christopher handed her a napkin and turned to Elijah. "What do you think, buddy?"

His son shrugged his shoulders but didn't

commit either way. How he'd love to know what was going on in that kid's brain. What did he think? Was he remembering the times they'd go with Julie, who sang the songs loudly but off-key? Did he remember the cups of hot chocolate and sugar cookies that they'd consumed while they'd waited in line to see Santa? Did he even care?

"What if we put up my Christmas tree tomorrow afternoon before we go downtown?" She peered at the children. "Maybe we could convince your dad to bring down the tree and ornament boxes from the attic."

"You don't have a real tree?" Elijah asked.

"My sister was allergic to pine, so we had an artificial one for as long as I can remember." She picked at her piece of pizza. "This will be my first Christmas without her, and I want to keep things as much like last year as possible."

Both children looked at her as she sniffled, but only Daisy put her hand on Aunt Sarah's. "It's okay to be sad and to miss her. I still miss my mommy."

"Thank you, sweetheart."

Christopher glanced at Elijah, who had

turned his gaze to his dinner plate and bitten off a piece of pizza as if he was angry at it.

PENNY GRABBED THE open bottle of red wine and rejoined Shelby and Jack in the living room of Shelby's condo. "Who wants a refill?"

Jack held up his empty glass. "Please."

"How is the black Lab doing after surgery?"

"He'll make it, but he's going to have a sore belly for a while. He won't look at another turkey carcass the same way."

"Poor guy." She finished off the bottle of wine. "Want me to get another bottle?"

Shelby shook her head. "After dinner. So what do you think of this dish?"

Jack and Penny exchanged looks, but didn't say a word. Instead, Penny took a seat on the sofa next to Shelby, but left her plate on the coffee table. "I'm not much hungry. I ate some pizza before I came over."

Jack shrugged. "I ate at Mel's shop earlier."

Shelby took a small bite. She instantly wrinkled her nose and placed her dinner plate on the coffee table next to theirs. "I know it's not very good, but I was hoping." She looked across at Jack. "You stopped over at Mel's?"

"She had ordered a book for me that I've been wanting to read, and it came in the other day. This was the first chance I had to stop by and get it."

"How did she look?"

Jack glanced between her and Penny. "The same as always. Did I miss something?"

Shelby shook her head. "Never mind." She picked up a notebook and pen. "I was hoping the other cousins would join us, but I guess they're busy with kids tonight. Christmas is coming up in a month, so we have a lot to do and not a lot of time to do it in. We have the tree lighting tomorrow night, so I figure we can meet at my garage at five, get a preview of the tree and walk over."

Penny raised her hand. "I'm working, actually, but you'll see me there."

"The fire chief roped you in as one of the elves?"

"Santa, actually." When her cousins laughed at her, she stared at them, with her mouth open. "I'll have you know that I will make a great Santa Claus. I'll have to put on lots of padding obviously, but I can pass out candy canes and charm little kids as good as anyone else."

"He couldn't convince anyone else?"

"He says it's part of my, um, training. That if I can learn to put others first, I might not make such impetuous decisions."

Jack gave her a pat on the shoulder. "I'm sure you'll be fine."

"Just don't tell Christopher's kids that it's me. I don't want to ruin the magic for them."

Shelby eyed her, but didn't say anything and turned back to her notebook. "Okay, next event is caroling at the senior home on Tuesday night. Are you working then, too?"

"I'm free."

Jack raised his hand. "I'm not."

"You close your clinic at four on Tuesdays."

"I promised Mel that I'd play Santa for story night at the shop."

Both cousins looked at him, and Penny asked, "How did she get you to agree to that one? You don't even like kids."

"Other people's kids are fine." He paused, then added, "Usually." He winced. "She caught me in a vulnerable moment earlier, and I said I would do it. It's no big deal."

"Do you want to reschedule caroling for Wednesday night, then?" Shelby asked.

Penny shook her head. "I'm working the next two nights after that. What about Friday?"

"That's the last committee meeting for the charity dinner at the Garden Room, which is the following Friday night." Shelby sighed and glanced at her notebook. "Why do we try to pack so much into the month?"

"Because it's Christmas, and it only happens once a year." Penny patted her cousin's knee. "We can go caroling without Jack. What about inviting Aunt Sarah to come with us this year? She might like that. And I know she's missing Nana something fierce."

"We all are."

They fell silent remembering the woman they had loved. The one who had encouraged their December festivities and the togetherness between the cousins. Who had smoothed ruffled feathers and dried tears. Who wouldn't be here for the first time this Christmas.

Penny wiped away a tear. "It won't be the same without her this year."

Jack cleared his throat and got off the floor

to walk into the kitchen while Shelby pulled her cardigan sweater tighter around herself. "Did Christopher say anything about what you got the kids?"

"They had a fashion show and tried on all the clothes. Daisy loved them."

"And the boy?"

Penny shrugged. "Christopher said Elijah liked them, but with that kid it's hard to tell. He doesn't exactly talk much about what he likes. Or doesn't like."

"From what I saw yesterday, he seems like the strong, silent type," Jack added as he brought a newly opened bottle of wine into the living room.

Penny drained the rest of her wine and held up her glass for Jack to refill. "I never thought about everything the victims of a fire really lose. And I don't mean just the material items." She swirled the glass and looked into its depths. "Pictures and things that held sentimental value." She looked up at them. "Those kids already lost their mom, and now they've lost things that belonged to her."

"You really like him, don't you?"

Penny frowned at Shelby's comment. "I'm talking about the kids."

"But when you talk about them, you're thinking about their father, too."

"You're not in my head, so don't pretend you know what I'm thinking."

Shelby turned to Jack. "You should have seen them at breakfast. Teasing and flirting."

"We did not flirt."

"Remember the rainbow ties? A person might as well be invisible."

"That's not true. In fact, I thought he might be interested in you." For a fleeting and jealous moment. "But then he met Mel, and I think she might be a better fit for him."

Jack frowned. "You're setting Mel up with the single dad?"

"You don't have a problem with that, do you?" Shelby stared at Jack. "After all, Mel is an attractive single woman who loves kids."

"I think the guy can get his own dates. Why don't you leave the matchmaking up to Aunt Sarah? She's a lot better at it than you."

"If I didn't know better, I'd call you jealous."

Jack raised his eyebrows at this suggestion. "Melanie and I are best friends. That's it. She can date whoever she wants."

Penny and Shelby exchanged glances, but

didn't say anything further on the subject. Finally, Penny sighed. "What about holding a fundraiser for Christopher and family once they find a place to stay? You know all the Cuthberts would come out to support it, as well as the rest of Thora."

"Can't we get through the Christmas toy drive first and then let Shelby plan another event? After all, you and I both know she won't be able to resist taking it over," Jack teased.

"I take over because no one else is willing to adopt a leadership role," Shelby protested.

"Speaking of leadership roles, word around the station is that the mayor won't be seeking reelection next year." Penny looked over at Shelby. "Could a certain cousin be interested in putting her hat in for the role?"

"Me? Mayor? I'm not sure about doing the whole politics thing."

Jack made a sound at the back of his throat. "Aren't you the one who keeps saying we need to have a better leader for the city of Thora? Just last week you were complaining about how the mayor should stop yapping about everything and actually do something."

"If he actually did something about all the

businesses pulling out of the community, we would see actual progress in the town." Shelby shrugged. "We need to be supporting our small businesses through tax incentives and other measures to ensure they thrive, which helps Thora prosper, as well."

Penny snapped her fingers. "Sounds like a campaign slogan to me."

Shelby chuckled. "We were talking about the fundraiser, not me running for mayor."

"Fine. We'll put a pin in that conversation for now." Jack pulled his cell phone from his back jeans pocket. "No offense to your cooking, Shelbs, but I need some real food. Who's up for Chinese?"

ON SATURDAY MORNING, Christopher brought down another box of Christmas decorations from Aunt Sarah's attic to add to the collection he'd already retrieved, and paused at the bottom of the stairs. Daisy ran up to him and frowned. "You're breathing hard."

"That's what happens when you get your exercise in." He carried the box past her and to the living room with the others. "This was the last one that said *Christmas*."

Aunt Sarah clapped her hands. "You're

a dear for doing all that. Usually I ask my nieces and nephews to help me, but they're getting busier and can't seem to find time for their favorite great-aunt."

He glanced at all the boxes. "Does all this ever get to be too much for you?"

"The Christmas decorations?" She shook her head. "I love doing this every year. Don't you?"

"My wife did all this stuff, and she was good at it. I try, but… What I meant was, this house and the upkeep and everything. Have you ever thought of downsizing or moving into an assisted-living complex?"

"The one like you work at, you mean?" She shrugged and opened several boxes until she found the one she wanted. "I've thought about it, and my sister and I talked about it before she died. But this is my home. I can't imagine not living here. And then where would the family go for Thanksgiving and Christmas? Or Easter?"

"They all have houses, too."

"But this is tradition, and that's hard to give up. You know exactly what I mean, don't you? Losing someone you love makes you want to hold on to those traditions even more." She pulled out a set of instructions and handed them to Christopher. "We'll need to separate all the branches by their stem color before we hook them into the tree stand. This paper shows the order."

Christopher scanned the instructions, then the box of evergreen branches she'd opened. "How old is this tree?"

"I think my brother-in-law, Jerry, replaced it back in 1980-something."

And it looked it. Some of the branches had bare spots, where the artificial needles had fallen off. "You ever think about getting one of the prelit models they have nowadays?"

"Prelit?" Aunt Sarah made a noise that told him what she thought about that. "What's the fun in having all the work done for you?"

By the time Christopher had sorted the different branches by stem color, Aunt Sarah had made hot chocolate for the kids and poured it into red and green mugs. Sipping her cocoa, Daisy sat on the sofa next to Aunt Sarah, who pulled a jumbled strand of Christmas lights out of another box and handed it to Elijah. "You look like you have a logical mind. Why don't you unravel these and plug them in to see what bulbs need to be replaced?"

Elijah didn't look excited by the idea but got on with the task. Daisy's face lit up. "What about me, Aunt Sarah? What can I do?"

"You and I are going to locate the Nativity and set it up on the coffee table. But first…" She walked to the stereo system and turned on a radio station that played nothing but Christmas music after November first. "We need a little music to inspire us."

They all set to work on their different assignments while carols played in the background. It reminded Christopher of his wife. Julie had loved everything Christmas and had decorated their house in the weeks between Halloween and Thanksgiving. She'd added to the collection of decorations every year until they filled a dozen red and green plastic bins that he stored in the eaves of the garage. While they may have lost everything else, at least they had been spared from the fire. "Aunt Sarah, would you mind if I brought some of our decorations here?"

Daisy clapped her hands. "Can the singing wreath be on my bedroom door?"

"I don't see why not. Chances are, you will be staying with me through the holidays,"

Aunt Sarah said and placed a wise man next to the crèche.

Once the tree was standing in the front window, Elijah helped Christopher place the strands of multicolored lights around the branches. They all stood back as Christopher plugged in the lights, and Aunt Sarah clapped her hands as they lit the room in reds, blues, greens and yellows. "Ooh, it's almost as good as the tree lighting tonight."

Aunt Sarah handed Daisy the star, and Christopher hoisted her up to fit it on top of the tree. They started to place ornaments, with Aunt Sarah pausing at times to share stories about the history of some of them. When she unwrapped a china angel and ran a finger down its cheek, she stopped. Daisy looked at her. "What's wrong, Aunt Sarah?"

"Someone gave this to me a very long time ago, and I always remember him when I unwrap her." She handed it to Daisy. "Why don't you find a special spot for this one?"

Christopher wondered if Aunt Sarah had had a special man in her life once. She'd mentioned that she'd come close to getting married. Maybe he had died early like Julie and left a void that no one else could fill in Sarah's heart.

And yet he wondered at times if he could find someone special again. Maybe she wouldn't fill Julie's place perfectly. But maybe she could add something else to his and his children's lives.

SHELBY HANDED OUT cups of hot chocolate to those who had gathered at her garage. Then they all began walking the short distance down Main to the tree lighting. Daisy had accepted a cup, but couldn't stand still without the cocoa sloshing over the sides, so Christopher held it while she danced in place. His daughter could find excitement in anything, but he knew that the appearance of Santa was at the top of that list.

He made small talk with Mel until Penny's cousin Jack joined the conversation. When Mel walked away, Jack asked, "So are you going to ask her out?"

"Who?"

"Mel. She's a nice woman. She loves kids."

Christopher opened his mouth to answer, but Jack stalked away. Wondering what had just happened, he turned to Shelby. "Did I say something wrong?"

"Don't worry about Jack." She looked him over. "But are you going to ask out Mel?"

"I wasn't thinking about it."

"And what about Penny?"

He frowned at her. "I'm not looking to ask anyone out. I'm not ready to yet."

Liar, his heart whispered. He ignored that small voice and handed Daisy her cup of hot chocolate.

"What does asking out mean, Daddy?"

"It's when adults want to get all kissy face," Elijah answered, scowling. "It's gross."

Christopher raised an eyebrow and to Shelby said, "Does that answer your question?"

"Some women like single dads and their kids. I wouldn't discount Miss Penny Cuthbert, no matter what she might say."

Aunt Sarah joined them and handed Daisy a napkin to wipe her mouth. "We're going to miss Santa's arrival if we don't start walking down to city hall."

"We wouldn't want to miss Santa." Shelby cupped her hands around her mouth. "All right, everyone. Let's get to city hall."

Christopher took a hand of each kid and joined everyone walking to city hall for the tree lighting. He must have been walking too slow for his children, as they raced ahead. Instead, Aunt Sarah joined him. "Shelby means well."

He stole a glance at her, wondering where that comment had come from. "Excuse me?"

"She's best friends with Mel, and she's trying to play matchmaker between the two of you."

"And you aren't with Penny and me?"

Aunt Sarah made a face. "Shelby's not as good at matchmaking as I am. Don't get me wrong. Melanie is a lovely girl, but you need someone with more spirit."

"Like Penny?"

"Your words, not mine."

Christopher stifled a chuckle and continued walking. "I appreciate what you're trying to do, but my children and I are fine as we are."

"Maybe. But it wouldn't hurt to add the right woman to your family."

"Aunt Sarah—"

But his words were cut off at their arrival at the large pine tree in front of city hall. It had been strung with thousands of unlit lights that swayed in the soft breeze of the evening, but it was still beautiful. Volunteers handed out song sheets to the crowd. At the stroke of seven, Thora's mayor stood next to the tree and held up his hands. "Welcome to the annual Thora tree lighting. Before we light the tree, let's sing some holiday favorites."

Christopher put his arms around his children as they sang songs he'd known since he was their age. Growing up with a single mom who worked two jobs, he'd had little experience with tree lightings and choir concerts. But he'd never felt deprived. There might not have been very many extras, but he knew he was loved and his mom did her best to provide what he needed.

When the song changed to "Santa Claus Is Comin' to Town," he could hear the blast of a fire-engine horn over the uplifted voices of the crowd. Turning his head, he saw the Thora fire engine pulling up to the curb. Christopher nudged his children and pointed to the truck as Santa pushed open the passenger door and stepped out. Daisy hopped up and down, clapping her hands excitedly. "Look! It's Santa, Daddy. He's here."

Santa had a dark green velvet sack over his shoulder, and he waved at the crowd as he approached the tree. The song ended, and he held up his hands much like the mayor had earlier to get everyone's attention. "Ho, ho, ho, and merry Christmas! I was passing by and heard a crowd singing my favorite song, so I asked the Thora Fire Department to drive me to the heart of the town. And here you are."

The mayor stepped forward. "Santa, since you're here, why don't you do the honors and light our town's Christmas tree?"

Santa placed a hand on his heart as if he was surprised by the request. "I could do that, but I'm going to need some help." He put his hand to his eyebrows. "Did I see Elijah Cuthbert out there?"

Elijah turned to Christopher, his mouth dropping open. Daisy tugged on his arm. "Santa called your name!"

Elijah's expression of wonder hardened to the same skeptical look that Christopher had become so familiar with, but he walked through the crowd to join Santa by the tree. Santa leaned down and whispered something in Elijah's ear, then ushered the boy to the large switch. "We're going to need you all to count us down. Five!"

The crowd joined in the countdown, and at the end, Elijah and Santa flipped the switch, lighting the tree. Oohs and aahs were heard among the crowd, and Daisy clapped her hands. Someone started singing "O Christmas Tree," and everyone joined in. Elijah stood next to Santa and sang along, giving Christopher hope that his boy might have some Christmas spirit in him after all.

This led to another Christmas carol, and Daisy tugged on Christopher's hand. "This was Mommy's favorite. She loved Christmas."

He nodded and blinked at the moisture in his eyes. He looked up to find Santa watching him from the front of the crowd. Santa gave him a bright smile, then winked.

After the mayor thanked everyone for coming, he reminded them that ornaments for the town's tree were available for sale, with the money going toward the toy drive. The crowd started to break up, some folks going to buy hot chocolate and others the ornaments, while still more people got in the line to see Santa. "Are we going to see Santa?" Daisy asked.

"We need to go get your brother first."

"Wasn't it amazing how Santa knew his

name and everything?" Daisy's eyes glittered with wonder, and Christopher nodded. "He knows everything, doesn't he, Daddy?"

"He knows all about little kids." And for a moment, Christopher had seen a glimpse of the kid his son had been before Julie died. He really missed that carefree boy.

Elijah approached them, and Daisy threw her arms around him. He grumbled, but allowed the contact for a moment before shrugging it off. Christopher put a hand on the boy's shoulder. "You did a great job, Eli."

"I guess."

"What did he whisper to you?" Daisy asked.

Elijah looked down at the ground and mumbled something. Because of the crowd around them, Christopher couldn't hear the response, so he crouched down to get to his son's eye level. "What was that? I couldn't hear you."

"He told me that good things can come after the bad stuff."

CHAPTER SIX

CHRISTOPHER STARTLED AT Santa's words given the events of that week. Good things after the bad? How had Santa known what they were going through? Would go through over the next few days, weeks, months? For a moment, he believed in the holiday magic, but then figured all of Thora had heard about their fire. He put his hand on Elijah's shoulder and ushered the kids to the line to visit with Santa before it grew any longer.

As they waited, Daisy asked aloud what she should ask from Santa. The doll that she had been talking about for the last few months? Or maybe a dollhouse to replace the one that had been burned in the fire? Elijah rolled his eyes at each request, but didn't offer any answers himself.

When their turn came, Daisy ran up first and took a running leap into Santa's arms. "Oh, how I've missed you," she said and laid her hand on his ample chest. "You don't know what we've been through."

"I might have an idea, Daisy," he responded and helped her get settled on his lap. "So what would you like most for Christmas?"

Daisy put a finger to her cheek, then leaned in to whisper in the jolly man's ear. He drew back his head and glanced up at Christopher before whispering into the little girl's ear. Daisy nodded solemnly at his words, then gave him a kiss before scrambling off his lap.

Christopher gestured to Elijah. "Your turn, buddy."

His son shook his head. "Dad, I don't need to sit on Santa's lap. I'm too old for that."

Santa frowned at him. "Don't tell me that I have an unbeliever on my hands." He peered at Elijah and crooked his finger at the boy. "Could we have a moment?"

Elijah sighed, but walked forward and stood before Santa. Christopher couldn't hear the words being exchanged, but his son nodded several times, then shook hands with Santa. "We've got a deal, then?"

"Sure."

Christopher gave Santa a smile as he

moved out of the way of the next child in line, but Santa stood. "Mr. Fox, I'd like a word."

Christopher felt like Daisy had when he'd called Elijah's name earlier. Santa knew his name? Feeling almost like he was eight again, he approached the old man and gasped when he saw the set of familiar eyes under the wig and beard.

PENNY GAVE CHRISTOPHER a smile when recognition dawned in his eyes. "Surprised to see me?"

"Frankly, yes. What are you doing?"

"My job for the night." She glanced over at his children, who were waiting for him with Aunt Sarah. "We're being watched, so keep up the pretense."

She knew that the last thing he would do was shatter his children's belief in Santa, so he nodded and dropped the volume of his voice to an intimate whisper. "You wanted to tell me something?"

She looked into his eyes, wondering how much she should share with him. "Daisy's Christmas wish."

"It was for the dollhouse, wasn't it?"

"It was for you."

When Christopher reared back, Penny felt her heart squeeze a little at the pain that entered his eyes. "She loves you so much, but she's worried. Her wish is that you would find your laugh this Christmas."

"I laugh."

"I'm just repeating what she said."

"And Eli?" He glanced to where his kids were watching them. "What did he say?"

"Hey, man. Give the kids a chance to meet Santa," someone in line shouted.

Penny looked over Christopher's shoulder at the waiting crowd. "He's right. We can talk later when there's no one waiting for me. I am the star of the show, after all." She tried to inject a little levity with her answer, but couldn't ignore that he was obviously hurting. She rubbed his arm. "Have a merry Christmas, Christopher."

Christopher nodded and walked away, glancing behind him once to look at her before joining his family. Penny gave him a nod, then focused on the long line of kids waiting for her. She lowered the tenor of her voice and asked, "Who's next?"

SHE DIDN'T GET a chance to talk to Christopher on Sunday due to her schedule. Once her shift ended Monday afternoon, she drove to her aunt's home with the thought of a long shower before dinner with the family. But it was only her aunt and herself who ate that night. "Christopher said he had an appointment with his children," Aunt Sarah explained when Penny asked about the two place settings at the kitchen table.

Disappointment tugged at her heart, but she gave her aunt a smile to hide it. "It will be like old times, then."

"You have to admit it's been nice having little ones in the house again." Aunt Sarah dished up the casserole, then took a seat next to Penny. "They certainly keep life interesting. And so does their dad, right?"

Penny poured ranch dressing over her salad. "I know what you're doing, and it won't work." Aunt Sarah put a hand on her chest, but the innocent act didn't convince her. "Christopher is a nice man, but nothing will happen between us."

"And why not?"

"You know why not. I'm not going to lose my heart again to another single father who's still in love with the mother of his children."

"Julie passed away almost two years ago. It was a tragedy, but life has to go on."

"He's still hung up on her." Penny placed the cloth napkin on her lap. "I can see the same signs that I ignored with Alan. The way his lips tip up at the mention of her name. The look of loss in his eyes when he shares a story about her. Or the way his children talk about her. He loves her."

"Certainly, he does. Death doesn't end love."

"So why are you pushing the two of us together?"

"Just because he still loves her doesn't mean he can't love again. And you would be a good match for him."

Penny couldn't keep back the bubble of laughter. "Why in the world do you think that?"

"Because he needs someone with your spirit to bring back joy to his life." She reached over and grabbed Penny's hand. "I know Alan hurt you. Being left like you were is a hard thing to get over, but you have moved on. You took the job here. You've reconnected with your family. And now you're ready to fall in love."

"And what about you? You never moved on."

Aunt Sarah's smile tightened into a thin line, and she let go of Penny's hand. "We're not talking about me."

"Why not? You were left at the altar, too, so you know what I've been through. You know what it's like to play back every moment that you had together, wondering where it went wrong. And to think you won't ever fall in love again."

"My situation was different. The war took him from me."

"And you never gave yourself another chance to find love. Even after he came back from Korea."

"So you want to be like me? Eighty-seven years old and alone in a big house?" Aunt Sarah peered into her eyes. "I had one great love, but I lost him. And now I face these so-called golden years by myself." When Penny started to protest, Sarah continued. "I know you kids watch over me, but it's not the same. I wouldn't wish this solitary life for you. You have too much life and shouldn't bury yourself away."

Penny grasped Aunt Sarah's hand in hers. "And so do you. You didn't die with Nana, but you certainly act like you did. She would hate to see you like this."

Her aunt blinked for a few moments, and Penny wondered if she'd wounded her aunt with her words. Finally, Aunt Sarah took a deep breath and let it out slowly. "I'll make you a deal. You keep an open mind about Christopher. And I'll live a little more."

BOTH THE FIRE INSPECTOR and insurance adjuster had confirmed what Christopher feared. The house was a total loss and would need to be rebuilt from the ground up. That meant they would likely be in temporary housing for a year or so until construction was completed.

If he wanted to rebuild.

At the moment, he wasn't sure whether or not rebuilding was the right option for them. To be uprooted from one home to go into a rental and then move again? The idea of it made his head ache. He flipped another page of the sports magazine as he sat in the waiting room of the counselor's office on Monday evening.

Elijah sat on the floor, his homework spread out on the coffee table. He'd already spent his time in the woman's office, and they waited while Daisy met with the counselor. Their monthly meetings with Dr. Shoemaker seemed to keep things status quo, rather than improve their situation, but Christopher didn't want to know what it would be like if they didn't have these sessions. Daisy's obsession with the cape and Elijah's silences could have fallen into something worse.

The door to the counselor's office opened, and Daisy trudged out and took a seat next to Christopher. Her eyes looked red, as if she'd been crying. He put his hand on her back before getting to his feet and entering the office. Dr. Shoemaker looked up from her notes, her glasses perched at the end of her nose. "I'm sorry to hear about the house fire."

He took a seat across from her. "We'll be fine."

"I don't doubt that. You have gone through one loss and have the tools to get through this, too." She set the notebook on her lap and peered at him. "How was Thanksgiving?"

"It seemed to be okay. What did the kids say?"

"I'm asking you how you felt about it. Not how the kids felt."

He stared back at her and shrugged. "It

was fine. My mom joined us at the Cuth-berts'." He told her about how he'd enjoyed the large family dynamic. "Reminded me of Julie's family."

"Elijah tells me that you met a woman."

His son had mentioned Penny? "It's not what you think. She's not a romantic inter-est. She was the firefighter that saved our dog from the fire."

"And she's living with you and her aunt?"

"For the time being." He wasn't sure what she wanted him to say. "She's developed quite a bond with Daisy."

"Your daughter probably mentioned Penny a half dozen times during our conversation." Dr. Shoemaker sat forward in the chair. "How does it make you feel to have another woman enter the family dynamic?"

"She hasn't entered anything. She's there, but she's not a part of our family." He crossed his arms over his chest and settled into the sofa. "In fact, she's pretty irritating. Telling me she's worried about my kids."

"Why is she worried?"

He shook his head. "It's nothing. She just thought that Daisy's Christmas wish about me meant something."

"What was her wish?"

He swallowed and paused before answering, "That I get my laugh back this Christmas and be happy."

"Aren't you happy?"

"Dr. Shoemaker, we're here to help my kids. What I am or am not doesn't matter in this equation." Why didn't people understand? It was the kids who had to be happy. The kids whom he had to focus on, not some self-indulgent need for navel-gazing. If his kids were happy, then by extension he would be, too. "We're here because of Daisy and Elijah's grief over their mom."

"And not yours over your wife? You lost her as much as they did."

"Dr. Shoemaker—"

"It's okay to be happy again. To laugh. Even to find love with another woman. Wouldn't Julie have wanted you to know happiness again?"

"The kids are what's important. That's why we're here. Not for me."

"No. You're right. That's a topic for another time." She crossed her legs at her ankles. "Should we call in the children now?"

He nodded, grateful for the respite from

the doctor's probing questions. She rose to her feet and walked to the door to call in the kids. He put his arms around them and pulled them in close for a group hug. For once, Elijah didn't pull away first.

Dr. Shoemaker watched them for a moment, then said, "I'd like each of you to say one thing you're looking forward to this holiday. Christopher, why don't you start us off?"

He cleared his throat, taking a second to think about the request. "Well, I'm excited about spending more time with my kids."

"Can you be more specific?"

"How about taking one night to drive around and see all the Christmas lights? Then going out for dessert afterward."

Elijah slumped beside him, and Christopher didn't have to see his son's face to know he'd rolled his eyes. Dr. Shoemaker looked at Elijah. "You don't think that's a good idea?"

"It was Mom's favorite thing to do."

"And you don't want to do what your mom liked to do?"

Elijah glanced at Christopher before giving a quick shrug of his shoulders. "I guess I do, but you asked what my dad wanted to do. Not my mom."

Dr. Shoemaker made a note, then asked him, "Why don't you tell us what you're looking forward to, Elijah?"

"Presents."

She gave him a soft smile and nodded. "Most children would agree with you. Anything more specific?"

"No." He scrunched his face into a scowl. "Just presents."

"Okay. Daisy, what about you?"

"My choir concert."

Dr. Shoemaker smiled. "What do you like about your choir concert?"

"That I have a solo. And that my dad will be there to hear me sing." She rested her head on his chest. "I like singing."

She was so much like Julie, who loved to sing, albeit his wife didn't have the voice for it. Christopher had often caught her singing when she thought no one was listening. He brought Daisy closer to his side. Fortunately, his daughter had a wonderful voice.

Dr. Shoemaker nodded again. "And now why don't we share something we're not looking forward to? Daisy, you first."

His daughter bit her lip before shrugging. "Nothing. I love Christmas."

"Elijah?"

"I'm not looking forward to Daisy's choir concert." His words held a hint of laughter, and his son stuck his tongue out at Daisy, who laughed. But then his face got serious. "I don't want to go to the cemetery on Christmas again."

"And why is that?"

"Because it just makes us all sad for the rest of the day."

Daisy nodded at her brother's words. "I don't want to go, either. Do we have to?"

Christopher had thought that visiting their mother's burial place and laying the wreath and homemade cards at her grave had been a comfort that first Christmas. Yes, there had been tears, but they had enjoyed the rest of the day without Julie's absence hanging over them.

Hadn't they?

Dr. Shoemaker raised her eyebrows at him, and he gave a soft shrug. "I guess we won't go, then."

"And what are you dreading this holiday?"

Spending another holiday without Julie. But he couldn't say that. Instead, he smiled.

"I'm like Daisy. I love Christmas and all that it involves."

"No, you don't," Elijah said. "You complain about how busy it is because of everything going on." His son glared at him. "But Mom loved Christmas. She always said it was the best time of year because people were a little bit kinder to each other. She loved the songs. The decorations. And especially the cookies."

"Can't your dad love Christmas, too?"

"He doesn't love it like Mom did, so he shouldn't pretend that he does. He's not Mom."

"I'm not pretending, buddy. I do love Christmas."

This time, Christopher didn't miss the rolled eyes. His son turned to Dr. Shoemaker, shaking his head. Dr. Shoemaker made some notes before shutting her book and smiling at them. "That's all the time we have for today. Remember how important it is to listen to each other. It will help. I hope you all have a good holiday."

Elijah hopped off the sofa and left the room before anyone else could get up. Trailing after her brother, Daisy walked out of the office, and Christopher turned to the counselor. "I really do love Christmas."

Dr. Shoemaker nodded. "I know that, and I think Elijah knows that, too. But right now, he's separating you from Julie. If she loved something, you can't, and vice versa."

"Why would he do that?"

"Because she's gone, and you're not."

PENNY LOWERED THE volume on the television once her aunt had fallen asleep. She picked up her phone, checked texts, emails and all her social-media apps while trying to rid herself of this restless energy. She should be relaxing after a long shift at the fire station, but she couldn't. Something was off, and she couldn't figure out what it was.

The front door opened and shut, followed by the tromping of feet on the stairs. She glanced at the ceiling and debated checking on the Fox family. Partly to make sure they were all okay. She knew that Christopher had learned about the fate of his house that afternoon, and she was curious to find out what he planned on doing.

The other part of her, the one with the feelings growing daily, wanted to see Christopher. Period. She'd missed him the last couple of days, yet she didn't want to admit that. But she'd promised Aunt Sarah to keep an open mind.

The program on the television changed, and Penny got to her feet. She placed an afghan over Aunt Sarah. Upstairs, she could hear voices coming from her old bedroom, and she paused outside, listening.

Christopher was reading a story to his children, using different funny voices for each of the characters. But he didn't do those voices very well. A smile played on her lips as she listened, and she lifted her hand to hide it.

The chapter ended, and she tiptoed away to stand in the doorway of her room to watch as Christopher and Elijah came out, and the single dad turned out the light but kept the door cracked open. Then he walked his son down to the other bedroom and repeated the bedtime ritual.

An ache spread in her chest. Christopher was a single dad, but he was also a good man. How many fathers would jump in with both feet when the mother of their children died? Her own dad had passed on much of the childcare responsibility to Nana and Aunt Sarah. Penny had seen wisps of him when he was off duty, but her childhood had been filled with being raised by someone other than her father.

"Are you okay?"

She looked up at the sound of Christopher's voice, breaking the melancholy she'd been drowning in. "Fine." She stepped out of the shadows into the lit hallway. "What did you find out today about the house?"

Christopher made a face. "It's a total loss. I'll have to either rebuild or move somewhere else."

"I'm sorry to hear that." She reached out and touched his sleeve. He glanced at her hand, and she dropped it.

"But you're not surprised," he said.

"No. I saw firsthand what the fire did to the house, remember?"

He ran a hand through his dark hair. "I don't know what we're going to do. I mean, I'm not sure what's best for Elijah and Daisy."

"You don't have to decide tonight."

He gave a bitter chuckle. "Right. The inspector said that the structure has been stabilized so that we can start going through the ashes to find anything that might have survived and we want to keep."

"I can help you with that."

He shook his head. "You and your family have already done too much. I couldn't ask you to do that."

"You're not asking. I'm volunteering. See the difference?"

He smiled at her, and the wrinkles at the corners of his eyes appeared. "Then I'll accept the help."

She smiled up into his face until she forgot why she was smiling. The close, intimate feeling between them broke when she pointed down the hallway. "I'd better go back downstairs. The last I heard, Aunt Sarah was snoring in front of the television."

He stepped aside for her to walk away, but she stood in place, watching him. "It's all going to be okay, you know?"

"Good things come after the bad stuff?"

"I heard that Santa said that."

Christopher nodded, smiling. "He did. And I hope he's right about that."

CHAPTER SEVEN

APPLAUSE BEGAN AS the last carol ended with a flourish. Penny took a bow and winked at an elderly gentleman sitting in a wheelchair watching the performance. He hadn't cracked a smile or clapped along with the songs as the others had. And Penny was determined to get Mr. Duffy to enjoy himself. Even Aunt Sarah had noticed him, but she'd gone out of her way to avoid him. Interesting.

Maybe her aunt wasn't as finished with romance as she claimed.

Once the younger Cuthberts started to pass out candy canes to their audience at the senior living home, Penny stepped away from the group and took a handful of the candy to her grumpy friend. She held out a red-and-white cane. "Sweets for the sweet."

Mr. Duffy harrumphed but took the candy cane. Penny crouched down to face him. "You didn't enjoy the singing?"

"Too sentimental for my tastes."

"You like what? More hard-rock tunes?"

"I'll have you know, in my day, I was known as something of a singer myself."

When Penny gave him a skeptical look, he opened his mouth and started to sing an Elvis classic. The others around them stopped talking and listened in. Once he finished, Penny joined in the cheers and clapping. "We'll have to recruit you for next year's caroling."

The old man grumbled, but she didn't miss his smile before he turned his wheelchair and left them.

"I don't think I've seen Mr. Duffy smile since I got here."

Penny recognized Christopher's voice instantly. "You're working late tonight."

"I need to take some time off tomorrow to go through the ashes before the contractor comes to tear the house down." He looked down at her ugly Christmas sweater and shook his head. "Not many people could pull off the tinsel look, but you…" He winced. "No. Not even you can make that sweater look good."

She blushed at the backhanded compliment.

"I'll have you know, I made this sweater myself."

"It looks like it."

She poked his arm, but smiled. Shelby walked over to them. "Christopher, how did we sound?"

"Great. My residents loved it." He looked at Penny. "As did I."

Shelby nodded. "Good. Now we'll start going room to room for those who couldn't make it down to hear us."

She went, and Christopher seemed awestruck. "Does she ever stop? I don't think I've ever seen her in any other speed except fast-forward."

"That's Shelby for you." Penny picked up her song sheets from the piano. "I guess I should join them."

"I think it was nice that you included your great-aunt."

"She says she can't carry a tune, but she does love playing tambourine."

"I was wondering if she'd like to have a tour of the complex, instead of going caroling."

"Why would she want a tour?"

Christopher shrugged. "In case she's looking to make a change. After all, that house is big for one person. Let alone a frail woman in her eighties."

"She better not hear you call her frail." Penny paused. "Has she said anything to you about this?"

"We talked, but she didn't say either way. I just thought that since she's here, I could show her the amenities we offer."

"You trying to kick my aunt out of her house?"

"I'm only offering her an option."

Penny stepped closer and whispered, "You leave my aunt out of this. She isn't ready to give up and move in here."

"Moving here isn't giving anything up. Our seniors live full, productive lives here."

"Save your sales pitch for somebody else."

"Why don't you let your aunt make up her own mind?"

"Because she'll sell the house that I grew up in, and then where would I be?" Penny grimaced. "But this isn't about me."

Christopher nodded. "No, it's not. It's about what's best for your aunt."

The thought of losing the house made Penny want to cry. And if she felt this way about the possibility of the house going to another family, how much more was Christopher feeling over losing his home suddenly to a fire? She put a hand on his arm. "I'm sorry about your house. I'll be there to help you tomorrow, but please don't mention a tour to my aunt right now."

"She'll move eventually. Isn't it better for her to make that decision while she can still enjoy the rest of her life?"

Penny glanced over her shoulder at her aunt. Had the family missed the signs that she was ready to leave the house? And would it be better for her to give it up? She approached her aunt, who had been watching them. "What did Christopher say to you that upset you so much?"

"Nothing."

"It's not nice to lie to your aunt."

She glanced over at Christopher. "We can talk about it later. Should we join the rest of the carolers?"

Aunt Sarah frowned. "I'd rather go home, if you don't mind. I'm not as young as I used to be, and I'm ready to call it a night."

Penny helped her aunt put on her coat, then texted Shelby to let her know they'd left early.

Once inside the car, Penny let the engine idle for a moment. Her aunt put her head on the headrest and closed her eyes. "Christopher does a nice job there, don't you think? The seniors seem to love him."

"Even cranky Mr. Duffy respects him." She glanced at her aunt, but she didn't have a reaction. Maybe she'd read the situation wrong earlier.

Aunt Sarah opened her eyes and cleared her throat. "I've been thinking."

Here it comes. Penny wasn't sure if she was ready to hear that she wanted to move into the seniors' home. "What were you thinking about?"

"I have friends who have moved into the home and love it. Did you see the calendar of activities they have? Or the menu of what they serve in the cafeteria?" Aunt Sarah gave a soft smile. "Imagine not having to cook again."

"But you love to cook."

"I used to. And since Christopher and his family have moved in, I have a reason to. But once they move out, and you after them..." Aunt Sarah shrugged. "Cooking for one person is decidedly dull. And pointless."

"Did Christopher ask you to move into the home?"

"No, but he did ask if the house gets to be too much sometimes."

"And what did you say?"

"It's no secret that I depend on other people to help me do things around the house." Aunt Sarah stared out the car window. "Maybe I should sell the house before I get hurt or sick."

"You're the healthiest person I know."

Aunt Sarah looked over at her. "I'm also eighty-seven, and my time grows short. I want to enjoy what I have left. Maybe Christopher is right about that."

"But Cuthberts have always lived in that house since Pops's granddad built it."

"Technically, I'm not a Cuthbert. Only related to one who married into the family, so your argument doesn't stand."

"You'd really sell the house?"

"I'd see if anyone in the family would want it first, but I'm starting to consider it."

CHRISTOPHER HAD GIVEN himself the entire day off to go through the burned shell of his house. Despite their words the night before, Penny had joined him in the futile search for anything that might be saved from the ashes. He moved the scorched bookcase from the living-room wall and shook his head. The books had burned along with the DVDs and CDs.

"What about this?" she asked.

He found Penny holding up a photo album. "How bad is the damage?"

She flipped a few pages. "Very minimal. Scorched edges, but the pictures inside are fine." She closed the album and handed it to him. "I'd say that's a good find."

He put it on the stack of the few things they had salvaged so far.

Once they finished sifting through the downstairs, Penny checked the steps before they walked up to the second floor. She pointed out weak spots to avoid, and they started in Daisy's room. The black scorch marks had created dark murals on the once pink walls. Most of her dolls and toys had burned or melted. He found a portion of Mr. Bear and pulled him from the rubble. "I bought her this the night she was born."

Penny stopped her inspection of the closet and faced him. "Do you think we could wash it?"

He shook his head and put a finger through

a hole that had burned through the face. "She hasn't played with the bear in years, and I think I'm more upset by this than she will be."

"I know this is hard, but sometimes you can find treasures that you never realized were here."

He cocked his head to the side as he looked at her. "Is there a metaphor in there?"

"You know what I mean. Like the photo album. That's irreplaceable."

He knew she was right. They moved next to Elijah's room but found very little that could be salvaged. The baseball bat and glove had been burned beyond recognition, while his trophies had melted into strange-looking sculptures.

In his own bedroom, Christopher found the dresser facedown on the floor. With Penny's help, they got it upright. He pulled open a drawer and sighed at the mess the burned clothes had left. He reached to the back of the drawer and pulled out a velvet bag. *Please let them be okay.* Opening the bag, he pulled out a strand of pearls and a diamond solitaire. Penny looked over his shoulder. "They survived the fire."

"They were my wife's. I was saving them

for the kids." The velvet bag would need to be replaced, but the jewelry was intact. He was truly grateful. "I thought they'd be gone."

Penny put a hand on his arm and smiled up at him. "Maybe Julie was watching over them for you."

"That is something she would do. They were important to her." He tucked the jewelry into his pocket so it wouldn't get lost. "I kept thinking to put them in a safe-deposit box, but put it off. Thinking I'd have time to do it later."

"Then it's a good thing they survived."

Christopher looked around the ruins of the bedroom he'd shared with his wife. "It's hard to believe that this is all gone."

Penny gently put a hand on his arm. "I'm really sorry. Is there anything I can do?"

He wished she could change it all to before the fire. To change it before even his wife died. He closed his eyes and took deep breaths. He'd done that since Julie died. Focused on breathing in, breathing out. Counted to ten. Then he'd be ready to face whatever it was that needed doing.

After reaching ten, he opened his eyes and saw Penny watching him. Shaking his head, he searched through more drawers in the dresser but found nothing worth saving.

"Have you decided what you're going to do?"

"No. The insurance company has hired a contractor to remove all the debris, but if I choose to rebuild, it won't start until after the New Year."

"Have you talked to the kids about it?"

This had to be his choice. They were too young to realize the implications of their options and what they meant. He had the knowledge and hopefully the wisdom to make the right decision. "Whatever I choose, I want to keep the kids in the same school. For that reason, I'm leaning on rebuilding. But that means about a year of living somewhere else temporarily, which doesn't sound very stable for them."

"It's a tough decision."

He nodded and moved to the closet. In there, the flames had burned through the walls and the ceiling. He could see patches of sky where he should see roof. Clothes that had once hung on hangers had been reduced to nothing, leaving the hangers empty. All of Julie's things that he'd had a hard time letting go of were gone. The wedding gown she'd had preserved to pass down to Daisy one day. The sweaters and jeans and dresses that he'd pushed aside to get to his own clothes for almost two years. He'd give anything to have them in his way now.

He turned and noticed Penny watching him. He took a deep breath and cleared his throat before she could read his thoughts. "There's nothing here to save."

"The floor is less stable in here. We should go back downstairs."

He nodded and patted the jewelry in his jeans pocket. At least he had that.

PENNY TOSSED CHRISTOPHER a bottle of water, then opened her own and took several long swigs as she watched him. He kept his back to her as he drank from his bottle, so she couldn't tell what he was thinking. Going through the remains of the fire couldn't be easy on anyone, but the sense of loss that had been emanating from him enveloped more than what little was left of the house.

She surveyed the kitchen, which had sustained the most damage besides the basement. Flames had burned through the floor, and she could see the basement below through the charred floorboards. "I don't think we can salvage anything in here."

He turned to her, and the look in his eyes made her insides melt. The need to touch him, to offer him what little comfort she might, propelled her forward, and she pulled him into a hug. "Go ahead and cry. The kids aren't here."

He clung to her and breathed deeply. "I thought I could handle this. I keep telling myself that it's just stuff. Just things."

She rubbed his back. "But it's memories, too. At least those can't be destroyed by the flames."

"But time has a nasty way of making you forget them. Memories fade."

She wished that was the case for her. She wanted to forget the pain that Alan had caused her. Wanted to forget the way she'd lost not only him, but also the relationship she'd been forging with his daughter, Callie. Did the girl still think of her like Penny did of her?

She rested her head against his chest and tightened her grip on him, drawing comfort for herself. "Some memories are best forgotten."

"If I had known that time was running

out so quickly, I would have spent every day memorizing how Julie's eyes crinkled in the corners when she laughed. How her laugh started high and ended in a low chuckle."

Penny looked up at him. "Sounds like you do remember that."

He backed away and shielded his eyes with one hand. "Enough of this. Let's finish what I came here to do and leave. I don't have time for this."

"You need to grieve this loss, too."

He stepped back, his gaze burning. "This isn't like losing my wife, so don't start with all that." He brushed past her to head back into the living room.

She followed him. "Christopher, I didn't mean to upset you. But these feelings aren't something that you can box up and put away. Or sweep up and throw into the trash. Your kids are worried about you, and frankly, so am I."

He tipped back his head and groaned. "Daisy's wish again? I'm happy enough."

"But is it enough for you?"

"I promised my wife that I'd put them first, and I have. I've kept that promise."

"Why is that promise so important to you?"

"It just is. Promises are meant to be kept."

"Did someone not keep their promise to you?"

Christopher shook his head and walked over to pick up the stack of items they'd been able to save, including the photo album. "I should get back before the kids get home from school."

"THANK YOU, BUT I don't think that will work out for my family." Christopher hung up the phone and marked the number off his list of possible rentals. Because of the dog, their options were limited. He reached down and gave Caesar a pat on the back before calling the next number.

The front door opened like it was an announcement of his children returning from school. The sounds were unmistakable. Caesar barked and left him at the kitchen table to greet the kids. Elijah was the first to enter, dropping his backpack and coat on his way to the counter, where Aunt Sarah had left out a snack. Christopher cleared his throat and pointed at the fallen items. "You can eat once you pick up your stuff and put it where it belongs."

"Whatever."

Elijah picked up his coat and bag and left the room, returning in a few moments with Daisy, who was wearing her cape. "Where's Aunt Sarah?" she asked.

"Penny took her grocery shopping."

"Oh." She spotted the snacks on the counter and walked over to them. "What are you doing home from work?"

"Trying to find us a new place to live."

"What's wrong with staying here? This place has the best food." She smiled at the snack.

He smiled at his daughter. "This is only temporary."

"What's tempomary?"

"He means it's just for now, not forever." Elijah rolled his eyes at his sister and bit into his carrot stick.

"Your brother's right. This is Aunt Sarah's house, not ours. We are her guests."

Daisy screwed her face up into a frown, but took her snack from the counter and placed it on the table next to his list. "Why don't we ask her if we can just stay here? She likes us, so I'm sure she'd say yes."

"That's not the way it works, dummy."

"Elijah, what have we said about using that word?"

His son sighed. "That it's not nice, and I shouldn't say it."

"And?"

He looked across the table at his sister. "I'm sorry I called you a dummy." He pulled the chair out from the kitchen table and took a seat. "I don't want to stay here. I want to go home."

"We can't live there anymore. We talked about this."

"I know. But I wish we could."

Mark a point in the column for rebuilding. The new house wouldn't be the same one, but it would be in the same place. It would be a little familiar.

"I was able to save some things from the house today." Christopher stood and retrieved the photo album from the family room, where he'd left it.

Daisy wrinkled her nose as he got closer. "That stinks like the time Mommy burned the popcorn."

"It does, but it will get better." He opened the book and pointed at his wedding picture. "Your mom was the most beautiful girl I ever saw. And you look just like her, Daisy. You've got her dark curly brown hair."

Daisy giggled and pulled the album closer to her. "She looks just like a princess."

"She did."

Elijah stared at the pictures, forgetting to finish his snack. When Christopher started to flip a page, his son stayed his hand. "Wait." He bent to get a closer look at the photo of Julie holding her newborn son. "Is that me?"

"You know it is."

Elijah ran a finger down Julie's cheek. "I forgot she had brown eyes like chocolate chips." He looked up at Christopher, and Eli reminded him of the little boy he remembered before cancer stole his mother. But he blinked, and the glimpse was gone. His son shook his head. "I've got homework to do."

"You can finish your snack first."

"Not hungry."

Christopher watched Elijah leave the room and head upstairs to the bedroom. Daisy sighed. "He doesn't like to talk about Mommy."

Christopher pulled her closer and rested his chin on top of her head. "Sometimes it makes me sad to talk about her. Elijah probably feels sad, too."

"But I like to talk about her." He grinned at his daughter as she turned to the next page. "Tell me why you named me Daisy."

"You know that story. I've told you a hundred times."

"So make it a hundred and one."

She smiled up at him, and he couldn't say no to that request. "Your mom's favorite flower was a rose. So that's what we were going to name you."

"Rose Christina Fox."

"Who's telling the story?" He kissed the top of her head. "Right. Rose Christina. But after you were born, your mom held you in her arms and said you looked like a Daisy. So that's what you became."

Daisy laid her head on his arm. "I love that story."

"I do, too."

CHRISTOPHER WALKED OUT to the car to help retrieve the grocery bags when they returned to the house with more food than Penny figured they'd need, but Aunt Sarah had insisted that the Foxes would be staying longer than originally planned. She looped several plastic bags over her wrists and started toward the house.

"You can make more than one trip, you know," Christopher said as he passed by her.

"I can handle it. I'm stronger than you think." She sped up to pass him before they reached the front door, then down the hallway to the kitchen. Placing her bags on the counter, she massaged the red welts on her wrists.

Christopher raised an eyebrow at her when he set down the bags he'd brought in from the car. He disappeared, presumably for another load. Once the bags were all arranged on the counter, Christopher left to make more calls while Aunt Sarah started to make dinner and Penny unpacked and put away the groceries. The pantry looked as if it was already full.

Penny held up a large economy-size bag of rice. "Where do you want me to put this? There's two bags this size already in here."

"Put it on the bottom of the other two. I'm thinking of making my cube steak over rice later this week."

"I don't know how much more I can fit in here."

"It will fit. Trust me."

Still skeptical, Penny emptied the grocery bags and found spaces for most of the items.

Those she couldn't, she left on the counter, and Aunt Sarah rearranged things to make them fit. With the groceries put away, Penny recruited the kids to help her set the table for dinner, but could only find Daisy. "Where's your brother?"

"Upstairs doing homework."

"Want to help me?"

"Sure!" Daisy jumped up from where she'd been playing with her dolls. "I can't do the glasses, though. Daddy said I might break them."

"Oh, you'll do just fine."

Together, they set the table, and Penny demonstrated how to make a fan out of the cloth napkin. Daisy applauded her effort. "That's so fancy."

"But easy to do, right?"

Daisy nodded and set about making the rest of the napkins into fans. Penny pointed upstairs. "I'm going to go get your brother, okay?"

"Okay, but watch out, 'cause he's cranky."

"Thanks for the warning." Penny left Daisy to finish the table and took the stairs two at a time. She'd bonded so easily with Daisy, but couldn't seem to find common ground with

Elijah. He kept her at arm's length for some reason.

She tried knocking on the door to the guest bedroom he was staying in. No answer. She knocked once more, then started to turn the doorknob. Elijah swung the door open. "I'm busy."

"Dinner will be ready soon, and I wanted to check on you."

"Why?"

Okay, so not off to a good start. She picked up the math book that was lying open on the bed. "Fractions, huh? I always got confused by those."

He took the book from her hands. "I don't need your help."

"Good. Because I wasn't offering."

Elijah crossed his arms over his chest. "What else do you want?"

"Like I said, I wanted to check on you."

"And score some points with my dad?"

That one caught her off guard. "Your dad has nothing to do with this." She took a seat on the edge of the bed. "Why don't you like me?"

"Why do I have to?"

"Most kids like me. I'm really funny when you get to know me."

"We're not going to be here long enough to make it worth it." He sat on the other side of the bed, his back to her. She stood up to leave, but stopped at the door when Elijah said, "I had a mother, and she was an angel. We don't need you."

She paused and went over to face him. "I'm not looking to be your mom, okay? I thought maybe we could be friends."

"I don't need any more friends. Now would you please leave?"

At least the kid was polite when he was throwing her out of his room. Penny stepped out and shut the door quietly behind her. She startled as she spotted Christopher standing in the hallway watching her. "I apologize for his attitude."

She held up a hand. "He's only being honest. He doesn't want to be friends with me."

"It's not about you. He doesn't like any woman close to Julie's age for some reason. We've been talking about it with the family counselor, but unfortunately, it hasn't improved his attitude."

"He lost his mom, so I can relate. I understand."

"I wish I did." He winced and crossed his

arms over his chest. "He's so angry and rude, and I'm ready to pull out my hair. He's nine, not even a teenager. I cringe to think what he'll be like at that point."

"It's okay."

"No, it's not, but I don't know what else to do with him. If Julie were here…"

"If she was, she'd be wondering what to do about his attitude, as well."

"Maybe you're right."

"I usually am." She smiled.

Christopher relaxed. "It must be nice to know all the answers."

"Hardly." She put her arm around his waist. "But I'm right about Elijah. He just needs time."

"And what about me?" Christopher moved closer, looking at her intently. "What do I need?"

Penny stared into his eyes and swallowed hard. If she stood on tiptoe, she could kiss him. Could see if these friendly feelings had something more behind them.

His mouth parted, and the tip of his tongue touched his bottom lip.

Just leaning a little closer… That was all it would take.

Christopher took a step back and cleared his throat. "Aunt Sarah had asked me to find you. She needs your help with something."

"Sure. Thanks." As she passed him, she told him, "It will get better, Christopher."

"I hope you're right."

AFTER DINNER, AUNT SARAH suggested watching a Christmas movie before the kids went to bed. Daisy and Elijah lay on the floor in front of the television while Penny and Christopher sat on the sofa. Aunt Sarah fell asleep in the recliner about twenty minutes into the movie, snoring softly. Christopher exchanged a look with Penny, trying not to laugh as the snores got progressively louder. "Is there any way to stop her?"

Penny shook her head. "The TV puts her to sleep every night about this time, and I haven't figured out a way to make her stop snoring."

"I can hear you," Aunt Sarah mumbled, but her eyes stayed closed. "I'm only resting my eyes."

"You're resting them loud enough for us to hear." Penny shook her head, and Christopher squelched a laugh.

The movie was one that he watched several times with the kids every year. He could quote most of it verbatim. It couldn't keep his attention. Instead, he sneaked looks at Penny while she watched the movie, laughing at parts. She was lovely to look at, but her friendly demeanor attracted him, as well. Sitting on the sofa next to her made it feel like they were together. He knew he shouldn't be thinking like that. He was in no position to be considering any woman, much less Penny. He wasn't ready. And he needed to keep his promise to Julie, anyway, about putting the kids first. Poor Elijah couldn't see Penny's good points, so Christopher would have to keep his distance from her.

But another part of him, one that had been dormant for a long time, seemed to be awakening with Penny's presence. She reminded him that he was a male who still had desires that wanted to be explored. That he could have a future that included more than his children. That he wouldn't have to be alone, but could have a partner to love and help him in his life's journey. It was the worst idea he could have had.

Penny laughed and reached over to pat his leg. "This cracks me up every time."

The touch was brief, but it set his nerve endings on alert. He wanted her to touch him again.

He didn't want her to touch him ever.

Closing his eyes, he rested his head on the back of the sofa. A nudge to his ribs, and he opened one eye to look at her.

"Resting your eyes, too?"

He grinned. "It's been a long day."

"You're not interested in the movie?"

"I've seen it a million times."

"It's one of my favorites." She held up her hand. "Wait. This is my favorite part." She repeated the dialogue and laughed along with the kids. When the movie finished, the kids went upstairs to get ready for bed. Penny stood and removed the disc from the machine to put it back in its case. "It wouldn't be the holidays if I didn't see this movie."

"I'm more partial to the classic Christmas movies myself."

She smiled at him. "We'll have to watch one of your favorites next time." He reached out and pushed one blond strand of hair behind her ear. Her smile faded, and she bit her lip as she kept her eyes on him.

He didn't want to look away, but he turned to find Elijah watching them with a scowl from the kitchen.

CHAPTER EIGHT

SATURDAY MORNING, CHRISTOPHER woke early
and quickly put the foldaway bed back into
the sofa and straightened the pillows. He had
more energy than he'd had in a while and
figured he'd make his famous pancakes for
everyone's breakfast. In the kitchen, he found
the ingredients and quickly stirred the batter.
In the refrigerator, he also found bacon. He
prepped a sheet pan of bacon and placed it
in the oven before greasing a griddle for the
pancakes.

He'd made two stacks of pancakes when he
heard the footsteps behind him. He turned,
expecting Aunt Sarah, but found Penny standing there in a hoodie and boxers. She yawned
and rubbed her eyes. "You're making breakfast?"

"Did I wake you?"

"The smell of bacon is the best alarm ever."
She took a seat at the counter on one of the

stools, propping one bare foot on the top rung. "Please tell me that you also made coffee."

"I can't start my day without a shot of caffeine." He poured a cup and offered it to her.

She took the cup and inhaled the aroma before taking a sip. "Ambrosia." She got off the stool and retrieved a carton of half-and-half from the fridge. "But I like it sweet and creamy."

The words reminded him of her. She was so sweet, trying to soothe and comfort his kids. She'd even tried to reach some kind of understanding with Elijah, who hadn't made it easy on her. Christopher topped off his mug with coffee before he returned the carafe to the machine. "What do you like on your pancakes?"

"Butter and maple syrup, of course."

He placed a stack of three pancakes on a plate alongside three pieces of bacon. "Let me know what you think of these pancakes. My kids will tell you that I'm famous for them."

She buttered the cakes, then poured a generous amount of syrup over them. Taking her fork, she nodded at him before slicing through the stack and putting a bite in her mouth. She closed her eyes as she chewed and swallowed, but she didn't say anything.

He couldn't wait any longer for her reaction. "Well?"

"That. Was. Amazing." She took her fork and stabbed more pancake. "You could get rich off of these if you decided to sell them."

Her words of praise pleased him, and he turned back to the griddle to pour three more circles of batter.

She took a slice of bacon and bit into the strip. "Where did you learn to make them like this?"

"I worked my way through college in a diner as a waiter, but I'd fill in behind the grill if they were shorthanded. The short-order cook eventually taught me his pancake recipe."

"Thank goodness he did." She finished her pancakes and eyed the other stacks waiting. "Do you think I could have a couple more of those before I have to leave for work?"

He put another stack of three on her empty plate. "I can always make more."

Aunt Sarah stepped into the kitchen, sniffing the air. "Do I smell bacon?"

Christopher smiled and prepared a plate for her, then set it down in front of her at the kitchen table along with a cup of coffee. After her first few bites, she sighed. "I'm putting you in charge of breakfast on the weekends. This is fabulous."

Shortly after, first Daisy, then Elijah showed up in the kitchen. Daisy cheered when he placed the plate of pancakes in front of her. "My favorite!"

Even Elijah's grumpy attitude mellowed slightly as Christopher fed them all pancakes until they were stuffed. He sat on a stool next to Penny drinking his coffee, satisfied with the way the morning was starting. He remembered other Saturday mornings with a sleepy Julie eating her way through a stack of pancakes while she also fed two small children and Christopher cleaned the kitchen. He'd missed those mornings. After she died, he didn't make pancakes for a few months until Daisy said she missed them. He'd made them like always, but he and the kids had struggled to eat them. The second time was easier. Then it became a Saturday-morning routine.

He stood, getting ready to wash the dishes, but Aunt Sarah insisted that she'd clean the kitchen since he'd worked so hard making breakfast. Penny piped up. "You might as well let her since she'll nag you until you do."

Aunt Sarah gave Penny the stink eye, but then shrugged. "I don't nag. I just insist that things go my way until everyone else agrees."

Christopher held up his hands and sat back down on the stool. "I won't argue, then." He swiveled around to face the kids. "If you're done eating, why don't you take your plates to the sink? Then it's time to get dressed."

The kids grumbled, but picked up their plates. When they left the room, Penny poked him in the arm. "The charity dinner is next Friday night."

He'd forgotten about the invite she'd given him. "I don't know if I'll be able to go."

"Why not? You don't work late on Fridays." She peered at Aunt Sarah. "Help me out here. You think he should go, don't you?" She turned back to him. "She'll nag you until you do."

"You seem to be doing a good job of it yourself," Aunt Sarah said from the kitchen sink, her arms in soapsuds up to her elbows.

"I just think you'd have a good time. You need to have a night to yourself. Even if it is in a room full of people." She smiled into his face. "Come on. Say yes. You know you want to."

It sounded tempting. He turned to look at his children. "You should go," Elijah said, surprising everyone.

"You think I should?"

His son nodded. "That way Grandma can drive down and watch us."

Daisy clapped her hands. "I love Grandma. Say yes, Dad."

He couldn't remember the last time he'd had a night out, and his children seemed to approve. "Why not?"

"I'D BE GLAD to drive down and watch them. We can make a whole weekend of it," his mother said later over the phone. "So this charity dinner... Is this a date?"

"Mom..."

"Christopher, it's been almost two years. You're a young, healthy man who shouldn't be alone."

"We've talked about this."

"Well, I think it's time that you move on."

"How do you move on from the love of your life?" Did she really expect him to forget Julie and fall in love with someone else? "I promised Julie."

"I'm sick of hearing you use that promise as an excuse."

"I'm a man who keeps my promises."

"Unlike your father, right? You are not like him."

But part of him feared that he was. How many times had he made a promise to himself to eat healthier or be more organized only to fall into old habits? The times he broke the promises to himself felt like all the times his father had promised to come see him and had never shown up. He well remembered sitting on the sofa, looking out the window at the driveway for his father's car that never arrived. "I keep my promises, Mom. I can't go back on that now."

She paused on the other end, then sighed. "What time do you need me to pick up the kids?"

Once he'd set that up, he called the kids into the kitchen. "Get your coats. We're going shopping."

Daisy clapped her hands as if they were off on an exciting adventure. But then, most things were for her. Elijah looked as if he'd rather eat worms. "Shopping? For what?"

"We need to buy some toys for that charity dance I'm going to."

Elijah's wariness switched to interest. "What kind of toys?"

"That's what I need you two for. We're going to buy toys for kids who might not get them otherwise." He knelt down in front of them. "I know things have been hard for us lately, but people have been generous to us. I want us to show that same giving spirit to those who need it more than us. Do you think you can help me?"

They drove to a downtown Thora store called the Whistle Stop that had a sign that promised "toys, toys, toys." Christopher gave Daisy the task of finding a toy for a girl her age, while Elijah perused toys a nine-year-old boy would like. They walked the aisles in single file since the store was full of other shoppers and the many shelves of toys.

Daisy got distracted with the superhero action figures, but changed her mind after she found a small chest of costumes. "This, Daddy. Definitely this one."

He noticed that a superhero cape was included with the costumes. No wonder she'd chosen it. He nodded and carried it as Elijah searched through the model cars. Less decisive than his little sister, he picked up one and looked it over before putting it back on the shelf. He seemed to gravitate toward the ones that required more work, like assembling and painting, rather than simply putting on decals. When he'd narrowed it down to two, Christopher put a hand on his son's shoulder. "These cost less than the costumes. Why don't we get both for the kids?"

Elijah looked up at him, and he felt as if he'd won the lottery by the awe in his son's eyes. "That would be great."

They carried their purchases to the register and had to wait in a long line before their turn. Once he'd paid for the toys, they walked out onto the sidewalk, and Daisy pointed across the street. "There's Mel's Books. Can we go? Please, Daddy?"

He agreed and held the children's hands as they crossed the busy street at the corner once the stoplight turned. With it being a Saturday afternoon, the streets were crowded with Christmas shoppers. On the icy pavement, Daisy let go and ran into the store, followed closely by her brother. When Christopher stepped inside, he noticed that the bookshop looked as busy as the toy store had been. He spotted Melanie bringing out a box set of novels for a customer and waved at her when she noticed him.

Glancing at his watch, he told the kids, "You've got thirty minutes. Then we'll meet right here at the coffee bar, okay?"

They nodded and sped off to the children's section, which had a mural of favorite childhood stories on the back wall, as well as small tables and chairs where kids could sit and read. He perused the table of new releases before finding himself in his own favorite section, mysteries and thrillers. One of his seniors had mentioned an author he might enjoy, so he searched for the name and read the back covers of several novels before deciding on one. "Find what you're looking for?"

He turned at the sound of Melanie's voice and held up the book. "One of my residents recommended her."

"That's her best, in my opinion." She looked him over. "I never figured you for the spy thriller type. I thought you'd be more literary."

"I like to live a more exciting life through my reading."

"I don't know. Raising your kids seems like a pretty great adventure."

"You've obviously met my daughter, Daisy, then." He shared a smile with the bookstore owner. He looked at her and wondered why he didn't feel the same tingles that he did with Penny. Melanie would be a better choice for him if he was interested in finding a wife. Quiet and unassuming. A better match with himself than the woman who had made several appearances in his recent dreams. "Speaking of my kids, I'd better find them."

Elijah had a book in his hand when Christopher found him at the coffee bar. "Where's your sister?"

"Coming!" she shouted as she ran up to them with two books. "Can I get the other one with my allowance?"

"Sweetie, you spent all of yours."

"Then my next allowance."

"You've spent that, too." He glanced at the titles of the books, deciding to return later to buy the one she didn't choose. "Why don't you put the other book on your Christmas list?"

She sighed as if such an undertaking would

be too much for her, but finally settled on one before running away to put the other back on the shelf.

They took seats at a table near the coffee bar, and Christopher bought the books along with hot drinks. Cocoa for the kids and a chai latte that he'd discovered he liked a few months ago. They set to reading their books and sipping their drinks. It felt like an almost normal Saturday morning. At least before the fire.

His life could be summed up in a few phases. Childhood. With Julie. Without Julie. And now after the fire.

"DADDY!"

Christopher jumped out of the sofa bed and ran up the stairs to Daisy's room. When he threw open the door, she was standing in her nightie beside the bed. "I frowed up."

"Do you feel like you have to be sick again?"

She nodded, and he led her quickly to the bathroom. He dampened a washcloth in the sink and put it on the back of her neck like his mom had when he'd been sick as a child. He rubbed her back, then gave her a cup of water to rinse her mouth with after she got sick.

Back in the bedroom, he removed her soiled nightgown and stripped the bed, stacking the linens near the door to take downstairs to the laundry room. Then he found another set of sheets and blankets in the hall closet and made up the bed once again before putting Daisy back under the covers.

Christopher put his hand on Daisy's forehead and sighed. He didn't need a thermometer to tell him that she was running a temperature. He'd noticed her glassy eyes at dinner the night before, but figured the girl was just tired. He'd been wrong. "I don't think you're going to school in the morning. Do you need anything before I wash your sheets?"

She shook her head and closed her eyes. He brushed her damp bangs off her forehead. He might not be good at some things, but he had learned to be a good nurse without hovering. Julie had hated that. Daisy sank farther into the blankets, and he figured she'd sleep the rest of the night. He'd check in on her after he started the laundry.

At the door, he picked up the linens. Penny appeared. "Is everything okay?"

"Daisy's got a stomach bug."

Penny looked past him into the bedroom. "Poor kid. Anything I can do?"

"I've got this." He adjusted the load in his arms. "Looks like I get a day off from work."

"You don't have to miss work. I can take care of her."

"I couldn't ask you to do that."

"I'm off tomorrow already, so why not me? No reason for you to take the time off."

"She's my daughter. I can't just leave her here."

"She'll be fine under my care. You don't have to do it all."

Christopher hesitated. "It's a generous offer, but—"

"I can do it. Trust me."

He knew he could trust her. That wasn't the point. "It's not that I don't think you can take care of her, but she's my responsibility."

"And you can't accept help from others."

He cocked his head to one side and stared at her. "That's not what I meant."

One of her eyebrows rose. "Really? Because you seem to think you have to do everything for your kids. But that's what I'm here for. To help you."

"I thought you moved in to help Aunt Sarah."

She gave a soft shrug of her shoulders. "I can help you both."

Christopher looked into the bedroom where Daisy was lying on the bed. He knew that he should stay home with her. Knew that he'd be thinking about her the whole time if he didn't. But Penny's offer to care for his daughter would take one burden off his shoulders. And the weight of everything was starting to wear him out.

He turned back to Penny and nodded. "Okay."

"Really? You'll let me take care of her?"

"You're not backing out, are you?"

"No." She smiled wide. "Thank you for trusting me."

"If there's one thing I can do, it's trust you with my daughter."

PENNY RAISED HER head from the side of the bed to peer at Daisy. She'd rested with the girl in case Daisy had needed her. Good thing, too, since Daisy had been up twice to be sick. She stood and pulled the covers over the girl's shoulders, then reached up to smooth the damp curls away from her face.

Daisy opened one eye to look at her. Penny smiled down at her. "Do you need anything, sweetie?"

"I'm thirsty."

"Are you hungry, too?" Daisy shook her head. "Okay, I'll be right back."

Penny ran down the stairs to the kitchen, where Aunt Sarah was sitting at the counter with the newspaper and a cup of coffee. "How's your patient?"

"Thirsty." Penny opened the refrigerator and considered the pitcher of orange juice before pulling it out. "Would this be too acidic for her stomach?"

"If you give her a glass with half juice and half water, she should be fine."

Penny poured some into a glass, then topped it off with water from the faucet. "She says she's not hungry yet."

"Take up some crackers just in case." Aunt Sarah looked up from the obituaries. "Playing nurse is not a fun way to spend your day off."

Penny shrugged as she grabbed a sleeve of crackers from the cupboard. "Christopher needed me."

"From what he said, you volunteered before he could ask you."

"Don't go down that road, Aunt Sarah. I was just doing the kind, neighborly thing."

"Seems to me that you're going above and beyond being a neighbor to him. I think you like him."

"Of course I do. He's a good father."

"And a good man."

"Penny!" A wail came from upstairs.

Aunt Sarah raised her eyebrows. "Duty calls."

Penny took the cup of juice and sleeve of crackers upstairs to her old bedroom to find Daisy fastening her cape around her shoulders. "You okay, sweetie?"

"I thought you were gone forever."

Penny handed her the juice. "Just sip this at first. And I brought you crackers in case you want to eat something." She took a seat next to Daisy on the bed and sighed as the girl rested her head on Penny's shoulder. "How is your tummy feeling?"

Daisy lowered the glass and shrugged. "A little better, I guess."

Penny put a hand to the girl's forehead.

"You don't have a fever, so that's good. You're going to be okay."

She started to rise off the bed, but Daisy put her hand on Penny's leg. "Don't leave me."

"I'm just going to get you another pillow and prop you up a little more. I'll be right back." She slid off the bed and retrieved the pillow from the hall closet. When she returned to the bedroom, Daisy nibbled on a cracker. "Aunt Sarah will make some chicken-noodle soup later if you're up to it."

"Mommy used to make that when we got sick."

Penny returned to the bed and took a seat beside the girl. "What else did she do?"

"She always read stories, and she'd sing silly songs to us." Daisy paused, then shrugged. "That's all I 'member."

"She must have been a good mommy."

"The best."

"I don't remember my mom."

Daisy peered at her. "Not one thing?"

"No. She died when I was just a baby. But my dad kept some of her things in a box, so when I got sad and missed her I would go up to the attic, open the box and look at them."

"Like what?"

Penny tried to recall. "Jewelry. Letters. Lots of pictures that my dad took of her." She smiled at the girl. "My dad says I look a lot like her, so sometimes I'll look at the pictures to see if he's right."

"Is he?"

"He usually is." Penny leaned over and kissed the top of the girl's head. "Sometimes when I'm sick, I feel better after I take a bath. What do you think we try that after you finish your juice?"

CHRISTOPHER HAD CALLED Penny several times throughout the day, and each time she had reassured him that everything was fine. But nothing could replace actually being there with his daughter. He left work early and hurried back to the house. He didn't even take off his jacket, but walked upstairs to the room Daisy was staying in. With the curtains and blinds closed, the room was dark, but with the hall light he could see that she was sleeping. He crossed the room to the bed and kissed her forehead, noticing that it was cool. Penny had been right. She would recover quickly.

He left the bedroom and hung up his coat

on the rack by the front door before locating
Penny and Aunt Sarah watching a soap opera
on the television. Well, Penny watched while
Aunt Sarah dozed on the sofa with Caesar
napping on her lap. Penny looked up from
the recliner. "You're home early."

"I wanted to make sure Daisy was okay."

"So the seven phone calls where I told you
she was fine didn't reassure you?"

He shrugged, then yanked off his tie before
sitting on the sofa next to the sleeping Aunt
Sarah. "It's not that I didn't believe you, but
I wanted to see for myself."

"It's okay. You're her dad, so I guess it's
expected." Penny looked him over. "Besides
worrying about your daughter, how was your
day?"

"I thought I had a lead on a house for rent
a few streets over from here, but they already
leased it." He rubbed a hand over his face.
This finding a new home was wearing on
him, making him more tired than usual. "I
checked with my real-estate agent for any
new listings, but she says that this is the slow
season. Very few people want to put their
house on the market before the holidays. She

might see some after the first of the year, but I was hoping to be settled by then."

"Aunt Sarah has said you can stay here as long as you need to."

"Weren't you the one who didn't want me and the kids to be a burden on her?"

Penny frowned. "You're still holding that against me? If anything, I think you all have been good for her. She's less lonely and more active. She loves to cook, and you've given her a reason to."

"I'm sitting right here and can speak for myself." Aunt Sarah opened her eyes and looked at them. "But Penny's right. Your family can stay here however long it takes for the right house to become available."

"I appreciate that offer, but I don't want to overstay our welcome." Bad enough they had already been living there two weeks. He couldn't keep imposing on Aunt Sarah's good graces. "I've got an appointment tomorrow after work to see an apartment complex that accepts dogs. It's farther away from the kids' school and my job, but I could make it work."

"You don't want an apartment."

"It's not ideal," he replied. "But I have to take care of my family."

"So stay here a little longer. Don't settle." Aunt Sarah reached over and patted his hand. "I'll be angry with you if you move out before you're ready. It hasn't been all that bad here, has it? I mean, sleeping on the sofa bed can be uncomfortable, but you haven't complained."

"It hasn't been bad at all. That's the problem. It's been amazing knowing that the kids are being watched after school. Then to come home to dinner all ready and on the table and I don't have to cook? You've loved and supported us through a difficult time in our lives." He shook his head. "But I can't depend on you."

Aunt Sarah looked wounded and he immediately regretted his words. "Not that you're not dependable. What I mean is that I don't want to get used to you being there because eventually I'll be on my own again."

"So what's wrong with enjoying the help for now? You've been on your own for so long. Accept our help."

"I do appreciate it. More than you know." The kids hadn't had any meltdowns over the last two weeks. Without the peace of mind he had knowing the kids were well looked after, he never would have made it through day one after the fire, let alone this long. Their kindness was something he knew he'd never be able to repay, but he'd try.

He put a hand on his chest. "If there's ever anything I can do for you, don't hesitate to ask me."

Penny chortled. "Don't tempt her. You never know what she might come up with. I hear there're more boxes she needs from the basement."

Everyone laughed.

CHAPTER NINE

THE DAYS BEFORE the charity dinner passed in
a blur between work and all the preparations
required for it. Shelby had given Penny a list
of things she needed to do, and she was barely
home between work and completing the list.

The day of the dinner dawned gray and
cloudy with a promise of several inches of
snow. Hoping that the meteorologist was
wrong about the amount of flurries, as well
as the timing—just before the dinner—Penny
put on the sparkly emerald green dress that
she always wore to this event. It was the only
night of the year that she'd wear it since sparkles weren't really her thing. But it always
pleased her nana and Aunt Sarah to see her
in it.

After putting her long hair into an updo
pinned in place with rhinestone clips, she carried the silver high heels downstairs with her,
rather than putting them on and attempting

to walk. Christopher opened the front door and breezed in from work, glancing up at her. His eyes widened, and he whistled. "Wow. I didn't know firefighters could look like that."

She waved off his compliment, but the butterflies in her belly danced with pleasure. "I'm happy to expand your world."

He took off his coat, brushed a few snowflakes off the collar and flung it over a hook on the coatrack by the front door. "Isn't it too early to be leaving for the dinner tonight?"

"We still have to get some things set up at the hall, so Aunt Sarah and I have to leave early." She bent down to put on her heels, but looked up at him. "Your ticket is on the table by the front door, and I'll save you the seat next to mine."

He hesitated, and she felt a prick of disappointment that he'd chicken out on his promise to her. But then he gave a short nod. "My mom is taking the kids out for the evening so they can get some Christmas shopping done, making me free for the entire night."

"I'm sure you could use the time off from dad duty." He frowned at her words, and she quickly explained. "I didn't mean that you don't love your kids or anything like that.

But it's nice sometimes to have an evening for yourself." His frown deepened. "There's nothing wrong with wanting some time alone, right?"

He gave a short bark of laughter. "Alone in a ballroom with hundreds of other people?"

She shrugged. "You know what I mean."

"I don't need time away from my family. My need to be alone ended the day I married Julie."

Right. The mention of his deceased wife put a damper on the butterflies. She squeezed past Christopher to pluck her coat off the rack beside him. "I'm sure you'll have fun tonight. And don't forget your promise for a dance."

He looked at her, and she knew she could lose herself by getting involved with this man. He was in his relationships all the way, and he would expect nothing less from her. She glanced away from him to put on her coat, but it got stuck on her elbow. Christopher reached over and helped her put it on, standing close enough for her to smell the faint scent of fabric softener on his shirt.

She swallowed as the butterflies started to take flight. She couldn't be attracted to him. Well, she could be, but she shouldn't be. She shouldn't get involved with him. He'd made it clear that his children would always come first in his life, and she wouldn't play second fiddle again.

No, it was better that she got rid of this attraction to him. Maybe she should accept Jack's offer to set her up with one of his friends. Another man might dim this hopeless crush she had on Christopher.

She took a step away from him. "I need to get Aunt Sarah."

"I could take her with me if it would be easier."

"I appreciate it, but she has things to do herself before the dinner, too."

Then she fled from the room to find her aunt and get as far away as she could from the tempting man in the hall.

"GRANDMA'S HERE!" DAISY yelled up the stairs.

Christopher didn't doubt that his daughter had been watching at the window, waiting to see his mom's car pull into the driveway. He checked his appearance in the bathroom mirror one more time, then paused. What did it matter what he looked like? He hadn't taken this much interest in his appearance since he'd been entering puberty and trying to impress a girl. Shaking his head, he opened the door and walked out into the hallway as Elijah exited his room. His son stopped short and stared at him. "Why are you all fancy?"

Christopher looked at the suit he wore. "Because it's a fancy dinner."

Elijah scowled. "You like her, don't you?"

"Who? Penny?" Christopher sighed and put a hand on his son's shoulder. "I think she's a nice woman. That's all."

"Whatever." Elijah shook off his touch and walked downstairs to join his sister and grandmother.

Trying to tamp down his temper, Christopher stood in the hall for a moment before joining his family downstairs. Daisy bounced over to him and wrapped her arms around his legs. "You look so pretty, Daddy."

His mom smiled at him. "You do look handsome. I already checked into the motel. Otherwise I would have been here earlier."

He nodded his thanks to them both, then glanced at his watch. "The dinner starts at seven, and I should be back by eleven or so. Ten, if I get bored."

"Don't worry about a curfew. The three

of us are going to be too busy having fun to notice the time." She pointed at his children. "Right?"

Daisy cheered, but Elijah didn't look convinced. In a flurry of activity, coats, hats and mittens were put on, then a rush to get out the front door. "Have a good time tonight, son."

"I will."

"Forget your worries and try to enjoy yourself. You deserve it, Chris." She put a hand to his cheek. "Drink a little. Eat a lot. And maybe dance with a pretty woman."

"Thanks, Mom."

She and the kids started to walk away, but his mom turned back. "I was thinking you and I could have breakfast tomorrow morning before I head home. Just the two of us."

"The kids—"

"Will be fine here. I already asked Sarah if she would keep an eye on them for a little while."

"She already watches them too much. I don't want to take advantage of her."

"I promised her that we would bring home a grilled cinnamon roll in kind." His mom reached over and straightened his tie. "You and I need to have a talk."

He was confused. "Are you okay?"

"Nothing like that." She took his elbow as they walked down the porch steps. "Now, I meant what I said. Leave the worries at home for the evening."

He helped her into the car and then watched her back out of the driveway and leave with his children. Snow had fallen since he'd returned home from work, so he had to clear off the windshield and back window of his car before leaving for the hall.

His mom might have said to leave the worries at home, but they followed him as he drove to the hall. When his mother said they needed to talk, he knew it was serious. Was she finally retiring? Maybe she would and move closer to him? Having Aunt Sarah and Penny help him with the kids had taken a burden off of his shoulders. One that he didn't look forward to facing alone again once he found a house.

Or maybe she would convince him to move closer to her. She was right that there were jobs and schools around where she lived. But then, that meant leaving Thora.

And Penny. That thought made his chest

ache more than leaving Thora. He couldn't imagine not seeing her again.

To drown out those maudlin thoughts, he turned up the volume on the radio.

IN THE LOBBY of the hall, three large Christmas trees, decorated in jewel tones of emerald, sapphire and ruby, greeted guests. These weren't the simple types of trees decorated with homemade ornaments or that held sentimental value, but tall and elegant ones with glistening icicles and perfectly placed gold and silver garland. He put a hand to his coat pocket to feel for the ticket, feeling out of place and thinking that if he left now, no one would notice.

A woman called his name and he searched for the source of the voice to find Aunt Sarah waving at him to come over. She looked as if she'd visited the hair salon earlier that day, with her mostly white hair in soft waves around her face. Dressed in an elegant black gown, she looked like a queen surveying her subjects. Christopher walked to her side. "You look amazing."

She twittered and slapped at his arm. "Don't be ridiculous."

"I expect you to dance with me. Then I'll be the envy of the entire room."

Her cheeks turned pink, and she took his elbow when he offered it to her. "You are a charmer."

"I used to be."

"You haven't lost it, young man."

At the doors to the ballroom, Christopher handed his ticket to Uncle Mike. "Sounds like they've moved your seat. You'll be at one of the family tables." The uncle nodded to Aunt Sarah. "Shelby said you'd know where to seat him."

"Right between me and Penny." When Christopher started to protest, she patted his arm.

"I'm not family."

"You almost are. We've been living together for two weeks." She glanced around the crowded room. "Maybe I shouldn't say that too loud. The gossips would have a field day if they heard a young man had moved in with me."

"A young man and his two children, who are better than any chaperones might be. As well as her great-niece."

She laughed and guided him to a long table

at the farthest end of the room. He recognized Cuthbert family members and waved to them. It did feel almost as if he had been grafted into the family, one he admired. He pulled out a chair for Aunt Sarah and asked her if he could get her something to drink from the bar.

With her drink order, he left her, greeting some people he knew from the kids' school and the senior home. The line at the bar was long, but he didn't mind. It gave him a moment to appreciate the work that the family had done in decorating the hall. Three more Christmas trees were surrounded by unwrapped toys on a stage that shared space with a three-piece orchestra playing Christmas carols. Servers in white shirts and red bow ties circulated among the guests with trays of appetizers.

Ahead in the line, a woman turned around and waved him to come forward. Dr. Shoemaker looked different in a pink off-the-shoulder dress. "I didn't expect to see you here."

"Likewise."

She introduced him to her husband, but didn't mention where she knew Christopher from, though the man could probably guess, considering her profession. The two men shook hands. Then the husband stepped forward to talk to the bartender. Dr. Shoemaker looked behind Christopher. "Are you here alone?"

"My mother has the kids."

"Of course. But you know that's not what I meant."

He pointed to the Cuthbert family table. "Penny invited me to join them."

"She did? Good for her. A night out without your kids is a good thing."

He shrugged, then motioned to the bar. "I think your husband is waiting for your drink order."

"He knows what I like. I'm more interested in talking to you right now." She tilted her head to peer at him. "How are you doing?"

"We're not in your office."

"Then consider me as a friend asking how another friend is doing."

He gave her a smile, but he knew it must have appeared forced. "I'm fine." When she looked closer at him, he sighed. "It's the holidays, so you know what it's like. I'm just trying to make it through."

She nodded. Her husband returned and handed her a stem glass with white wine. "I do know. And I also know that you're doing your best. Merry Christmas, Christopher."

"Merry Christmas to you and your family, too."

When he returned with both his and Aunt Sarah's drinks, he found that the family table had filled with more people. He spotted Penny chatting with one of her cousins—Jack, the veterinarian. While Aunt Sarah looked like a queen, Penny looked like a fairy princess. He'd seen her earlier at home, of course, but seeing her now made his heart thump a little faster. The moisture in his mouth had disappeared, and he sipped his beer to help.

He was in over his head. He just knew it.

A few minutes after seven, Shelby accompanied Aunt Sarah to the stage and the microphone that was set up there. Sarah smiled at the crowd. "Good evening, and welcome to the forty-first annual Cuthbert family Christmas toy drive. Usually, it's my sister, Lila, who stands here, but as you know, we lost her earlier this year."

Aunt Sarah paused, and Christopher could see that her words had upset her. Shelby put her arm around her aunt and continued, "We want to thank you all for your presence here tonight, as well as the generous gifts you brought. There's still a chance to give with the cards and envelopes available on your tables. Please contribute to helping more kids enjoy a holiday they'll always remember. Thank you again for your generosity, and enjoy your evening."

There was a warm round of applause, and then Shelby helped Aunt Sarah back down the stairs. When she returned to her seat, the older woman took her napkin and dabbed at her eyes. "I didn't know how hard it would be without her here."

Christopher nodded and put a hand on her arm. "Believe me, I know. Every first was difficult without Julie."

"And the second?"

He shrugged. "A little easier, but I still miss her."

Sarah took a sip of her ice water, then looked over toward Penny, who was on the other side of him, chatting with Shelby. "Maybe you need someone new to help you miss her less."

"Aunt Sarah, we've talked about your matchmaking."

"I can't help it if I see two people who suit each other so well." She nodded at Penny. "She needs a man who is grounded and stable. A man who will love her completely."

"That man isn't me."

"But it could be."

ONCE DINNER ENDED, the three-person orchestra was replaced with a DJ who played contemporary music, and the dance floor soon filled with merrymakers. Shelby took the empty seat beside Penny. "I'd say this year's dinner was a success."

"It absolutely was. You wouldn't let it be otherwise."

Her cousin shot her a wry smile. "I don't control the world."

"But pretty close." The music pulsed through Penny, and she bobbed her head to the rhythm. "I like the DJ this year. Definitely an improvement on the past one. At least this one plays music from this century."

"You know how Nana liked things her way, and she fought me every year on the music. But now I get to do things differently."

The two grew silent, remembering the woman they'd loved. Jack joined them, bringing over his drink. "The dinner's going well. You should both be happy. What's wrong?"

Penny scooted out the chair next to her, and Jack took a seat. "We're thinking about Nana."

"Oh." He put an arm around Shelby's shoulders. "She would have hated all the changes you made, but in the end, she'd be proud of the work you and Aunt Sarah did."

"I hope you're right." Shelby sighed and nodded to the catering manager, who beckoned her from the door to the kitchen. "Duty calls. I'll catch up with you both later," she said and walked away.

"Remember that friend you were telling me about? The one who said I looked cute?" Penny asked Jack.

"Tony? What about him?"

"I'd like to meet him."

Jack reared back at her words. "Really? Last I heard, you weren't interested in dating anyone."

She shrugged. "Things change."

Jack glanced over to where Christopher sat talking to Laurel. "This wouldn't have anything to do with Aunt Sarah's houseguest, would it?"

"If you don't want to give Tony my number, you don't have to."

Jack narrowed his eyes at her. "Tony's a nice guy. I'd hate to see him get pushed aside when you finally realize that it's really Christopher you want."

"You know what? I can get my own dates." She glanced around the room and found a group of men talking on the edge of the ballroom. "I'm ready to dance."

She left Jack and approached the group. "What does it take to get a dance with one of you guys?"

One of them turned to her and looked her up and down before nodding. "All you have to do is ask."

She led him to the dance floor and the DJ changed to a fast-paced song that was currently reigning on the radio stations. The guy had solid dance moves, and she felt a little awkward dancing beside him. She could hold her own, but she wasn't as smooth or as sophisticated as this guy. She leaned toward him. "What's your name?"

"Dave."

"I'm Penny."

Talking wasn't necessary after that as they

danced. After the fourth song, she held up a hand. "I need a break to catch my breath."

What she really needed was a break from him. He seemed nice, but he'd had a heavy hand with the aftershave, giving her a headache. One of her cousins took her spot as she exited the dance floor. Some fresh air would do her good.

Once outside, she took a big gulp of the cool night air. Closed her eyes and let the breath out slowly.

"Everything okay out here?"

CHRISTOPHER HAD WATCHED Penny leave the ballroom and had followed her. Penny opened her eyes and smiled at Christopher. "Just taking a little break."

"I saw you on the dance floor." He couldn't take his eyes off her. Instead, he'd sat and watched in jealousy as someone else had held her in his arms. "You're a good dancer."

"I'm passable, but I enjoy it."

"You looked like you were. And your friend seemed to be enjoying himself, too." Christopher had noticed how many times the guy had reached out to touch her. And each time, he'd wished that he could be the one she was dancing with.

"He's not a friend, but he was available to dance." She reached up and tucked a couple of stray hairs back into the sparkly clips he'd noticed earlier. "I should go inside."

"I'm available."

She turned to him, but didn't say anything. He held out his hand toward her. "I did promise you one dance."

She looked at his hand, then up at him. For a moment, he thought she might turn him down. But then she put her hand in his. He led her to the dance floor and took her in his arms. She felt right as he held her, and feelings he thought he'd buried with his wife resurfaced. It had been so long that he'd held a woman in his arms. And not just any woman, but one he cared for.

Because deny it all he might, Penny had captured more than just his interest.

She rested her head on his chest, and he closed his eyes, swaying to the beat of the song. "You know, seeing you tonight reminds me of a song back in the day. But instead of wearing red, you're wearing green. And you look gorgeous."

She lifted her head to peer at him, a sad look in her eyes. "Christopher…"

"A friend can pay another friend a compliment, right?"

"Yes. We can be friends."

"Dipping you."

He braced her back and dipped her low, then pulled her up. She laughed with pure joy, like she was a kid. "Do that again."

After dipping her a second time, she squealed as he pulled her upright. He liked hearing her laugh and rested his cheek against her forehead. "Like I said before, you're a good dancer."

She shook her head. "Not as good as you."

"My mom insisted that I take lessons when I was little." He grimaced at the memory and the names and taunts that had come from some of his classmates. "Then I had to take karate to defend myself against the bullies. Elijah used to take lessons, but when Julie got sick, it got pushed to the side. Now he says he's not interested."

The song ended, and he let her go with some reluctance. "Thank you for the dance."

She gave him a smile, then slipped away.

He watched her leave the room and regretted not asking for one more dance.

THE NIGHT WORE ON, and by ten o'clock Penny was ready to end the evening. She'd danced with a few guys and had watched Christopher take turns dancing with her cousins, including Shelby. She'd tried to ignore the feelings of jealousy that rose in her chest, but failed.

Luckily, Aunt Sarah was ready to leave, too, so Penny gave her excuses to her cousins with promises to call later in the week. She gave the valet her ticket and gave her aunt a hand with her coat while they waited for the car. Aunt Sarah tugged the lapels of her jacket around her. "It was a lovely evening, but I, for one, am glad it's over with."

"You and Shelby did a wonderful job."

Her aunt turned to her. "You and I both know that Shelby did the majority of the work. I'm too old for this kind of thing. It's time to hand the reins over to her permanently."

"You're only as old as you feel."

"Then I must be a hundred and forty-two tonight."

When the valet pulled up with the car, she

tipped him, and she and her aunt got going. Turning to her aunt, she pulled out of the parking lot. "I don't know about you, Aunt Sarah, but I'm ready to get out of these fancy duds and into my yoga pants."

"You said it, Pen."

Back at the house, Aunt Sarah headed straight for her bedroom, while Penny went to the family room. The woman there rose to her feet when Penny entered the room. "You must be Penny. The kids told me all about you. Well, Daisy, at least, didn't stop talking about you." She thrust her hand out. "I'm Denise, Christopher's mother."

Penny could see the resemblance instantly, especially in the eyes. "He's told me a lot about you."

"All good, I hope."

"Well, you did make him take dance lessons."

Denise covered her eyes. "He told you about that? He'll never let me live it down."

"After dancing with him tonight, I have to thank you for insisting on the lessons. He's very good."

His mother looked pleased at her words.

"Then I'm glad I made him take those lessons."

"You had a good time with the kids tonight?"

"The best. I miss them. I've been debating taking an early retirement and moving down here to be close to them."

"You should. They're amazing. Even E's mood sometimes wouldn't persuade me otherwise. But then, you know that already." Penny shook her head. "They've definitely made my time here more enjoyable."

"And my son?"

Her son made her confused. And wanting things that she shouldn't.

But instead of saying that aloud, she gave a shrug before continuing. "If you'll excuse me, I'm going to change into something more comfy. My feet are killing me in these shoes."

Once Penny changed and returned to the family room, Christopher had come home, as well, and had settled on the couch next to his mother, his tie loose and suit jacket off and hanging over the end table. He stood when she entered the room, but she waved to him to sit down. "You don't have to stand on my account."

He took a seat again. "You look a lot different now," he teased.

Penny tugged at the hem of her University of Florida hoodie. "This is the real me. Not the version of me you saw earlier tonight."

"I know. As beautiful as you were, I like this version better."

She was about to shoot a comment back when his mother stood. "I'd better say goodnight and get back to my motel." She turned to Penny. "It was nice to meet you. I like having the face to match up with the name."

"Likewise."

Turning to Christopher, she gave him a quick hug and kissed his cheek. "I'll pick you up tomorrow morning about eight?"

"Sure thing. I'll walk you out to your car."

When Christopher returned a moment later, he yawned and pulled the tie from around his neck before plopping down on the couch. "Some night, huh?"

Penny nodded from the recliner. "I should let you get to sleep. It was a long day, and now you have early plans for tomorrow."

"Don't leave. Not yet."

She looked over at him. "Did you have a good time tonight?"

He tilted his head back and closed his eyes. "More than I thought I would. You?"

"It was interesting."

He opened one eye and looked at her. "Interesting how?"

Interesting because dancing with him had been the highlight of her night. Interesting because seeing him dance with other women had been hard. Interesting because despite her insistence that they were just friends and could only be friends, she had started to want more from him than only friendship. But she didn't say any of that, only shrugged. "Oh, you know. Planning and working so hard for months on this one night, and then having it all over in a few hours."

"Kind of like a wedding." He glanced at her and winced. "Didn't mean to bring up a touchy subject."

"It's fine. I'm over it."

"Your aunt would like to see you dating again."

"Let me guess. She wants me to start dating you." She grinned. "I love the old woman, but she's got to stop with this matchmaking."

"She thinks we're a good match."

"We are. As friends."

"Penny, don't you think there's something more than friendship going on between us?"

She started to protest, but knew he was right. "But we can't pursue anything with each other. It's too complicated."

"I know that, too." He closed his eyes, and she took that as her cue to leave. She was almost at the door when she heard him speak. "It's too bad, really. I think I could be good for you."

"Good for me?" She turned back to look at him. "If anything, I'd be good for you. You need to loosen up a little more. You'd be lucky to have me as a girlfriend."

"Somehow I think you'd be trouble."

"The best trouble of your life."

He chuckled and nodded. "Thank you for dancing with me tonight."

"Seemed to me that you had plenty of partners to dance with."

"Jealous?"

She laughed as if the idea was ridiculous. Because it was. They could only be friends. She had no right to be jealous of him enjoying himself with other women.

Even if the idea made her want to weep, not laugh.

He stood and approached her. "Would it help if I said I wished I'd been dancing with you instead?"

"You can't say stuff like that."

"Why not? It's the truth."

"The truth only makes it more complicated."

"Maybe for a minute tonight, we can forget the complications and admit that we wish for something more."

She looked into his eyes, and the butterflies from earlier that evening seemed to nudge her forward. She rose on tiptoe to kiss his cheek. But as she did so, he turned toward her so that they met lip to lip. Her eyes closed at the kiss, and she wound her arms around his neck to draw him closer.

"Daddy?" a voice called from upstairs.

Penny jerked away. "You better go."

He nodded and squeezed her shoulder before leaving the room.

CHAPTER TEN

THE WAITRESS FILLED their mugs of coffee as Christopher peered at his mother, wondering if she'd really meant what she'd just said. When the waitress left, she gazed at him. "I'm serious, Chris. After talking to the kids last night, I don't think that you staying alone is the answer to keeping your promise to Julie."

Not this again. "What did they tell you?"

"That they haven't seen you smile like you used to until the last couple of weeks. That despite everything going on with your old house, you seem happier." She poured cream and two packets of sugar into her coffee and stirred. "You never promised Julie that you would stay single. Only that the kids would come first."

"And they have."

"I'm not disagreeing with that. But you have put them so much into the forefront that you've lost yourself in the process."

"You don't need to worry about me."

"You're my son, so of course I worry."

He stared into the depths of his coffee as if he could find the right words to say there without hurting his mom. Finding none, he simply nodded as if he agreed with her. But she didn't know. Sure, his mom knew more than most since she'd also been a single parent, but she was wrong on this issue. And she didn't know what it was like to add grief to that mix.

"Sweetie, you're not doing anyone any good by being miserable."

"That's the thing. I'm not miserable."

She raised one eyebrow at him like she used to when he'd told a fib. "Daisy cried when she told me that she misses your laugh. She misses the dad you used to be."

"I can't be him anymore. There's too much going on." He ran a hand through his hair and knew he needed to get it cut before it became shaggy. But then, he remembered when the kids needed haircuts and not himself. "Mom, I appreciate what you're trying to do. Honestly, I do. But we're doing okay."

"Okay, yes. But wouldn't it be better to be

doing well? To be living a life with more joy and peace?"

"You've drunk the Christmas hot chocolate."

She cocked her head to one side. "There's nothing wrong with wanting to be happy and at peace. Julie would have wanted that more than anything. But you're letting this one promise hold you back."

"Back from what? Getting involved with another woman?"

"Not just another woman. Penny."

Her name hung in the air while the memory of their kiss last night played in his mind. He shouldn't have taken it that far, but the whole evening had woven its magic around him until kissing Penny had been all he could think of. But she'd been right. Their complicated lives kept them apart. "Penny agrees with me that we shouldn't be together."

"How does she know? For that fact, how do you?"

"Because she doesn't date single dads, and I don't date, period."

The waitress dropped off their plates of food, stopping the conversation momentarily. Christopher knew his mother, however, and the conversation wasn't over. She put salt and pepper on her eggs as he put his napkin into his lap. They ate in silence for a few minutes.

"You two have it all wrong."

"Here it comes."

"I'm serious, Chris. Penny is a wonderful, beautiful woman who loves your children. And they adore her. Well, Daisy does. And Elijah will come around eventually." She looked over at him. "He misses Julie something fierce. He still won't talk about her?"

Christopher shook his head. "Not with me. He might with the counselor, but she hasn't said."

"You need to get him to talk."

"You think that I haven't tried? He won't open up to me." Christopher glanced around at the other diners, realizing he'd raised his voice. He closed his eyes and took a deep breath. "I'm not angry with you, Mom. It's the whole situation. I thought we were getting to a better place, and then the fire took everything away."

"Not everything. You still have each other."

"I know that I should be grateful that we survived and the dog was saved and that the insurance will cover our costs." He hung his head. "But sometimes I get so angry that I want to punch something and rip it apart with my bare hands. To get my knuckles scraped up so that at least I have a physical scar from all of this inner turmoil. And it's not just the fire. It's also losing Julie to cancer after the years of treatment that couldn't save her. It's having everything be on my shoulders, and I'm so afraid I'm failing at being a good dad."

He felt his mom's hand on his own, and he raised his head to see the tears gathering in her eyes. "You are not failing."

"You're biased because you're my mother."

"I'm not biased about this." She squeezed his hand. "I've known bad fathers, including yours. You are nothing like him."

"But if I'm making my kids miserable, how good can I be?"

"They are grieving, and not because of anything you are doing. Sweetie, you are an amazing father. You always put them first." She held up a hand when he started to speak. "And not because of that promise. But because you love them and would do whatever you had to for them." She scooted closer to him. "You're also a great man who is going through a lot right now. So it's okay to be angry."

She leaned into him. "But I'm afraid that you're going to miss out on something wonderful for you, and for the kids, if you don't find the courage to be happy again."

AT THE HALL, Penny wrapped ornaments in Bubble Wrap and repacked them into their special crates, which would be saved for next year's toy drive dinner dance. The day after a big event always felt a bit depressing to her. As if all the anticipation was spent on a mere moment in time and she was left feeling blue and out of sorts.

Or maybe that was just her reaction to Christopher's kiss.

She'd built up in her head what it would be like. The reality of it had left her moody and angry. It had been a good kiss, so that wasn't it. But it had been a onetime thing. It couldn't happen again.

"Stop moping and get these ornaments put away," Shelby said from the other side of the Christmas tree. Her cousin's head popped into view and she glared at Penny. "And don't tell me that's not what you're doing. I can see."

"I don't have anything to mope about."

"Then why the orange-dog eyes?"

Penny smiled at the term. Growing up, Shelby thought melancholy meant a melon-colored collie. The cousins had all adopted the orange-dog phrase to break up those gloomy moments ever since. "It's nothing."

"Good. If it's nothing, get to work. I promised the manager we'd have the hall cleaned up by noon."

Shelby put a full crate of ornaments on top of the others as Penny wrapped a maroon-colored ball. "I don't like focusing on what-ifs, you know?"

Shelby groaned and looked at the ceiling. "If we talk about it now, can you get back to work right after?"

"Why am I the only cousin helping you out with cleaning up the joint? Where are the rest of them, anyway?"

"Jack's working. My sister is who knows where with who knows who. And the others said they'd be here by ten. You're the only one I could get to commit to this early in the morning."

Penny pulled another ornament from the

tree, a bright red one that had silver sparkles. "And there's nothing to talk about."

"Good. Get back to work."

Penny wrapped the ornament, but stopped to look across the hall to where the dance floor had been last night. "Maybe in another world we could have been together, but we live in this one."

"You're killing me, Penny." Shelby took the ornament from her hands and tucked it into the nearest crate. "You're trying not to talk about Christopher, right? All this mooning about is over him?"

"I'm not mooning." Shelby arched her right eyebrow at this, and Penny sighed. "Let me rephrase that. I'm trying not to moon over him because nothing can or will ever happen between us."

"My spidey sense tells me that something has already happened."

"It was nothing. Let's get back to work."

"No, it was something, but you wish it were nothing."

What Penny wished for could fill the room. When she was younger, she'd wished that her mother would come back from heaven. Then she wished that her father would notice her.

She wished she'd find a man who loved her, then wished she'd never met him when he broke her heart. "Wishes are fickle things."

"Only the wisher is fickle. The wish is sincere at the moment it's made."

"You sound like Nana when you talk like that."

Penny could see Shelby swallow and then she nodded, but didn't say anything. Instead, Shelby bent over the crate of ornaments to rearrange them. Penny guessed that Shelby wished that Nana would come back, too. Penny sure did. She'd left six years ago for school and had missed out on the last years of her grandmother's life. Not that she knew they were the last years at the time, but phone calls and emails were a poor substitution for being present.

"Can I ask you a question? Was there ever anyone that you wanted to be with, but circumstances kept you apart?"

Shelby faced her. "You remember Josh? I had a thing for bad boys in those days."

Despite being a few years younger than her cousin, Penny did remember Shelby's high-school crush, who had broken her heart. "I'm talking as an adult, not high-school stuff."

"We all have to move on and deal with things as they are, not the way you wish they could be."

"So you're saying I should what? Forget Christopher?"

Shelby glanced away. "I haven't forgotten Josh. So, no, I'm not saying you can forget. But if you truly can't be with Christopher for whatever reason, then move on. Don't waste years wondering if you could have done something to make it happen."

"But what if there is a chance?"

"He's still a single dad. And you swore those off." Shelby reached out and touched her hand. "What does Christopher think?"

"That we can't be together. For different reasons than mine, but they're still obstacles. Mainly two named Elijah and Daisy."

"Daisy loves you."

"And Elijah can barely tolerate my presence."

"I think he's like that with most people, so I wouldn't feel too hurt."

"Do you think I'm the reason my dad never got married again? That I kept potential girlfriends away, somehow?"

"The reason Uncle Mark stayed single is

because he was already married to the fire-house, and no woman could come between them."

DAISY CLUNG TO her grandmother's legs. "Please don't go back home. You can stay here with us until Christmas."

His mom leaned down and kissed his daughter's wet cheeks. "I wish I could, but I have to work on Monday. But I'll be back Christmas Day." She looked beyond Daisy at him. "Should I plan on a motel again? Or do you think you'll have a new place by then?"

Aunt Sarah piped up. "You'll camp here, even if they've moved out. There's plenty of room for you."

Mom smiled and walked over to hug the older woman. "I just might take you up on that. After all, no one has beaten me at Scrabble until you."

Aunt Sarah nodded and patted his mom on the shoulder. "Don't forget to take a bag of Christmas cookies for your ride back."

"And you wonder why I look well-fed." Christopher handed his mother her coat and then the plastic bag full of decorated sugar cookies the kids had made with Sarah.

His mom put a hand on Elijah's shoulder. "Are you too old to hug your grandma?"

Elijah didn't answer, but put his arms around her waist, resting his head against her chest while she kissed the top of his head. "There's my sweet boy."

After his mom left, Christopher returned to the house to find his children had scattered to their rooms. Aunt Sarah sighed. "It's always hard to say goodbye to family."

"It's only for a couple of weeks."

"I was thinking I'd make pork chops and buttered noodles for dinner. Do you think the children would like that?"

"I think they'd eat anything you made." He glanced at the living room. "Did Penny say when she'd be home?"

Aunt Sarah gave him a smile that held an air of self-satisfaction. "Did you two have plans for tonight?"

"No. I was just wondering."

"Hmm." Then Aunt Sarah left the room, humming a Christmas carol.

Just because he asked where she was didn't mean anything. They'd said last night that they couldn't be anything more than friends. He'd meant it and knew that she had, too.

Despite this crazy attraction, they had to be adults and put that aside.

But he started to question his reasoning when Penny joined them for dinner. Had she always looked so shiny? Did her eyes light up when she talked every time? And had her mouth always been so tempting before?

"Daddy, I asked you about my choir concert." Daisy waved her hand in front of his eyes. "Did you hear me?"

He shook his head to clear the thoughts distracting him. "What about your concert?"

"I said I have a solo, and I want Penny to come. Can she?"

"That's up to her, sweetie." He looked across the table at her. "Did you want to come with us?"

"I'm back to work tomorrow. When is the concert?"

Daisy bounced in her chair. "Wednesday night. Please say you can come."

Penny spoke to Aunt Sarah. "I get out of work at five that night. We could go together, if you'd like?"

Aunt Sarah looked over at Daisy and nodded. "I don't think we have much choice on this one, do you?"

Daisy clapped her hands. "I will sing the bestest that I ever have. Just for you."

She said it with her eyes on Penny, and Christopher wondered if he was going to have a problem with her connection to the woman. Daisy would be heartbroken if Penny chose to stop having contact with her. Should he set up some boundaries?

But when he saw his daughter so happy, he didn't think he could come between them.

"Maybe you could put makeup on me?" She glanced at him and then at Penny.

Christopher couldn't believe his ears. "You're too little for makeup. We've talked about this."

"Mom would have let me."

Elijah rolled his eyes. "You don't remember Mom enough to know what she would have let you do."

"I do, too. I remember that she had the prettiest eyes. And she used to make me laugh when she blew bubbles on my tummy." She screwed her mouth to the side, thinking. "And she said I could wear makeup when I got older. Well, I'm older now."

"She meant a lot older than you are now, Daisy."

"But Ashley's mom said she can wear mascara for the concert. And Lakeisha gets to wear lip gloss to school all the time."

How did his daughter get old enough to have friends who wore makeup? She was six. "Well, I say that you're too young. When you're thirteen, we can talk about it again. But not now."

"You're the meanest daddy in the whole world."

Daisy threw her napkin on the table and stormed out of the room. Feeling as if he'd once again failed as a parent, Christopher put his head in his hands. He felt a hand on his elbow and found Penny looking at him. "I said that to my dad at least once a week, but I didn't mean it," she said.

"I should talk to her."

He started to rise out of his seat, but Penny encouraged him to sit down. "Let her cool off. Six is too young for cosmetics, so you're in the right. She wants to be like her friends."

"She does have a solo."

"Don't cave, Christopher. It won't make things easier on you."

He peered at Penny. "When did you get to be an expert on kids?"

"I watched my ex-fiancé get manipulated by his daughter all the time, so I learned a couple things." Penny glanced at the ceiling. "She's probably sitting on her bed, waiting for you to come up and give in to her request."

Aunt Sarah nodded. "I never had a child, but I helped Lila enough to raise Penny and know that if you give in to this now, it will make things worse down the road."

"But she should come down and finish her dinner."

"In my house, if you leave the table in a tantrum, you're finished eating." Aunt Sarah stood and took Daisy's plate into the kitchen.

Christopher still wasn't convinced. He glanced at Penny, who nodded reassuringly. "I went to bed a few times without finishing my dinner. I had a tendency for dramatics at the table, and Nana was determined to teach me better habits."

"And did it work?"

She smiled. "Eventually."

Aunt Sarah returned to the table and glanced at Elijah. "Are you finishing your dinner?"

"Yes, ma'am." He put a large forkful of

noodles in his mouth and chewed them as if to prove his point.

Aunt Sarah nodded.

THE LAST CALL on Penny's shift Wednesday came at a few minutes after four. Hoping that the circumstances would only need something simple, she jumped on the truck and checked the first-aid kit for the fourth time that day. They'd had quite a few calls requiring medical services for some reason. A heart attack. A fall down basement stairs. A car accident that required them to cut away the passenger-side door. There'd been no fatalities, so that was all good in her book.

The fire truck pulled up in front of an apartment complex. The chief gave the unit number over the walkie-talkies. "The neighbor said that there was a strong smell of gas coming from the apartment, so proceed with masks on."

Penny put on her mask and the hat over it. She grabbed the kit as they ran up the three flights to the indicated door and rapped on it. No answer. Johnson announced their presence and knocked again. He shook his head, then raised the ax to ram it into the door.

After several attempts, the door opened to reveal an empty apartment. Johnson took off his mask and sniffed the air. "False alarm."

"We should check the apartment just in case."

"I'm telling you. It was probably a kid thinking they were being funny."

Penny shook her head and started to search the apartment, but found nothing. She returned to the living room. "It's empty."

"Like I told you. This is someone's idea of a joke." He put a hand on the splintered door. "The landlord's not going to like that." He took out his walkie-talkie and relayed the information of the false alarm.

They took the stairs much slower than they had running up. Johnson turned to her at the landing on the second floor. "Why did you insist on checking the apartment?"

"What if there had been someone in there who needed us? It only took a minute or two to check."

He peered at her. "Did you learn that with your fancy degree?"

"No. I was on a call in Tallahassee that appeared to be a false alarm. My partner found a woman unconscious in a closet when he searched the rooms." She shook her head. "I have the experience to back up what I'm talking about. Maybe if you'd listen to me for once, you might realize that."

Johnson grunted and walked down the last flight of stairs. Trying to hold her temper, Penny followed him to the truck and climbed in the back, wanting to put some distance between her and her partner. What might be seen as being impulsive to others was actually combining her learning with experience.

Once they returned to the station and the report for the files had been written, it was later than she'd expected. She'd hoped to have enough time to go back to the house, shower and eat dinner before Daisy's choir concert. If she was lucky, she could swing through a drive-through for a bite to eat and then get to the school, hopefully before the singing started. She called Aunt Sarah to let her know she'd have to meet them at the school.

"Cuthbert," Mac called as she walked out of the locker room. "You have a minute?"

Great. What had Johnson told him? She followed the fire chief to his office. "Good call on searching the apartment before writing it off as a false alarm."

"We didn't find anything."

"This time. You and I both know that it could have gone in a different direction. It's our job to ensure that it was all clear." He moved to the other side of the desk. "Johnson asked to be assigned a different partner."

"Because I insisted that we search?"

"Because you need a stronger partner who can teach you what you don't already know."

Penny raised her hands. "I don't get it, sir. You tell me I'm too impulsive and need to trust my partner, and now you say that I was right to question him? How do I tell the difference?"

"That's what having a stronger partner will do for you. Teach you when to follow your instincts and when to depend on your training." He glanced at the roster. "I'd like you to work with Luke Roberts. He'll teach you everything you need to know."

Penny nodded, remembering how highly her father thought of the man. "Yes, sir."

"You'll make a great fire chief one day. But I need you to learn how to be the best firefighter on our team first. Understood?"

CHRISTOPHER DROPPED DAISY off at the choir room, then rejoined Elijah and Aunt Sarah in front of the gymnasium. One of the older students handed them programs as they entered and searched for four seats together. He glanced at his watch. The concert started in ten minutes, and Penny still hadn't arrived.

"She'll be here." Aunt Sarah removed her coat and plopped it on the chair beside Christopher. "She promised."

He nodded and took his seat, flipping through the program. Each grade would be singing two songs, and his heart swelled at seeing his daughter's name listed as a soloist. Glancing at his watch again, he said, "Maybe I should go stand out front so she can find us?"

Aunt Sarah nodded. "Go. Elijah and I will save your seats."

The parking lot filled with cars as parents and students streamed into the school. Five more minutes. Where was she? Anticipation at seeing her filled his chest, and he wondered if the connection between them was the one he should really be worrying about, instead of Penny and his daughter. When had Penny become so important to his family? To him?

And could she find a place within that family? Would she even want one? She seemed to agree with him that they could only be friends. Even if he had started to question whether that was what he truly wanted.

He ran a hand through his hair. Talk about jumping the gun. They'd never been on a date, and here he was, trying to imagine what it would be like to be married to her.

Could he be married to a woman with a dangerous job like firefighting? Losing Julie had nearly destroyed him, and he was still feeling her absence. What if he was to get involved with Penny and lost her to a fire? He couldn't handle losing another woman whom he loved like that.

Wait. Loved?

He'd loved Julie. Had known it the moment she'd walked into his sixth-grade science class. The fact that she didn't go out with him until three years later never changed his feelings for her. She was the most beautiful girl he'd ever seen. She made him laugh like no one else and her confidence was infectious. Around her he felt as if he could do anything.

But loving Penny? What he felt for her wasn't like what he'd had with Julie. So it couldn't be love. Right?

A familiar car pulled into the parking lot,

and Penny popped out of it and ran toward the school. "The fire chief called me into the office after the last call, and I rushed to get here. Am I late?"

He swallowed hard, knowing that while it may be different from what he'd had with Julie, he loved this woman. "No." The word came out sounding like gravel. He cleared his throat. "You're just in time."

He held open the door to the school for her and they both entered. What was he doing? He had no business having these feelings for her. They were inconvenient and couldn't go anywhere. Penny wasn't the right woman for him.

He ushered her to their seats and was relieved when the lights dimmed and the fifth graders came out to stand on the risers. Sitting next to Penny, he could sense when she laughed and sighed. Her hand was lying on her knee, and for a moment he thought about picking it up and holding it in his.

But he kept his gaze forward and listened to the children singing, hoping that his feelings weren't being telegraphed on his face.

When Daisy's grade walked out and took their places on the risers, Penny leaned toward him. "There she is. She looks so confident."

The pianist began to play the first bars of the song, and Daisy grabbed the microphone like a rock star while she waited for her cue. Her voice rang out sweet and pure over the audience, and he had to shake his head. That was his daughter sounding like a natural. When her solo ended, she returned the microphone to the stand and stepped back to join the rest of her classmates to finish the song.

Penny leaned closer to him. "She was fabulous."

He turned and looked at her mouth, so close. Then he lifted his eyes to stare into Penny's. She looked back at him, wide-eyed and aware of him. He was about to reach out and touch her cheek when the song ended, and the audience applauded. He saw Daisy step forward and give a small bow before rejoining her class for the second song.

Somehow, he got through the next hour, clapping when appropriate. But his mind was far from the concert. Instead, it was on the woman sitting next to him. She had sat back and angled her body away from his. Taking her cue, he sat closer to Aunt Sarah.

When the concert ended with all the children singing "Silent Night" and holding battery-operated candles, Christopher was the first to stand, applauding the efforts of the children and the choir director. The lights in the gymnasium turned up once more, and he bent to grab his coat from the back of his chair. He also held out Penny's coat for her to put on.

Penny nodded her thanks and he realized he couldn't take his eyes off of her. "We were going to go for dessert. Would you like to come with us?" She hesitated, but he wanted her to be there as much as he'd wanted to keep from touching her before. "Please. Daisy would be heartbroken if you didn't."

She grinned and agreed. "To be honest, I'm starving. I'm surprised the growls of my stomach didn't interrupt the concert."

"I have to go pick up Daisy from the choir room."

"I'll stay here with Aunt Sarah and Elijah while you do."

He nodded, wanting to say something more. Something that would try to explain these feelings that seemed to be swirling around them, but he couldn't find the right words. Instead, he moved past her to go find his daughter.

THE SMELL OF grilling onions made Penny's mouth water as she perused the menu. While the others ordered pie or ice-cream sundaes, she craved protein, especially if it was covered in cheese. When the waitress turned to her, she ordered the cheeseburger platter with onion rings. She noticed that Christopher smirked and shook his head. "What? I didn't have time for dinner before the concert."

Daisy looked at her dad. "Can I get a cheeseburger, too? I was too nervous to eat dinner before."

Christopher nodded and turned to Elijah. "You want a cheeseburger, too?"

The boy shrugged, and Christopher nodded to the waitress. "He'll take one, too. Aunt Sarah?"

"Well, I wasn't going to say anything, but a cheeseburger sounds pretty good."

Penny held up her hands. "See what a good influence I am?"

Christopher laughed at this, and the children turned to him, mouths open. The waitress left with orders for five cheeseburgers instead of desserts, not knowing the big moment that had just occurred. Elijah was the first to speak in the stunned silence. "Dad... you just laughed."

Christopher looked at each of them. "I guess I did."

Daisy smiled brightly at him. "I got my Christmas wish early. Laugh again, Daddy."

He reached over and touched her cheek. "I'll try to laugh more, okay? You don't have to use your Christmas wish on me."

Penny unwrapped her straw and rolled the bit of paper between her fingers. Being with Christopher's family should feel strange, as if she was on the outside looking in, but instead she felt comfortable. As if they did this all the time. She put her straw into her ice water and took a long sip.

"You were wonderful, Daisy," Aunt Sarah said, beaming at the little girl. "You looked like an angel up there."

Daisy fluffed the white dress she was wearing. "That was the point. I was supposed to be like the angel telling the shepherds about the baby. But Mrs. Leavy wouldn't let me wear wings or a halo. She said I had to suggest an angel, not be one."

"You're always my angel," Christopher said, smiling. "I'm so proud of you."

"Thank you, Daddy. Do you think Mommy could hear me from heaven?"

Christopher's smile dimmed slightly, but he nodded. "I'm sure she did. She'd be proud of you, too."

Daisy smiled and wiggled in her seat, pleased at his words even as Elijah scowled. Penny wondered why any mention of his mother seemed to anger him. She knew he was going to counseling, but it didn't seem to be working. He was always angry. Always aloof. And not just to her, but to his own father and sister. She'd seen him have a moment with his grandmother last weekend where he'd actually looked happy, but it had been fleeting, his smile soon replaced by the usual frown.

After they ate and Christopher paid the bill, they went to their cars. Daisy walked next to Penny and took her hand. "Can I ride home in your car?"

Penny glanced over her head to Christopher, who nodded. "How about you, E? Feel like riding with me, too?"

"No, thank you."

At least he'd been polite when shooting her down. Penny directed Daisy over to her car and buckled her into the passenger seat. They listened to Christmas carols on the radio during their drive, singing loudly. When Penny pulled into the driveway, Daisy sighed. "I like you. I wish you could always live with us."

"We don't have to live together to be friends." Penny glanced over at the girl. "I'd like to be your friend."

"I think you're the best friend ever." Then she opened the door and ran up the sidewalk to the front porch, where Aunt Sarah unlocked the front door.

Christopher waited for her at the door. "Thank you for making her night by coming to the concert."

"I had a great time, to be honest. She's got quite the voice."

He nodded. "Unlike her mother. Julie didn't have the ear for it." He looked up and down the street. "I've got to get the kids into bed now, but will you be up for a little bit? I think we need to talk."

Ugh. Those dreaded words. The last time

she'd heard those had been the night before the wedding that never was.

But she gave him her best smile. "Sure. I'll wait in the family room for you."

"Actually, I thought maybe we could take a walk through the neighborhood. It's not as cold tonight, and I'd like to look at the lights on the neighbors' houses."

A walk in the dark lit by Christmas lights sounded too romantic to be a brush-off. She nodded, and he gave her a smile before entering the house.

She followed him inside and took her coat off since it was likely he'd be putting the kids to bed for at least a half hour. More, if they convinced him to read extra chapters of the story they'd been enjoying. Part of her was tempted to climb the stairs and sit at the top to listen in to the storytelling, but she decided that giving them their space was the better choice.

She walked into the family room to find Aunt Sarah settling on the sofa with Caesar on her lap along with a crocheted afghan. Pointing the remote to the television, she flipped channels until she found an old sitcom and decided on that.

"Did you want to watch something, sweetie?"

Penny sat in the recliner. "No. Christopher and I are going to take a walk when he's done getting the kids into bed. Thought we might enjoy some of the Christmas-light displays. Especially the Moores' at the end of the street."

"A walk, huh?"

"I guess he wants to talk."

Aunt Sarah gave her a mysterious smile and started to pet the dog. "That's a good sign, I think. And about time, too."

"It's just talking, Aunt Sarah, so don't start making any wedding plans."

Aunt Sarah put a hand on her chest. "Who, me?"

"He hasn't even asked me out."

"But he will."

"What if I don't say yes? I still haven't changed my mind about single dads, you know."

Aunt Sarah scoffed. "You already have, and you know it." Penny couldn't disagree. She couldn't because Aunt Sarah was right. Christopher was a fine man who loved with his whole heart. They might have some issues, but they could work it out.

Wait. Was she really considering getting involved with Christopher? Maybe Aunt Sarah's romantic ideas were starting to rub off on her.

Christopher stuck his head into the family room. "Ready for that walk?"

Penny stood and leaned over to kiss Aunt Sarah's cheek. "We'll be back soon."

"Don't do anything I wouldn't do."

They shared a smile, and then Penny followed Christopher to the coatrack. Christopher again helped her into her jacket. She looked up at him to thank him and found herself staring into his eyes for longer than was prudent. He reached past her to grab his coat, breaking the spell.

Opening the door for her, Christopher let her pass him onto the front porch. Then he asked, "Where to?"

Penny pointed to the end of the cul-de-sac. "The Moores always put up a fantastic Christmas-light display. Why don't we try that direction?"

They walked side by side in silence for a while. When they reached the empty lot where Christopher's house used to be, he paused. She put her hand in his. "Have you decided to rebuild?"

"I'm getting estimates first about what it would cost to rebuild. But part of me doesn't want to wait a year to move into a new place."

She squeezed his hand. "You can always decide to buy a house elsewhere and move in right away."

"I've been talking to a real-estate agent about possibilities, but I haven't found what we need just yet." He shook his head. "That's not what I brought you out here to talk about."

"So, let's talk."

He looked at her and let go of her hand. "I don't know if I have the words to say what I want to. The words or the courage."

She swallowed as she looked back at him. It sounded like bad news to her. "Then let's walk a little more. Maybe seeing the lights will inspire you." She shivered, suddenly feeling as if the temperature had dropped.

They strolled a little farther and stopped in front of the Moore house. They had chosen a *Nutcracker* theme this year, with small speakers playing the music as lights flashed in sync with the song. The mouse king and nutcracker squared off as fairies and children surrounded them.

She and Christopher stood watching it for

several minutes. Then he took her hand in his again. She leaned against his arm, and he moved it to put it around her, drawing her close to his side. "It's beautiful," she said. "They've done a lot of different displays, but they always put a lot of work into this."

"It takes work, but it's worth it if you want to make it happen."

She peered up at him. "You're not just talking about the lights, are you?"

He turned so that he faced her squarely. "I've been telling myself that there are too many things keeping us apart. That we have too much to overcome."

When he paused, she leaned forward. "But?"

"But I can't stay away from you. It's like you're a flame, and I'm the moth who can't resist you." He put his hands on her shoulders. "And the part that tells me we won't work out is being drowned out by the part that just wants to be with you."

She put a hand on his chest. "I told myself that I couldn't be with a single dad. Not after what happened with Alan. But you're making me change my mind."

"Are you serious?"

She nodded and reached up to put a hand to his cheek. "I want to be with you as much as you want to be with me. And I know that there are some things we'll have to work out, but I'm betting we can if we do it together."

He smiled at her. "I was hoping you'd say that."

She lifted on tiptoe and pressed her lips to his. He pulled her closer and deepened the kiss, wrapping his arms around her. She didn't seem to feel the cold anymore.

CHAPTER ELEVEN

CHRISTOPHER TOOK A deep breath as he checked
his reflection in the mirror. He hadn't been
on a first date since he had been fifteen, and
he couldn't remember feeling this nervous
then. Shaking his head, he opened the bathroom door and stepped out into the hallway.
Daisy ran out of her room and looked him
over. "You look pretty, Daddy."

He picked her up and kissed her on the
cheek. "Thank you. I needed that."

"Where are you going?" she asked as he
placed her back on the floor.

"Penny and I are going out to dinner."

"Can I come, too?"

"It's an adults-only dinner. No kids." When
she pouted, he ruffled her hair. "And after
we eat, she's going to help me pick out some
Christmas presents for you and your brother."

"I still want to go."

"Aunt Sarah said she's making your favorite macaroni and cheese for supper, and if you ask nicely I'm sure she'll play a game with you after."

This seemed to satisfy her, and she took his hand in hers. They walked downstairs together to find Penny sitting on a stool in the kitchen as Aunt Sarah stirred the macaroni on the stove. Whatever they'd been talking about before Christopher entered the kitchen stopped when he entered. Penny looked over at him and smiled. He found himself smiling back at her.

Daisy put her arms around Penny. "Daddy said I can't go with you guys. That it's adults only."

"He's right." She rubbed the girl's shoulder. "No kids tonight."

"But I can play a game with Aunt Sarah after dinner."

Daisy looked over at the older woman, who nodded. "But we're not playing old maid again. You beat the pants off me last time."

They all shared a chuckle. Christopher looked over at Penny. She was lovely in a navy blouse and jeans. "Are you ready?"

She nodded and slid off the stool. They got ready to go and headed for his car. He opened the door for her, and she smiled up at him before entering. "I can't remember the last time I was out with such a gentleman."

"It's all part of the dating experience when you're with me."

Once she was inside, he shut the door and ran around to the driver's side, eager to get away from all his responsibilities for just one night. He started the car and let the engine idle until it warmed up a little more. "I was thinking we could go to the new Mediterranean restaurant that opened last month. How does that sound?"

"Great. I've been wanting to go."

The radio station played Christmas carols as they drove in silence. He'd always been able to talk to her, so why was it so hard to find something to say? This was Penny. She had become a friend above all else. At a stoplight, he closed his eyes and silently cursed himself. He was going to mess this up before it even got started.

He felt a hand on his, and he opened his eyes to find Penny looking at him. "It's okay. I'm nervous, too."

"I can't even remember the last time I was out with a woman, Julie included. She was sick for so long that much of our time was spent at home." He paused. "I'm not supposed to talk about her on our date, am I? See. I don't know what the right etiquette is anymore."

"I tell you what. We agree that we can talk about Julie and Alan, although I'm sure my words won't be as complimentary. They were a big part of our lives that they can't help but be on our minds tonight."

"Alan didn't know what a treasure he had when you were with him."

She smiled at him. "Thank you for saying that."

"I mean, you're beautiful and funny and kind and good at your job. What was he thinking?"

"I can only say that he told me that he felt that his daughter deserved to grow up with both of her parents in the same house."

"So they're back together?"

"A friend of mine told me they broke up again about a month after they reconciled, but Alan still hopes that they can make it work."

Christopher whistled. "He's either really determined or very naive."

Penny laughed and settled back into the

seat. "Maybe you should have been the one to give me a pep talk four months ago when he texted me to tell me that he didn't want to get married. I remember I was in my bedroom after the rehearsal dinner and showing my cousin my wedding dress. Shelby had to read the text to me, and she wasn't as nice as you."

"He broke up with you in a text? I take it back. He's a coward."

She shrugged. "It's water under the bridge. Looking back, I could see the red flags that I chose to ignore because I was in love with him. I thought my second thoughts were nerves and not signs that I needed to get out."

"I'm sorry that he hurt you."

She leaned back on the headrest and looked over at him. "Did you ever have reservations about Julie?"

"I knew that I'd marry her as soon as she smiled at me and loaned me a pencil in sixth-grade science." He lost himself for a moment, remembering the way that her smile had made him feel invincible. He would do anything for her when she shot him that grin. How he missed it still. He cleared his throat. "Don't get me wrong. She wasn't perfect, but

I loved her with everything that I had. And part of me always will."

PENNY REPLAYED CHRISTOPHER'S last words before they arrived at the restaurant. He'd always love Julie. Even with dating Penny, his wife would always own a piece of him that she couldn't touch. She had simply murmured something in response to his declaration. Then they'd pulled into the parking lot, and the subject had thankfully been dropped.

With Alan, she'd been competing with the very-much-alive mother of his child. But she couldn't compete with a memory. Maybe she was right to think that this wouldn't work out between her and Christopher. Maybe she should let him down easy at the end of the night. Because she was done being second to anyone, period. She wanted to be first in his life.

She closed her eyes for a second and sighed, then lowered her menu to see Christopher smiling at her from the other side of the table. He was so handsome. So smart. So good. And her reasons for stopping this relationship before it started fled from her mind.

They ordered their meals, and Christopher

asked for a bottle of red wine for them to share. When it arrived, she took a tiny sip and the first thing she noted was that it was sweet. Second, it sent shots of warmth from her chest to her fingertips. And last, it tasted very good. She nodded at the sommelier, who poured more into her glass, then more for Christopher.

When the sommelier left, Christopher raised his glass of wine in the air. "To new beginnings."

She clinked her glass against his and took another sip, this one longer than her first. "I don't think I've ever liked a wine as much as this one." Or maybe it was the man she was drinking it with.

"It was one of Julie's favorites."

Oh. She tried not to let those words diminish her pleasure. She was starting to regret her words in the car about talking about Julie and Alan.

Christopher winced. "I'm sorry. I'll stop bringing her up."

"It's okay." Even though it wasn't. She searched for a change of subject. "Aunt Sarah has really gotten attached to Caesar even though she always claimed that she wasn't a dog person."

"He has that effect on people."

"You might have a fight on your hands when you find a house and move out."

"Actually, she's asked me to stay on longer. At least through the New Year. But between you and me, I don't think she'll be at that house for very long."

Aunt Sarah hadn't said anything to her about this. "You're still planning on her moving into your seniors' home?"

"Only if that's what she wants." He paused, as if thinking of how to say the right words. "The house is getting to be too much for her."

"So she's said. But I don't think she's as convinced to move as you think she is."

They fell silent until the waitress brought freshly baked pita bread and a trio of dips, including hummus. Penny took a piece of the bread and dunked it into the bean dip that glistened with olive oil and a squeeze of lemon. Popping the piece into her mouth, she chewed and felt her eyes drift closed at the exquisite taste.

"Looks like you like the hummus."

"More like love it." She pushed the bowl

toward him. "You should try it. And the pitas are still warm from the oven."

"You know how to sell it." He dipped an edge of the pita bread and bit into it. "Very good."

"When I lived in Florida, there was this little Mediterranean restaurant across the street from my apartment. Alan and I would often get carryout from there and take it back to my place. Or I would pick up tubs of hummus and tabbouleh to have in my fridge."

"I haven't had much Mediterranean in the past, but I like it so far."

Penny tipped her head to the side to look at him. "If you're not a fan of the food, why did you suggest coming here?"

He looked as if he'd been caught in a lie. "Aunt Sarah might have mentioned that you wanted to try this place."

She reached across the table and took his hand in hers. "That is so sweet of you."

"I wanted you to enjoy yourself."

"But what if you didn't like the food?"

"Penny, I could be sitting across the table from you at a fast-food restaurant and be enjoying myself just because I'm with you." He smiled and gave her hand a squeeze. "I know I talk about Julie too much and it makes you uncomfortable. I'm trying to get better at that."

She could see that he meant it. "I know." She scooted her chair so that it was closer to his side of the table. "Now you have to try this *toum*. It's a garlic sauce with a strong bite, but I personally love it."

She tipped a piece of the pita into the white dip and fed it to him. He took a bite, and she watched as his eyes widened, and he nodded. "That's really good. What is this other brown dip?"

Throughout dinner, Penny explained the different kinds of Mediterranean food, sharing her meal with him. She loved feeding him pickled turnips, which he didn't care for, and the chicken shawarma, which he agreed was the best part of their meal. The awkwardness from earlier had disappeared, and Penny couldn't remember a date she'd enjoyed more.

CHRISTOPHER HADN'T HAD a date like this in his life. Of course, he'd been a teenager when he'd last been dating Julie, and he'd grown up considerably since then. He knew what a mature relationship involved and also how to romance his partner and make her feel special. He'd enjoyed learning from Penny about the different food and how to eat it. When she'd fed him from her hand, he couldn't take his eyes off her as he savored whatever she'd given him.

He fell in love with her in the middle of this restaurant, and it didn't scare him. Instead, he couldn't wait to get to know her better and explore where this relationship could go. He only hoped that she felt the same way.

"So what does that mean? That your fire chief wants to pair you up with a stronger partner?"

"It means that he wants me to get practical experience to go along with my education by pairing me with someone who will actually teach me. That I'm finally on the right track and have a chance of seeing my goal of one day running a firehouse myself."

He raised his eyebrows at this confession. "You want to be fire chief?"

"Sure. I'd be phenomenal when I get the chance. I'm determined, capable. I've worked hard to get this far." She cocked her head to one side and peered at him. "You don't agree?"

"To be honest, I don't know much about what that involves. But I do know that you could make it happen if you want it to."

"You'd be okay being with a fire chief?"

He took her hand in his and rubbed his thumb along the side of it. "I've thought a lot about it. At one point, your being a firefighter did give me pause, but you've come to mean so much to me, to all of us, and it's who you are. How could I turn away from all of that? What would that make me if I did?"

She reached up and touched his cheek. "Who are you, Christopher Fox? I don't think I've ever met a man like you."

"Alan didn't approve of your career plans?"

"He figured that he'd be chief, but I could be his second in command." She shook her head. "I want to be in charge, you know? I can be a good leader and I'd love to get the chance to show it." She paused. "What about you? Is the seniors' home job your dream career?"

Christopher laughed at the thought. "Hardly. It was a steady job, though, when I needed one. And it provided the health insurance that Julie needed for her treatments."

"So if you could have any job, what would it be?"

He'd never been asked that question, and it took him aback. Julie had assumed that the only dream he needed was her and their family. "When I was a kid, I dreamed about having my own business. Being my own boss and in charge."

"You're in charge of the home."

"But I'm not the boss. I still have someone to answer to. But when you have a family and responsibilities, you don't get the luxury of quitting your job to go out on your own."

"What kind of business would you want?"

"That's the thing. I don't know because I never got to think about it seriously. I had bills to pay, and then a family, and then Julie got sick." He shrugged. "I haven't had time to explore the possibilities."

"So what's stopping you now?"

"They're named Daisy and Elijah. You might have met them. I barely have the time to read a book for myself, much less think about a different future."

She squeezed his hand. "But isn't that what you're doing with me? Looking at different possibilities?"

"You're more than a possibility, I hope."

His cell phone buzzed, signaling that he

had a text, but he ignored it. He wanted to keep the evening going, and it had been a long time since he'd had an evening out. But when the phone rang for an incoming call, he checked the screen. Aunt Sarah was calling. "Sorry, Penny. This could be about the kids."

He pressed the button and put the phone to his ear. "Hi, Aunt Sarah."

"Christopher, it's an emergency."

He sat straighter in the chair. "What's wrong?"

"It's the kids. They're missing."

CHAPTER TWELVE

CHRISTOPHER BURST INTO the house after Penny to find Aunt Sarah sitting at the kitchen table, her eyes stained red with tears. "What happened?" Christopher asked her.

"I don't know. We had dinner, and everything seemed to be okay." She dabbed at the corners of her eyes with a dish towel. "Daisy said she was going to the bathroom, and Elijah was going to do homework before we played a card game. But then they didn't come back. I've searched everywhere I could, but they're not here. I'm sorry."

Christopher sat on a chair, unable to remain standing. His children were missing. Where would they go? And why run away, if that was what they had done? Had his date with Penny really upset them that much? He rubbed his face. "It's not your fault, Aunt Sarah."

Penny put a hand on his shoulder, and

he glanced at her. "We'll find them. They couldn't have gone far." She nodded as if to reassure him as she turned to Aunt Sarah. "Did they say anything at dinner? Were they upset about something?"

Aunt Sarah glanced at Penny, then looked Christopher in the eye. "They didn't like that you went out on a date."

Penny's hand slipped from his shoulder, and he frowned. He should have known that he was moving too fast for his children. He should have ignored the attraction and kept his friendship with her intact. Instead, he had impulsively thought he could have it all. That his children would welcome another woman into their family. But their disappearance had proved him wrong.

Christopher stood and nodded. "Okay. We'll split up and search. I'll check the old house in case they went back there. Penny, can you search here?"

Aunt Sarah spoke up. "I already did. They're not here."

Penny grabbed her aunt's hand. "I know you did, but I might be able to search in hard-to-reach spots that a little kid might fit into."

Christopher glanced at his watch. "It's eight

thirty. We'll meet back here at nine and call the police if they aren't found. Text me if you find them, and I'll do the same."

Aunt Sarah raised her hand. "And I'll stay in case the kids come back. You two get moving."

Penny headed for the basement door. "I'll start at the bottom and work my way up. See you at nine, if not before."

Christopher raced down to the lot where their house had once stood. He walked to the cement slab that had been his front porch and called Elijah's and Daisy's names, but no answer came. He didn't think they would hide in the dark here. The place gave him the creeps, and he was the adult. Christopher ran a hand through his hair. Where would they go? Maybe the garage.

The garage door creaked as Christopher pulled it open and peered into the darkness. "Daisy? Elijah?"

There was a shuffling sound. Then his son stepped forward. "She's not here, Dad. It's just me."

Christopher snapped on the light switch by the door and winced at the harsh light. He ran to Elijah and pulled the boy into his arms. Elijah clung to him, and Christopher closed his eyes, thankful that he'd found him. "Why did you leave the house? And where's Daisy?"

"I don't know where she went." Elijah sniffled and wiped his face. "But I had to come here."

"Why?"

"Because I wanted to find Mom's things." He looked around the garage and pointed. "I know you kept some of her stuff, but I can't find it. And I have to find it."

"Why do you have to find it right now?"

Elijah stared up at him, but didn't answer. Christopher gave him a nod, figuring that if his son was determined enough to come here in the dark to look, then it was important. "I need to let them know I found you." He texted Penny to let her know Elijah had been found, but he didn't know where Daisy had run to. "We'll find your mom's stuff. Don't worry." They moved aside different boxes and bins, searching the garage.

"You ran away to find Mom's stuff, but why did Daisy run away?"

"She didn't like you going out with Penny." Christopher knew enough about his son to know that there was more that he wasn't sharing. "What else?"

"That's it."

Christopher gazed at his son until he lifted his eyes to meet his. "Honest, Dad. She was upset about the date."

"I thought she liked Penny."

"She loves Penny, but…"

Christopher waited for his son to continue. When he didn't, he asked, "But what?"

"Maybe Daisy wanted Penny all for herself. You know how she is about sharing."

"That doesn't seem right. Daisy wouldn't run away because I was friends with Penny, too."

"Maybe she doesn't want Penny to replace Mom." Elijah paused to swallow, then whispered, "Maybe I don't want you to replace Mom."

Christopher knelt beside his son and put his hands on his shoulders. "Penny could never take the place of your mom."

"I'm not talking about Penny." Elijah turned away.

These were more words than his son had said in months. Christopher yearned for him to open up more, but knew that he couldn't push him. That only seemed to make him grow silent. So he stayed on his knees, watching Elijah until he was ready to say more.

Elijah turned to face him. "I'm talking about you."

Christopher frowned. "Me?"

"Mom was the one who did the funny voices when she read stories to us at bedtime. She was the one who liked looking at the Christmas lights and listening to Christmas music. Not you. Mom." Elijah took a deep breath, as if he'd been holding all this in for months, which he had. His son's eyes filled with tears as he looked at him. "I don't need you to be Mom. I need you to still be Dad."

Christopher pulled his son into his arms. "I'll always be Dad, even when you have kids of your own. That will never change."

"Then stop trying to be like Mom."

Had he tried to become like Julie? He'd wanted to help the kids get through their grief and had taken on the things she'd loved to do. How was he supposed to know that he wasn't helping Elijah, but hurting him instead? He put a hand on the back of his son's head. "I'll make that promise if you make me one. We need to talk about Mom more, even if it makes us sad. Especially then. It's the way we remember her, and then we won't forget."

"That's what Dr. Shoemaker says."

"She's a smart lady, and we should listen to her, don't you think?" Christopher pressed a kiss in the curly hair above Elijah's ears. "I miss her, too, buddy. Every day, I miss her."

"I'm starting to forget her voice."

Elijah's quiet admission brought a fresh batch of tears that dampened Christopher's neck as he drew the boy into a tight hug. In Christopher's limited experience, those he'd loved and lost didn't disappear all at once, but in pieces. He had already forgotten the taste of Julie's kisses and at times struggled to remember her smell. Now, with the fire taking most of the belongings he'd kept of hers, the memory of her would fade quicker. "We'll find her stuff. I promise."

Straightening, he turned on the flashlight feature of his cell phone and held it high to try to locate the bin. He recalled putting it toward the back with the idea of saving it for his kids until they were older, but this seemed like a perfect time to share the contents with them. Taking a few steps forward, he paused to move several bins to make a path to the back of the garage. The light fell on the purple bin, and he moved forward to retrieve it.

PENNY READ CHRISTOPHER'S text and sighed in relief. One child had been found, and they would soon find Daisy. There weren't many places a six-year-old could get to. She turned the flashlight on and moved it over the boxes in the basement. They had been long ago organized by Nana, but the last year had seen things being put where it was convenient instead. Shaking her head at the disarray, she pushed aside a box. "Daisy? Are you down here, sweetie?"

No answer. Not that Penny had expected one. Daisy didn't like dark places that could contain spiders, and she doubted she'd be so upset over the date to overcome her fear and come down here. She bit her lip and tried to think of where Daisy would hide. When Penny had been the girl's age and been upset, her place to run had been the attic.

Penny straightened and took the stairs two at a time. When she ran through the kitchen, Aunt Sarah glanced up at her. "Did you find them?"

"Christopher found Elijah at the old house.

And I have an idea where Daisy would go. It's where I would go if I was upset about losing my mom."

"The attic." Aunt Sarah shook her head. "I didn't think of there. And I wouldn't be able to climb those rickety stairs if I had."

"Don't beat yourself up. This isn't your fault." She swallowed and closed her eyes. "I'm afraid it's all mine."

Before Aunt Sarah could protest, Penny left the kitchen and ran up the stairs to the second floor, then opened the rarely used door to the attic. It squeaked, and the light switch snapped as she turned it on. The stairs creaked under each footstep. "Daisy, I know you're up here."

A sniffle answered her, and she went to where her mother's boxes were stacked by the dormer window. She had to shift the army trunk that had belonged to Pops, and there seated on the floor was Daisy, her knees brought up to her chest. Her head rested on her knees as she sobbed. Her heart breaking for the little girl, Penny dropped to sit next to her. Unsure if the girl would welcome her touch, she hesitated reaching out to her, but couldn't deny the impulse.

Daisy looked up at her, her eyes red and swollen. Overcome with a strong protective affection for Daisy, Penny pulled the girl into her arms and rubbed her back. "What's wrong, sweetie? You can tell me. It's okay."

But Daisy shook her head and buried her head in Penny's shoulder. Penny rested her head on the girl's and continued to sit quietly until Daisy could share the burden on her heart. Remembering Christopher's admonition to text when the children were found, she typed him a quick text, letting him know she'd found Daisy. She put her phone on the floor beside her. "We were so worried about you. Aunt Sarah didn't know where you were, and she got really scared."

"Sorry."

"Needing time to yourself is okay, but you need to let an adult know before you go."

"I know."

Penny pressed a kiss to the top of Daisy's head. "I'm so glad you're safe."

Daisy pulled away to look into Penny's eyes. "You are?"

"Of course I am. You mean a lot to me."

Daisy rubbed her eyes with the corner of

her silky cape. "I thought that my daddy was going to take you away from me."

"Is that what this is about?" She was in unfamiliar territory here. Sure, she'd been friendly with Alan's daughter, but they hadn't had a connection like she did with Daisy. Not sure of how to proceed, she took a deep breath and thought about her words before speaking. She pulled the girl even tighter to her and rocked back and forth with her. "I'll always be your friend."

"But what if you marry my dad? Then you'd be my mom, not my friend."

"I'm not going to marry your dad."

The words were out before she could take them back. The truth to them hit her heart, and she took a long breath before letting it out. Christopher had been right. The kids weren't ready for him to be dating. As much as she might want to be with him, she had to put his children first, just as he'd been doing before they had tried to pursue something. She frowned at the ache associated with that thought, but knew what she had to do.

She smoothed some of the curls away from the girl's forehead. "I'm not going to be your mother."

The girl seemed to wilt as she pressed her cheek against Penny's chest. "I want us to be friends always. Just you and me."

"I can be friends with you, as well as Elijah and your dad, because there's room in my heart for all of you, not just you."

"Elijah, too? He hates you."

"I don't think it's me that he hates."

"He misses Mom, but he won't talk about her."

"And you need to talk about her, right?"

Daisy looked up at her and nodded.

Penny smiled at her, then stood and held out her hand to help the girl to her feet. "You came up here because you knew this was where I would go when I was sad and missed my mom." The girl nodded again. "Do you want to see some of my mom's things that I saved?"

She led the girl to a hatbox covered in decoupage of floral paper. Inside there was a small jeweler's box that had a gold necklace with a cross made of diamonds. "My dad gave this to my mom the year I was born. She only wore it a few times before she died because Dad said she thought it was too fancy."

She pulled out an envelope stuffed with letters. "These are letters she wrote to me before I was born." Penny looked at the envelope and sighed. "I haven't thought of these notes in years. They are full of her hopes and dreams for me."

"I'm sad that you don't remember your mom."

Penny put an arm around the girl's shoulders. "It's okay, Daisy. I had my nana. And Aunt Sarah, of course. I always felt lots of love."

Daisy dropped her gaze to her lap. "I only remember a little of my mom. And some things I can't remember at all."

Penny sat down beside the hatbox and pulled the girl onto her lap. "What do you remember?"

"She loved to laugh, and she had the best laugh of anybody in the whole world. It would fill the room, and you had to laugh with her." Daisy tilted her head back to lean on her chest. "Even when she was sick, she would laugh with us. But she got really quiet at the end."

Penny tightened her arm around the girl. "That must have been hard on you."

"Yes. I wanted to save her, but I couldn't." She crumpled into more tears, and Penny rubbed her back and let her cry.

The sound of heavy feet on the attic stairs alerted them both to Christopher's arrival. Daisy raised her head, then ran to her father, throwing her arms around him as he scooped her up and held her tight. "Daisy girl, you scared me."

"I know. I'm sorry, Daddy."

He glanced at Penny over Daisy's head and nodded at her, mouthing his thanks. She tried to smile, but the pending conversation between them settled heavy on her heart.

Christopher kissed both of Daisy's cheeks, then placed her back on her feet. "You need to go downstairs and wash your face, then get into your jammies. We're going to have a little family meeting before bedtime tonight. You, your brother and me. Okay?"

He was excluding her already, and Penny knew she shouldn't mind, but she did. And he was right. It had to be the three of them together. It was time for her to gracefully bow out of the picture before things got worse.

The girl bobbed her head and left the attic. Christopher peered at her. "How did you know she'd be up here?"

Penny pointed at the hatbox. "I mentioned

once that when I missed my mother, I'd come up here and look at some of her things."

"Smart thinking."

She nodded. "Listen, Christopher, we need to talk."

"We do. But I need to talk to my kids first. Maybe we can meet by the Christmas tree downstairs after I get them into bed?"

THE KIDS PILED onto Elijah's bed after brushing their teeth and dressing in their pajamas. Christopher placed the bin he'd brought from the garage at the foot of the bed and opened the lid. "We're not doing a story before bed tonight." He glanced at his son, who nodded. "Instead, I thought we could hear from your mom."

The kids frowned at him as he pulled out his old cell phone, the one he'd had before Julie had died. He found the charging cord and plugged it into the phone and the wall before turning on the power. It took a while to load, but it finally shone bright in his hand. He checked the old voice-mail messages and found the one he wanted, then pressed the date and put the phone on speaker.

"Hey, babe. I know you're on your way

home with the kiddos, but I wanted to tell you how much I love you, love our family. The three of you mean the world to me." Here Julie paused, and when she continued her voice sounded strangled. "My best day ever was the day that I walked into your class-room and sat next to you. I wish we could have more time together, but it doesn't look like we're going to get it. Never forget that I love you. Always."

Christopher put the phone in his lap. "I saved the message because I didn't want to forget your mom's voice." He put a hand on his son's knee. "So that you wouldn't forget, either."

Elijah nodded, his cheeks wet with tears. Daisy picked up the phone and pressed the voice mail to play it again. They sat on the bed together, listening to the message twice more before Christopher put the phone back into the bin. He then took out two journals— one red, the other purple. He gave them to his children. "Your mom wrote in these for you before she died. She asked me to make sure that you got them when you were ready. I haven't been sure when that would be, but

I've realized that you will know when that is even if I don't."

Elijah opened the red leather-bound journal and ran a finger along the words written in ink. "What did she write?"

Christopher shook his head. "She didn't tell me. But I know she loved you both. If she could have stayed with us, she would have."

"I wish she was here."

Christopher nodded at Daisy. "I do, too. She would have loved seeing you sing last night."

Elijah looked up from the journal. "Can I keep this with me?"

"Absolutely." He tried to smile, but the effort seemed to be too difficult. "Elijah, I'm glad you said something tonight because I had forgotten these were in the garage. The fire might have taken things from us, but we still have these from your mom."

Daisy poked her head into the bin. "What else is in here?"

"Letters she wrote me when we were in school. Her favorite red sweater. Things that I wanted to keep to remember her."

One by one, he pulled out items and laid them on the bed. They talked about each one, sharing memories. Christopher knew it was a school night and growing late, but his children needed this tonight. Needed to remember their mother.

Maybe he did, too. Julie was always there in the back of his mind, but after his date with Penny and losing his children, he needed to bring out these memories to remind him why he had loved her. Why he always would love her.

And why he needed to let Penny go.

He looked at his children. "We're going to be okay, the three of us. Do you know why?"

"Because you've got our back," they both said together.

He smiled and leaned forward to kiss them each on the forehead. "No matter what happens, I'll always have your back."

Daisy gave a big yawn and eased down in the bed next to Elijah, who snuggled against her. "Can I stay in here with Elijah tonight?"

Christopher nodded as he put Julie's things back into the bin, then placed it at the end of the bed for them to peruse another day. After pulling the covers over his kids, he leaned down to kiss first one and then the other. "Good night, my precious babies."

"I'm not a baby," Daisy murmured, half-asleep already.

She'd always be his little girl, no matter how old she got. He slipped out of the room, shutting the door partway. Pausing in the hallway to make sure that they were asleep, he wiped his eyes and took a deep breath.

Downstairs, he found Penny sitting in the dark with only the lights from the Christmas tree turned on. She seemed lost in thought, and he wished he could stand there and watch her. But they needed to have this conversation, and the sooner, the better.

He walked toward her, and she turned to face him. "How are they?"

"Fine. Asleep. Thank you for finding Daisy."

Penny nodded. "I guess we should talk, huh?"

"Want to take a walk?"

"I'll go tell Aunt Sarah that we won't be long."

CHAPTER THIRTEEN

HAND IN HAND, they walked to the Moore house, staring at the lights for a moment. What a change a day had made. Last night, they'd been full of anticipation, but that had now turned to anxiety. Penny knew what was coming. What had to happen. They couldn't be together. Period. End of story. Time to move on.

And yet it made her heart ache at the thought. For a moment earlier that evening, she thought she could fall in love. Had fallen in love. But it was over before it really began.

"Chris—"

"Penny—"

They stumbled over their names at the same time. Penny reached up and touched his face with her mittened hands. "It's okay. I know what you're going to say. I was going to say the same thing."

"If things were different. If we were different." Christopher shook his head. "I have to think of my kids and it's more than just the promise I made to Julie. You understand?"

She dropped her hands and stared at the ground. "More than you know. Tonight really showed me that we were right from the beginning. None of us are ready for anything more than friendship between the two of us."

Christopher took a step closer to her and put his hands on her shoulders. She looked up at him. "So why does this hurt so much?" he asked.

"Don't say things like that." He wasn't making this any easier.

"It's the truth, isn't it? I look at you and see what I want right in front of me, but I can't have you. Doesn't that make you want to cry?"

Tears formed in her eyes at his words, but she shook her head. "No. It's better that we found this out now rather than later, when there are emotions involved."

He took a step back. "I don't know about you, but my emotions are already involved when it comes to you."

"Christopher..."

"Don't tell me not to say it because I may never get another chance."

His eyes reflected the Christmas lights behind her. Red, blue, green. She knew she should walk away before things got out of hand as they stood at that precipice. She needed distance to protect her, protect her heart. But walking away wouldn't hurt less. She looked up at him, hoping her eyes could say what she could not.

Christopher grimaced. "I've never loved another woman besides Julie before. And I never expected to fall in love with anyone again. But here you are. And it's going to kill me to let you go, but I have to."

Arrows pierced her chest, and she put a hand over her heart as if that would shield it from the pain. She knew what she had to do. "I think under the circumstances, it's best if I move out of my aunt's house. Tonight."

"No. If anyone should leave, it's us. You're her family."

"And you have nowhere else to go." Penny shook her head. "I should have moved back in with my cousin long ago, but I was enjoying myself too much living with you all." She took a deep breath. "So I'm going to say goodbye here and walk back to the house and pack. Give me five minutes before you follow me. Please. Let this be the end of it here."

She started to leave, but Christopher reached for her and turned her around. "I still want us to be friends."

"We will. Eventually. But right now, we should keep our distance." She looked up at him, wanting to tell him so much more. Wanting to share everything that was in her heart, as he had, but she knew it would only hurt them both. "Goodbye, Christopher."

She stood on her tiptoes to kiss his cheek, but he turned and kissed her fully on the mouth. Unable to help herself, she wrapped her arms around him and returned his kiss with all the love and passion she had for this man. She didn't want to let him go, but she had to leave him. After several minutes of sweet torture, she dropped her arms from him and stepped away. Then she turned and ran back to the house.

CHRISTOPHER WATCHED AS Penny left. The crush of his heart now couldn't compare to his feelings after Julie died. Then, he'd been bereft and felt so lost. With Penny, he felt as if someone had packed up his feelings and stored them away for later, when it would be safer to bring them out. He felt empty. And the burden of being a single dad weighed him down even more. He'd had a glimpse of what it might be like to have a partner helping him, and now it was gone.

He turned back to look at the Christmas lights, which blazed. He put a hand to his eyes, shielding them from the brightness of the display. What had once been beautiful and inspiring now seemed garish and overdone.

Although he'd done the right thing, he still clung to second thoughts. Maybe the kids needed more time and they would have accepted Penny into their lives. Maybe he and Penny could still find a way to work things out between all of them.

But those thoughts were followed by a cold hard reality. The truth was that he had to put the kids first, and they weren't ready for a new woman in their lives. He wasn't sure that even he was ready. He thought he might be, but if this was what it felt like, then maybe he should stay single. Alone.

It had been a night full of roller-coaster moments, and he longed to go back to the house and sleep. To deal with the fallout tomorrow. He'd had a breakthrough with the kids and their grief had healed, even if a little. The next counseling session should prove to be interesting.

And yet he'd lost something he'd wanted. Something he needed, even if it was too late to realize that now.

His steps back to the house were labored and slow, as he didn't want to start over with a life without Penny. But he'd bounced back from loss before. He could do it again.

AUNT SARAH SAT on the side of the bed watching as Penny packed what little she'd brought with her into the duffel bag. "Are you sure you can't stay?"

"I've overstayed my welcome as it is."

"Nonsense. You're always welcome here." She pulled out one of the T-shirts that Penny had flung into the bag and took her time refolding it before placing it back in gently. "This has to do with Christopher."

"No, it's about me."

"I shouldn't have talked about the date in front of the children. It wasn't their business, but I was too happy for the two of you.

You'd finally realized what the rest of us have known for the last couple of weeks." She frowned and gestured to the open doorway. "You shouldn't let this come between you two. It will blow over, and the children will be fine."

"Like I said, this is about me." Penny pulled more jeans from the dresser drawer and hugged them to her chest, but they served as a weak shield for the emotions overtaking her. "I never should have gotten involved with a single dad. You would think I'd learned my lesson the first time."

"So this is really about Alan."

Penny stopped packing and looked at her aunt. Had she been projecting some of her feelings that had been left unresolved from Alan onto Christopher's shoulders? She shook her head. "This has nothing to do with him."

"Shelby said you could move back in with her?"

"Actually, she has her niece Harper staying with her, so I'm moving in with Jack temporarily. But I really think it's time I found my own place after the New Year."

"What about this house? Would you consider buying it?"

Penny dropped the jeans and peered at her aunt. "So you've decided to sell up and move?"

"I think I'm ready to." She looked around the bedroom, and her eyes became liquid. "It's going to be hard to say goodbye to this place, but if I knew it was going to family... Would you think about it?"

So many memories were associated with this house. Penny agreed with her aunt—it would be easier to see it stay in the family than to watch strangers take possession of it. But she wasn't the right person to buy it. "Actually, I think there's a better solution."

THE SENIORS' HOME had once helped him stop thinking constantly about Julie after she died, but it no longer worked as the solution. Now he was dragging his way through his Monday morning and counted down the minutes until he could leave for the day. At breakfast, Aunt Sarah mentioned that Penny had moved in with her cousin Jack. Part of him knew it was for the best, but another larger part of him ached for her presence. Seeing her smiling face in the morning before he left for work had helped him through his day. But now he felt out of sorts. Angry. After he had snapped at his assistant, Brenda, a second time, she glared at him. "What has gotten into you?"

"Nothing."

"You need to get a cup of coffee and get that nothing out of your system." She glanced at the clock. "You have ten minutes before your next appointment, so you'd better move."

"I don't have an appointment this morning."

"Last-minute call, but she insisted that you would agree to see her."

He frowned. "See who?"

"Me." Aunt Sarah stood at the office door and unwrapped the scarf from around her head. Tiny curls graced her head, as if she'd just left the salon. "I know I'm earlier than the agreed time, but you can squeeze me in."

"Of course." Aunt Sarah hadn't mentioned that she would be seeing him when they'd had breakfast a few hours earlier. He waved his arm toward his office. "Come on back. Can I get you something to drink? Coffee? Water?"

"I think your receptionist mentioned you needed a coffee break. Why don't we take this meeting to the cafeteria?"

He nodded and took her coat, folding it

over the back of one of the chairs in front of his desk, then held out his arm for her to take. She placed her hand in the crook of his elbow and walked with him down the hall. "I appreciate you agreeing to see me on such short notice."

"You don't need an appointment to talk to me."

"I'm here on official business, so I thought it best."

They reached the cafeteria, and Christopher opened the door for her to enter first. She glanced around the expansive room, taking in the pretty Christmas decorations, as well as the large tree lit with twinkling white lights. Its boughs were hung with ornaments that the craft classes had been making the last few weeks.

He ushered her to an empty table. "Coffee or tea?"

"Tea with honey, please."

He left her at the table and got their drinks. Sandra from the kitchen offered a plate of Christmas cookies. After thanking her, he took the snack to the table. He placed the mug of tea in front of Aunt Sarah, then sat beside her. "You mentioned official business."

"It's time that I sold the house and moved in here."

The words made him choke on his sip of coffee, and he used a napkin to wipe his chin. "I thought you said that the family wasn't really prepared for this."

"Whether they are or not, I'm the one who's living in the house, and I say that I'm ready."

"Have you told them?"

"I told Penny a few nights ago, so I'm sure it's spreading around the rest of the family by now." She picked up a sugar cookie and had a bite. "Talking to your receptionist earlier, I know that you have several options for me. I'd like to see them before I make my final decision."

"Absolutely. We can set up a tour. I'll do it myself."

She smiled at him. "I hoped you'd say that."

"I have rooms that are available now, as well as some that will be vacant in the next few weeks. When did you plan to move?"

"Beginning of next year, I think. It will give the Cuthbert family one more Christmas at the house before it's sold." She reached out to touch his hand. "I know the real-estate market can be volatile, but I think I've already found the buyer."

That was quick. When Aunt Sarah decided on something, she moved fast. "That's good news. Who?"

"You."

"That's great to hear." He frowned. "Wait. Me?"

"The house is wonderful to raise a family in. My sister raised her boys. We raised Penny there. Now it's your turn."

"Aunt Sarah…"

She held up her hand. "Hear me out. You've been looking for a house that would keep the kids in the same school, maybe even the same neighborhood. You don't think you want to wait to rebuild, but nothing has come up that fits all your needs." She gestured in a way that suggested all his problems had been solved. "Voilà. You buy my house."

"That's sweet to offer, but I can't."

"And why not? You'll have the money from the insurance company from your old house for the down payment. And you already know that it's a good home for the right family."

"I don't know that the right family is us." Overwhelmed by the offer, he asked, "And what about your family? Shouldn't you give someone a chance to buy it first?"

"I offered it to Penny, but she turned me down."

At the mention of her name, he frowned and stared into his coffee cup. "This was her idea to offer it to me."

He stated it as a fact, rather than asking a question. Aunt Sarah looked at him. "That doesn't make it a bad idea."

He ran a hand through his hair. "I don't know about this, Sarah."

She patted his hand. "I know. It's a lot to think about, but you take your time. Consider your options. And in the meantime, show me the rooms here." She grabbed another cookie. "But after our snack break. I can't pass up a good cookie."

BORED AT JACK'S apartment, Penny drove to the Cuthbert Motors garage and parked her car next to her cousin's. Walking across the parking lot, she waved at Eddie, who had been working there since her uncle Mike had started the business. In the office, she found Shelby peering at the computer on her desk.

She looked up at Penny as she closed the door. "How are you doing today?"

"Fine." She shrugged. "Why wouldn't I be?"

"Because you broke up with Christopher."

"We weren't really involved yet, so it's no big deal. Why is everyone acting like it is?"

"Do I really need to say it? Denial is a dangerous thing."

"I'm fine. Really." She gave her cousin a smile as if to prove it was so, but the frown on Shelby's face didn't change. "I might be a little sad that we can't be together, but it's not like it was with Alan. There's no history here to get over. It was a moment, and it's done. Let's move on."

"Oh, sure. Move on from falling in love just like that."

"I wasn't in love."

Shelby peered at her like she didn't believe her. "If that wasn't love, then I'd hate to see when it does happen for you. He was perfect. Is perfect. Are you sure that the two of you can't work this out somehow?"

"No. It's done." Penny glanced at her watch. "What time are you off tonight? It will probably be my last chance for a couple of weeks, what with my schedule at the station, so I was thinking an impromptu cousins' dinner. Maybe that Italian place by Jack's apartment?"

"How are things living with him?"

"He's a caring vet who tends to bring home his patients. How do you think it is?" She shuddered. "I walked into the bathroom to take a shower this morning and found an iguana in the bathtub."

"It could always be worse."

"Never say that. Seven work for you?"

"Fine. Seven. But I'll have to bring Harper with me. My sister, Laurel, claims she needs some time for herself. My guess is that it's a new boyfriend."

CHRISTOPHER STARED OUT his office window, Aunt Sarah's offer on his mind. She was right about it being the perfect house for a family. Maybe even for his family. But there was something about the whole thing that felt wrong. He had a gut feeling that she would offer to sell it to him at a price lower than market value out of a sense of charity. He couldn't take advantage of her like that. He wouldn't.

He found the number for his real-estate agent and dialed it. When she answered, he told her the situation, asking that she find out the true market value of the property. She agreed to get back to him in the next couple of hours.

Satisfied that he was going to get some answers, he turned to his next task. Aunt Sarah had liked one of the vacant rooms and submitted an application for possession. Entering her information into the computer, he knew she would enjoy living at the complex. She had been lonely in the big house by herself, and his family moving in had highlighted how much she missed having company.

Though Christopher didn't think she'd anticipated how much his family would take up her time. For that matter, he hadn't anticipated how much it would mean to have her help and her company. It was nice to have another adult to talk to. To have someone he could depend on. Things would definitely change once he was alone with the kids again.

Alone. He winced at the word. But looking back, that was exactly what he had been. His days never changed. He fed the kids before school. Went to work. Came home and fed the kids again. Then baths, story time and off to bed. Only for him to clean the house and go to bed himself before repeating the same thing the next day.

There had to be more to life than that. Penny had shown him that he didn't have to go it on his own. And now she was out of his life, and he was alone. Again.

Brenda popped her head into the office. "Don't forget that today I'm leaving early so I can pick up Heather from the airport. Are you going to be okay without me?"

He nodded. "Go. And say hello to your daughter for me."

"She's still single, you know."

He waved her off. While he didn't look forward to being alone, he also wasn't ready to jump into another relationship.

The rest of the afternoon passed without incident, and he got the information from the agent about Aunt Sarah's house. Armed with facts and figures, he could determine his family's future.

Unfortunately, it was without Penny.

PENNY DRAGGED HER fork through the creamy Alfredo sauce, but didn't twirl any of the fettuccine onto it. After the antipasto salad and freshly baked bread, she wasn't hungry. Truth be told, she hadn't been hungry for that, either. When the waitress stopped at the table, she asked for a take-out container for her meal.

"I thought you said the breakup was mutual." Jack pointed to her full plate. "But you don't have an appetite, and you've been moping all night."

"I'm not moping."

Shelby shot Jack a look. "She's definitely moping."

"Why are you moping?" Harper asked.

Penny glanced at the girl and shook her head. "I'm really not." Then she looked at her two cousins. "Do we have to discuss this in front of the child?"

"She's four. Who's she going to tell?" Jack wiped his mouth with the cloth napkin and placed it next to his empty plate. "If it was mutual, why are you acting as if he broke your heart?"

"We went on one date. One. There's no broken heart." She knew in her head that they had ended things before it could get serious. So why was her heart aching as if it had been broken? Why did she find herself longing to shut herself in a room alone and cry until everything inside her had been wrung out? "I'm fine."

Liar, her heart whispered.

"Do we have to keep talking about him?" Penny asked.

Shelby wiped Harper's mouth, which was ringed with red tomato sauce. "What would you rather talk about? The fact that you're avoiding the family for Christmas by working?"

"I'm not avoiding the family."

"I remember your dad working the holidays after your mom died."

"This isn't the same thing. I'm trying to give the guys with families time off to spend with them. It's actually a pretty noble thing that I'm doing."

"And avoiding the family at the same time." Shelby stared at her hard, and Penny squirmed slightly in her chair. "But I'll give you a pass since your heart is bruised."

"For the umpteenth time, my heart is fine."

Harper cocked her head to one side. "Who hurt your heart?"

"Nobody, sweetie." Penny glared again at her cousins. "Subject change, please."

Jack shrugged. "How about we talk about Aunt Sarah selling the house and moving into the seniors' home?"

That brought Christopher to the forefront of her mind again, since she knew her aunt would be offering to sell him the house. Couldn't she get away from everyone mentioning that man to her? Couldn't they let her get over him?

Shelby and Jack discussed what would happen with the house while Penny put her dinner into the container to take home. Maybe she'd be hungry later. Or she could eat it for breakfast in the morning before she had to start her shift.

When the conversation stopped, she looked up at her cousins, who were watching her. "What? What did I miss?"

"Jack said that Aunt Sarah offered to sell the house to Christopher."

"I know. It was my idea." She shrugged it off. "You can say his name without me breaking down into sobs."

"Will you be okay if he moves into that house?"

She held out her hands. "I'm fine. I'll be okay. Got it?" Her cousins nodded, and she stood. "I'm going to run to the restroom."

"I gotta go, too," Harper said.

Penny held her hand out for the little girl, and they walked to the front of the restaurant, where the restrooms were. She opened the door to let Harper enter first. "Do you need help?"

"I'm a big girl."

Figuring that answered the question, she waited for the girl to enter a stall and close the door before choosing one for herself.

Once she finished, she waited for Harper to come out of the stall. Several minutes passed with no word. "Are you okay?"

"My tights are all squished and won't come up."

"Can you open the door for me?"

The stall door opened, and Penny could see that the tights were twisted near the girl's ankles. She helped her get them straight, then pointed the little girl to the sinks. "Wash your hands now."

Harper complied, but couldn't reach the paper towels. Penny handed one to her. "Do you like staying with Aunt Shelby?"

"I guess. She has a lot of rules."

"Your mom doesn't?"

Harper shrugged. "Do you like staying with Jack?"

"I guess. Except for the lizard."

Penny gave Harper's face a once-over with a damp paper towel while the girl squirmed. "There. Now we can see your face."

"You'd be a good mommy."

The words hit Penny in a soft place, and she nodded while trying to swallow her emotions. But the dam had been broken, so the tears came out. Harper patted her arm as she cried about her lost chances.

The bathroom door opened, and Shelby stepped inside. "What is taking you guys so long?" At the sight of Penny's tears, she shut the door and pulled her cousin into a tight hug. "It's going to be okay, Pen."

"I do love him. And I love his kids. What if I just threw away the best chance I have at finding happiness?"

"There will be other opportunities."

"But none like Christopher." She pulled several paper towels from the dispenser and dabbed at her eyes. "I really am fine."

"You will be."

IT WAS A LONG week without Christopher. On the afternoon of Christmas Eve, she went to see her father, who was waiting for her in the fire chief's office. Penny glanced around the office, but it was just her father there. "You wanted to see me?"

"Sit."

"I'm supposed to be working on a new training module for the New Year."

Her father pushed a chair toward her. "We need to talk first. Please."

She took a seat, and he pulled a chair from behind the desk to sit beside her. He looked tired. Weary and worn. Older than he was. What if he was sick and that was why he wanted to talk to her? They might not have been close all their lives, but he'd always tried to do his best for her. "Are you okay? Did you see the doctor recently?"

He frowned at her and ran a hand through his hair, a gesture that reminded her of Christopher. He often did that when he was stalling for time before he said something that she might not like. "This isn't about me."

Her temper flared. "I've been following protocol and not making any hotshot moves, so the chief has nothing to complain about me to you."

"This isn't about that, either. In fact, Dale said he's been impressed by your attitude lately. You're becoming a team member."

"So what is this about?"

"It's Christmas Eve." When she didn't say anything, he continued, "And you're working not just today, but tomorrow, too."

"I requested it so that those with families could have it off to celebrate." She held up her hands. "I don't see the problem. You used to do the same thing."

"Not out of the goodness of my heart, Pen. I used work to avoid the holidays." He reached over and took her hand. "All those Thanksgivings and Christmases away from you, I'd take back now if I could. I should have been there celebrating with you."

She swallowed, but kept her eyes on him. "I had Nana and Pops. I made it through just fine."

"After your mother died, I was lost for many years. I couldn't handle the grief and used work to avoid it. Even if it meant being away from you." He reached out and touched one end of her hair. "You look so much like her."

It was something she'd heard all her life. She didn't have a memory of her, though, and had to rely on pictures to see it. "What's the point of this talk, Dad?"

"You may look like your mother, but I'm afraid that you act more like me." He dropped his hands and looked at them. "You can't use work to avoid life."

"I'm not avoiding anything."

He peered up at her. "Are you sure about that? I know that you and Christopher decided to break up."

"Aunt Sarah called you."

"Of course she did. She's worried about you."

"There's nothing to worry about. I'm fine."

"No, you're avoiding the grief just like I did for all those years. You moved up here from Florida and threw yourself into the job to avoid the pain of the wedding that didn't happen. And you're doing the same thing over Christopher now." He shook his head. "Baby girl, I don't want you to wake up when you're fifty wondering what might have happened if you had taken a chance on finding your happiness. You don't want to end up like me. Go after Christopher if he's what you want."

"Why didn't you date after Mom died?"

"Because I don't think I can go through that kind of pain again."

She raised her eyebrows at him. "And yet you're asking me to do that. To pursue a man who can't be with me and will leave me in anguish."

"If I could do it all over again, I wouldn't have stayed alone. I wouldn't have used the excuse of my job to keep me from the people who mean the most to me. I would have been a better father."

"So what's stopping you now?"

"Maybe I'm afraid it's too late."

She looked at her father. Really looked at him and saw that he was right. She might look like her mother, but she resembled her father in temperament. "It's never too late for us. I didn't come back here to Michigan just to escape the mess of my life in Florida. I came back because I needed you. Still need you. And I don't think we can avoid each other anymore."

"I don't know how to be a father."

"Well, I'd say you're doing a pretty good job at the moment."

"I'll make you a promise if you make one,

too." He scooted to the end of the chair so that they were knee to knee. "I will make an effort to spend more time with you."

"And what do I have to promise?"

"That you won't give up on love just because it got tough."

BEDTIME ON CHRISTMAS EVE hadn't been a trial like most nights. Even with all the excitement of seeing Julie's parents earlier and the large Cuthbert family party after, the kids had been obedient and taken their baths without complaint. Then with their pajamas on, they'd settled into their beds and had quickly fallen asleep. If only every night could be as easy getting them into bed.

With them asleep, Christopher pulled out the gifts he'd been storing in Aunt Sarah's garage, then settled in front of the Christmas tree, watching the lights. Aunt Sarah came in from the kitchen and handed Christopher a Christmas mug of hot chocolate before sitting on the sofa beside him. "It looks like it's going to be a good Christmas."

"I think it will be. This year reminded me that it's not the things, but the people. It took a fire to remind me of that."

"A hard lesson, but a good one."

He pulled an envelope off the coffee table and handed it to her. "Here's an early Christmas gift for you."

She frowned, but opened it. Inside, it held a sales contract to buy the house. She gasped and held it to her chest. "This is what I was hoping for, but you're offering way too much."

"I consulted a real-estate agent for the fair market value of the house and contacted my insurance company to confirm the downpayment amount. If you agree to our terms, we can close on the sale next month."

"I know you and your family will be as happy here as the Cuthbert family was for years. A house like this deserves the sounds and active bustle of children. That's been missing for too many years."

"I hope you're right."

"And you know what else this house needs? The right woman to complete your family."

Christopher had known she wouldn't give up on her matchmaking even after his disastrous breakup with Penny. "There's nothing wrong with my family the way it is."

"Except for the fact that you're alone."

"I don't need to have a wife to be happy. My kids can be enough for me."

"But—"

"Sarah…"

"Did I ever tell you about Henry?" When he shook his head, she nodded. "I met him the summer of 1952. I had just graduated high school and was working as a clerk in a men's store. Henry came in to buy a suit for his brother's wedding, and I fell for him as he bought not just a suit, but two shirts and three ties. I think he bought anything I showed him just to keep talking to me. We became inseparable after that day."

She paused, and Christopher waited for her to continue her story. Her voice quavered when she did. "And then he enlisted to fight the Korean War. He refused to marry me before he left because he didn't want to leave me a widow if the worst should happen. We fought bitterly because of it, and I refused to see him off on the train."

She swallowed and stared at the Christmas tree. "I eventually forgave him, and we wrote letters while he was away. He came home on leave at Christmas and gave me a promise ring. If I could just wait until the war was over, we could be together."

"What happened to him?"

"He came home missing a leg. I told him it didn't matter to me, but he refused to marry me. He'd changed and become bitter. Left me standing alone at the altar with no explanation." She shook her head. "Over sixty years later, and I still miss him. I had other chances to marry, but I let my memory of what Henry and I had stop me. So I've been alone ever since. And trust me, there's no warmth in that."

"Julie's death isn't keeping me alone."

Aunt Sarah looked at him. "But the promise you made her is."

AT DAWN ON Christmas morning, the feet on the stairs signaled the arrival of Daisy and Elijah. Christopher gave a soft groan, but put on his slippers and walked into the living room, where they sat in front of the Christmas tree, still lit from Santa's visit the night before. "Merry Christmas," he said as he leaned down to kiss each child.

Daisy wrapped her arms around his waist.

"Merry Christmas, Daddy. Can we open presents now?"

He looked at the faces of both of his children, each hoping that he'd agree. "How about you each open one from Santa, then help me get breakfast started?"

They glanced at each other with crestfallen expressions, but nodded. He poked around the tree and handed one present to Elijah, then gave Daisy a brightly wrapped gift. Sitting on the sofa, he watched them tear into the wrapping and exclaim at the gifts. Daisy hugged the doll that Penny had chosen for her. "She's so beautiful. And I can brush her hair. And feed her. And change her."

"Almost like a real baby."

Daisy looked up at him. "She is real."

"Of course."

Elijah pored over the instructions of the model car he'd received. "This one is going to take us a lot longer to build, Dad. We might want to start on this after breakfast."

Daisy poked under the tree and brought out another gift. Christopher held up his finger. "Just one gift, Daisy."

"This one is for you."

Christopher took the present as she handed

it to him. His name was on the tag, but it didn't say who it was from. He opened it to find a beautiful silver picture frame. The picture showed him with his children as they stood in front of the Christmas tree. He remembered Penny snapping the picture, and him saying that he had pictures of the kids but not with them all since he was usually the one behind the camera. He hugged the picture to his chest. "I love it."

"She knew you would."

Elijah stood and joined Christopher on the sofa. "I miss Penny. Don't you?"

This admission made him put his arm around his son. "I thought you didn't like her."

"She's funny, and she made you laugh like Mom used to." Elijah lifted his head to look into his eyes. "Penny brought back your smile, but now it's missing again."

Daisy sat on the other side of Christopher. "Eli and I have been talking about it, and we think that you should ask Penny to be your friend again."

Christopher shook his head. "She is my friend."

"Then why isn't she here? Why are you so sad?"

He tightened his arms around his children. "We're doing okay, aren't we? We have each other. And it's Christmas, the best day all year. We only need the three of us."

"But you need Penny, too." Elijah glanced at his sister, then at Christopher. "Mom would have liked her. She would have wanted her to be a part of our family."

That seemed impossible. Julie hadn't talked much about his life after her. She'd talked about the kids, of course. But not about how he would go on living without her. She couldn't have known how lonely it would be. How he still reached for her at night in that space between dreams and reality.

Christopher kissed the tops of both of his children's heads. "Penny has her own family. And she'll always be our friend."

"But you love her." Daisy rested her head on his shoulder. "Mommy used to say that she loved both Elijah and me just as much, but differently. You love Penny as much as Mommy, but it's different, too."

Out of the mouths of babes.

Could this mean his children would accept

Penny as more than a friend? Perhaps one day welcome her as their mother? Could he have everything he wanted, starting with this Christmas? And why did that make him want to begin that new life right this moment?

He stood and looked at his children, still in their new Christmas pajamas. He clapped his hands together once. "Everybody upstairs. Get dressed. We have somewhere to go."

CHRISTMAS MORNING STARTED with an early call out to a house where the tree lights had a short fuse and started to smoke. The homeowner quickly called 911, and the fire truck arrived before the smoking turned to flames. Then they got a call for a woman with chest pains. The firefighters responded ahead of the ambulance, since they had been closer to the woman's address. Penny applied her basic training skills and took her vitals before the paramedics arrived.

When they got back on the truck, Penny needed a break. And maybe some food. A generous citizen had dropped off bagels and juice last night for their breakfast, and Penny dreamed of a salt bagel slathered with cream cheese and raspberry jam.

The truck pulled into the station, and Penny checked the first-aid supplies since the next call could come at any moment. The rest of the crew had headed into the kitchen already, and she was the last to enter. She noticed that Barnes sat at a table with a large stack of pancakes, and she frowned. They hadn't been back long enough for anyone to make breakfast. But her nose told her that bacon and sausage had been fried, too.

Aunt Sarah waved at her from the stove next to a familiar tall figure who was pouring batter onto a griddle. Seeing him made her heart squeeze. So close, yet so far away. A small hand fit in hers, and she looked down to see Daisy in a frilly red dress, her cape tied at the neck. "Merry Christmas, Penny."

Penny leaned down and gave the girl a hug. "Merry Christmas. Was Santa good to you?"

"He got me a doll, and she's amazing. She even wets her pants."

"And what else did he bring?"

Daisy shrugged. "We're going to open the rest later. Daddy said we had to come here first."

Penny looked up to find Christopher still flipping pancakes, but sneaking glances at her. Daisy tugged at her hand. "Daddy wants us all to be friends again."

"And what about you and your brother?"

"It's different without you. And Elijah misses you, too. But Daddy most of all."

Penny again looked up to find Christopher's eyes on her. "I guess I should go and talk to him."

She let Daisy lead her to the stove, and Elijah smiled at her as he handed her a glass of orange juice. "Merry Christmas, Penny."

He didn't scowl at her. Didn't shy away when she gave him a hug. "Merry Christmas, E."

"You're the only one who calls me that."

She let him go and looked at him. "Is that okay?"

"I think so. Does that mean I can call you P?"

She gave a smile at his broad grin. "It will be like our own secret nicknames."

The boy nodded and returned to his serious task of pouring juice into cups without spilling any onto the counter. Penny moved down the buffet line to stand in front of Christopher. He smiled at her. "Two pancakes or three?"

She couldn't smile back, but stood there staring at him. She'd missed him so much, and those feelings overwhelmed her. Biting her lip to keep it from quivering, she tried to keep calm. "Three, I guess. I know how good these are." Though she doubted she'd be able to eat them. "What is this?"

"It's called breakfast."

"I know that, but why are you here? I thought we agreed to keep our distance for a while."

"You stated that, but I can't agree to that. Not anymore."

"Why not?"

He looked her in the eye. "Because when I realized that I need you, that we need you, in our lives, I didn't want to stay away anymore."

"You need me?"

Christopher handed his spatula to Aunt Sarah and walked to stand in front of Penny. Putting his hands on her shoulders, he stared into her eyes. "I loved Julie, and I'll never stop. And I tried to ignore what I felt for you. What if you didn't feel the same way? What if you left me, too? Could I go on with my life like before?"

Penny swallowed hard, unsure of what to think or say. "What about the kids? Julie left big shoes for me to fill."

"They reminded me that I can love you, too, and it can be different from what I felt for Julie. And you don't need to be Julie. We just need you to be Penny."

"Wait. You love me?"

He rested his forehead against hers. "I love you desperately, Penny Cuthbert."

She smiled, though the tears coursed down her cheeks. "And I love you back, Christopher Fox."

Penny glanced behind her at the audience who seemed to be watching the show they were giving, then smiled, her heart full of joy, and pulled Christopher into a kiss that promised a forever future.

EPILOGUE

AT THE END of January, the Cuthbert family helped fill the moving van with Great-Aunt Sarah's furnishings for her new home at the assisted-living center for seniors. Christopher had closed on the sale of the house a few days before, and he was ready to start this new life in the grand home.

Christopher joined Aunt Sarah on the sidewalk as she stared up at the house, and he put an arm around her shoulders. "Are you going to miss it here?"

She gave a watery laugh. "From the sounds of it, Penny's already planning the next Cuthbert family Easter dinner here in a few months. I have a feeling that I'll be spending time here soon enough."

He nodded and sighed. "I wouldn't have it any other way."

Penny walked out the front door, a box

in her arms. "Wait. You forgot this in the kitchen."

Aunt Sarah waved her off. "It's a house-warming gift for the two of you."

Penny opened the box and pulled out a ceramic cookie jar that had their initials intertwined and stamped into it. Penny's cheeks colored. "I'm not moving in with Christopher and his family."

"Not yet," Christopher said and put his other arm around Penny's waist. "I figure the kids need a few months to get used to us as a couple first. But then I'm gonna marry you and I hope then you'll be here with us."

Penny beamed, her eyes wide. "You are? You do?"

"I'm thinking by the end of summer. Here. In the backyard. We can have an arbor and—"

"Sounds good to me." Penny hugged him tight and then said to Aunt Sarah, "What would you say about being my maid of honor?"

"I'm too old for that kind of thing," Aunt Sarah said, but she looked pleased at the request.

"Since when are you too old for anything?" Christopher asked. "Besides, you're the one who first saw what took the two of us so long to accept."

"And what is that?"

"That we are better together," he answered and squeezed his soon-to-be wife.

Penny reached up to kiss his cheek, but he turned his head to kiss her mouth. Something he planned to do every day for the rest of his life.

* * * * *

For more feel-good romances from
Syndi Powell and
Harlequin Heartwarming,
visit www.Harlequin.com today!

Get 4 FREE REWARDS!

We'll send you 2 FREE Books <u>plus</u> 2 FREE Mystery Gifts.

Love Inspired Suspense books showcase how courage and optimism unite in stories of faith and love in the face of danger.

FREE Value Over **$20**

THE WESTERN HEARTS COLLECTION!

RUNAWAY
JUDY CHRISTENBERRY

WHO IN
WYOMING

DO YOU TAKE THIS

19 FREE BOOKS in all!

COWBOYS. RANCHERS. RODEO REBELS.
Here are their charming love stories in one prized Collection:
51 emotional and heart-filled romances that capture the majesty and rugged beauty of the American West!

YES! Please send me **The Western Hearts Collection** in Larger Print. This collection begins with 3 FREE books and 2 FREE gifts in the first shipment. Along with my 3 free books, I'll also get the next 4 books from The Western Hearts Collection, in LARGER PRINT, which I may either return and owe nothing, or keep for the low price of $5.45 U.S./$6.23 CDN each plus $2.99 U.S./$7.49 CDN for shipping and handling per shipment*. If I decide to continue, about once a month for 8 months I will get 6 or 7 more books but will only need to pay for 4. That means 2 or 3 books in every shipment will be FREE! If I decide to keep the entire collection, I'll have paid for only 32 books because 19 books are FREE! I understand that accepting the 3 free books and gifts places me under no obligation to buy anything. I can always return a shipment and cancel at any time. My free books and gifts are mine to keep no matter what I decide.

☐ 270 HCN 5354   ☐ 470 HCN 5354

Name (please print)

Address   Apt. #

City   State/Province   Zip/Postal Code

> ### Mail to the **Reader Service:**
> **IN U.S.A.:** P.O. Box 1341, Buffalo, N.Y. 14240-8531
> **IN CANADA:** P.O. Box 603, Fort Erie, Ontario L2A 5X3

*Terms and prices subject to change without notice. Prices do not include sales taxes, which will be charged (if applicable) based on your state or country of residence. Canadian residents will be charged applicable taxes. Offer not valid in Quebec. All orders subject to approval. Credit or debit balances in a customer's account(s) may be offset by any other outstanding balance owed by or to the customer. Please allow three to four weeks for delivery. Offer available while quantities last. © 2020 Harlequin Enterprises ULC. ® and ™ are trademarks owned by Harlequin Enterprises ULC.

Your Privacy—The Reader Service is committed to protecting your privacy. Our Privacy Policy is available online at www.ReaderService.com or upon request from the Reader Service. We make a portion of our mailing list available to reputable third parties that offer products we believe may interest you. If you prefer that we not exchange your name with third parties, or if you wish to clarify or modify your communication preferences, please visit us at www.ReaderService.com/consumerschoice or write to us at Reader Service Mail Preference Service, P.O. Box 9062, Buffalo, NY 14269. Include your complete name and address.

50BWH20